MW00653579

GOOD FENCES

A SCORTCHED EARTH NOVEL

BOYD CRAVEN

Copyright © 2015 Boyd Craven III

Neighbors, a Scorched Earth Novel
By Boyd Craven

Many thanks to friends and family for keeping me writing! Special thanks to Jenn, who has helped me with my covers from day one and keeps me accountable!!!!!

TABLE OF CONTENTS

1

The last hymn ended, and I grabbed my hat and headed out of church before the huge line up of people boxed me in. I was in almost the very last pew and was therefore one of the first to shake hands with the pastor.

"Brian, are you coming back later on for the pot-luck?"

"No sir, I've got a ton of work to do around my place before I can even think about it. If I get done early, I'll try," Brian said smiling, but regretting not being able to attend.

"Well, I heard McKayla's niece is attending…"

I felt my cheeks burn and Pastor White smiled and smacked me on the shoulder. I put my straw hat on, tipped it to him and left before I could make an ass of myself. Stepping outside of the church, the heat of the day hit me like a physical blow. It was eighty five degrees with almost one hundred percent humidity. The nor-

3

mally blue Michigan skies were hazy. I wiped the sweat off my brow and immediately went to my old Chevy and climbed in, proud to have the restoration finally finished. It was a '68 step side, the only flashy thing I owned now.

☣ ☣ ☣

I used to be like everyone else, I had a wife, expensive cars and a condo right inside of town. I'd totally been what I'd grown to hate back then. Too much money, too fast. No appreciation in life. It all changed in a thirty second incident that would forever re-shape my life.

Cathy and I were headed across town to go get some Chinese takeout when, in a flash of lights, a squealing of tires, and a horrible crunch, my world got turned upside down, in a literal fashion. I lost consciousness. When I came to, the car was on its side. Cathy wasn't moving and her head was at a funny angle. I checked for a pulse and found none. I started to scream and blacked out again.

I remember them carrying me up the embankment we'd rolled down, on a back board, the sky shockingly beautiful for such an ugly day. I caught a glimpse of a kid sitting on the back of an ambulance being questioned by two uniformed police. I recognized that kid, but I was too grief stricken to call out, to ask him if he was ok. I may have even hit that kid in my cartwheel that ended Cathy's life. A bolt of pain shot through my ribs as the paramedics rolled me into an ambulance and shut the door.

I spent a long time in the hospital, probably longer than I should have. I didn't want to talk to anybody and, with Cathy gone, I had a lot of dark thoughts. I'd broken

4

my ribs from bouncing off the steering column and the police had failed to mention that I hadn't been wearing my seatbelt. Probably because if I had been like Cathy all buckled in, the crumpled roof would have killed me too. This oversight on their part was probably an act of kindness, but it was one I appreciated. It would have been a reminder that she was gone and I wasn't.

It turned out that the kid was the one who had caused the accident. He was texting and driving and blew through the stop sign at the intersection, t-boning my car. The result was pretty predictable, but what wasn't was his father's reaction. His father was my boss, and ran the largest construction business in the Tri-County area. I had started working for Landry construction when I was eighteen, and stayed for almost fifteen years - until they let me go after the accident.

Mr. Landry had a lot of connections at the city and state level; he had to. When the prosecuting attorney was insistent on bringing his son up on vehicular man-slaughter, George Landry had that quashed and the at-torney removed from the case. The DA then assigned somebody else, who offered George Jr. a sweetheart of a deal, where he'd relinquish his license until his eigh-teenth birthday, take driver's education all over again and then re-apply for his license. No charges as an adult, no acknowledgement that he killed my wife.

I was almost insane with rage when I heard the news. I was trying to get my wife buried, and one thing you never think about in your early thirties is what to do when a loved one dies. I was in absolute shock at how much things were costing, and I had the money to do it, but I needed to fill out the forms for her life insurance. Nobody was surprised when my life insurance policy showed up as having been canceled a month before the accident. Landry was good at cooking up the paperwork like that, the cheap bastard. So I bore out my grief almost alone; Cathy's family was larger than mine, but not by a lot. There were ten of us there for her service.

The final straw was when I sued the insurance company for damages and injuries. Nothing was going to get my wife back, but it'd taken me over a month without a paycheck to heal up, arrange the funeral and have the service. The day the suit was filed, I was served my termination papers within the hour. No severance package and, just like my wife's life insurance, my short term and long term insurance had been cancelled a month back as well. Not by me of course, and I knew the paperwork had been forged and back dated. All he had to do was tell me no, and fax it to the insurance company and it could have been legit. Typical George.

I survived with help from some of the members of the church, and moved back to my parents' old farmstead on the outskirts of town. A couple of the church moms would stop by every couple days with casseroles and side dishes, and check to see if I had empty booze or beer bottles lying about. I wasn't a drinker by any means, but in those days it was tempting. With the love and support of my church family I was able to open up the once shuttered farmhouse and get it livable again, one room at a time. I'd inherited it and paid to have it looked after, but I didn't want to do much with it at the time I had inherited it.

Now that I didn't have a job and nothing to do, I walked the property that had once been much, much larger as a kid. Slowly, my body and mind healed. I bought the '68 step side pickup and started repairs. I read a lot of my father's books, some of them on hunting, trapping and homesteading. That had gotten me re-interested in things, and was a great diversion in my grief. I decided to re-open part of the farm up for me to get a few chickens or pigs and goats. Grow a garden. Things I hated 20 years ago, but it was all I could think about now.

I found construction work at a new company, and life went on. When the insurance companies sent me a settlement offer, I took it. It'd taken a year, but I was ready to not have any more reminders.

Those long walks and solitary moments on the farm had reminded me why I wanted to flee the countryside and move into the city. But it had all changed. I couldn't have stayed in the condo, so I donated all of Cathy's things to the church and one of the members sold it for me at about what I owed on it. That hurt too. The market wasn't good and I kept waiting on Murphy to kick me in the balls again, before I reminded myself that not everything was about me. Two years on, life was moving on and so was I.

☣ ☣ ☣

McKayla was the Pastor's kin somehow. She had been trying to play matchmaker with me for almost a year now, after waiting a respectable amount of time for me to grieve. The only problem was that I wasn't interested. She was pretty enough, but both Kristen and I were embarrassed by everyone trying to push us together. We'd talk on the phone about once a week, even went out to dinner and a movie. She was a great gal, but she wasn't for me and neither of us had the heart to tell our families that the platonic feelings were mutual.

I'd figured I'd call her in an hour or so, that way I could share the embarrassment and ask her if she was ready to break the news to her family. I downshifted the truck as I turned the corner and groaned as I saw a state police cruiser and a township police cruiser waiting in the driveway. Not again.

"Gentlemen," I said, turning the truck off and getting out, "what can I do for you?"

"Mr. Cartwright, we've got a nuisance complaint and we figured since both township and ours got a different one, we'd come out together," the Statie said.

"Oh, and what's the complaint?" I asked, looking to see which cop was going to answer.

It was the township cop who answered, "Well, there's a complaint about the smell on the western end of your property and, well, a noise complaint."

"And what do you have?" I asked the state trooper.

"Cruelty to animals, insufficient housing. Also on the western side of the property," he said, and it was all I could do not to start cursing aloud.

"Oh, you mean the parcel where my barn sits, the parcel that I denied selling to George Landry, the parcel where I keep the goats and the pigs? The parcel next to the new housing development of McMansions? The subdivision they built on the west side of the farm where the complaints are?" I tried to keep the hate and anger out of my voice, but it was difficult.

For his part, the township cop looked embarrassed, but the state trooper hadn't been out here before on one of the calls and had no idea what was going on.

"Yes sir," he said, pulling out a sheaf of papers and handed them to me, "and the entire Home Owners' Association signed it."

I almost went through the roof when I saw a friend's name on it. It was Randy; he'd been out to the farm numerous times, and was the guy who got me interested in prepping in the first place. My best friend. WTF?

"Well gentlemen," I said, trying and failing to keep the anger out of my voice, "let's go take a walk."

Reluctantly, they followed me towards the barn. I knew I was going to make a mess of my shoes and slacks I wore to church, but I was pissed. If I hadn't wanted to get rid of these two cops and call Randy, I might have changed first. Instead, I was walking the dirt path from the house to the barn in my fancy loafers. I paused and then pushed the big roll up door open, letting them inside the barn where I had a door on the opposite side where we could get to the goat and pig runs.

"Oh... That stinks," the state cop said.

"Yeah, that's manure. People take a shit, pigs make manure," I snarked, walking across the room to the smaller door where we could enter the fenced in field.

"Oh I know, I just didn't think it'd be that strong of a smell. It's no problem," the state cop said.

I caught the township guys' eyes and he shrugged in a noncommittal fashion.

"Well, here's housing when they aren't outside. They all have indoor runs about four times the size of what's required. Then they have about forty acres apiece to run and play about in," I said calming down.

"What about water?" The township cop asked.

"It comes from a well," I told them, annoyed.

"There's no power in here, unless you ran it underground," the state cop said, turning on a hose I used to spray out the cement.

The water turned on to his surprise and he quickly shut it off.

"I don't need power out here in the barn," I told him.

"Oh, so the water is run from the house?"

"Oh for the love of Pete, why does it matter?" I nearly

9

shouted, startling both of them.

"So that's a yes?" The trooper said, checking off something on his metal clipboard.

"No, it's a no."

"Then how do you get water?"

"I told you, from a well. Now, can we finish this up guys?" I asked, my face burning with anger.

"How do you power a well if there's no water?" The township cop asked, curious.

"See that windmill out there?" I asked him, pointing out the window set into the side of the barn.

"Yes?"

"It draws water up into a holding tank that keeps things pressurized. When the tank is full, the overflow goes to two ponds out back." I told him.

"Ok, got it. My grandparents had something like that when I was a kid," the local said.

"Now, you want to go check out the animals so I can finally change out of my church clothes?"

They both looked at me and had the good grace to not mention anything else. I opened the door for them and they walked out first, so I could close and shutter the door against it popping back open. I showed them the goats, who were happily climbing on a stack of pallets I'd put back there for that purpose, and then we walked in search of the pigs and found them in their favorite wallow for the hot part of the day.

"So, are you satisfied guys?" I asked them as we were walking back.

"I don't see anything here actionable," the state boy said, "Me neither, though the windmill is what they were complaining about," the township cop said.

"Thanks guys, and I'm sorry. I've been dealing with that HOA and Landry for two years now. They built up all those houses right on the edge of the fields and then complain that a farm actually farms. This has got to be what, my fourth visit by you guys?"

"Fifth," the local cop said.

"Fifth. Landry is pissed I won't sell off my parents' property and he hates me anyways," which was very true, his name was the first one from the HOA to be signed on the complaint.

He'd built his large house on the hill overlooking my western 40 acres. That's why I moved the pigs over one pen. In hindsight, it was a jerk move but I had been planning on rotating them that way in two years when I had more grow outs. The pigs would have been there sooner or later as I rotated the land use, and next spring they would go where the goats were.

"Ok, well, I'm sorry to have bothered you," they told me, before getting into their cruisers and leaving.

I stalked into the house to change and then I was going to call Randy. I was opening the screen door when the sound of crunching gravel caught my attention. It sounded like the police were coming back up the long driveway. I turned, exasperated, only to see a cube van, with Randy's Plumbing monogrammed all over it.

"Well, shit," I spat and waited.

2

I must have worked my anger out talking with the cops, because my conversation with Randy started off civil and remained so. I showed him the complaint the HOA had sent the cops, and the copy they had handed to me and his expression went from bewildered to pissed off.

"Hold on a sec." Randy pulled out his cell phone and hit a couple buttons.

"Hey hun, did you sign a complaint for me from the HOA? No? Ok, thanks hun, bye." Randy hung up the phone and turned to me.

"Somebody forged my signature."

I believed him. He lived two houses away from George Landry, and his house had also butted up to the fields, but his was closer to the goats and his twin daughters would often try to coax some of the goat babies close with carrots. It's how I became friends with him to begin with.

GOOD FENCES

"I bet you he's trying to force me to sell him the property," I muttered.

"You're still zoned agricultural here, right?"

"Yeah," I answered, "but I'm sure he can get the zoning changed once he gets it. He's a vampire around these parts. It's bad enough that his bastard of a son lives right next to me."

"Easy now," Randy patted me on the shoulder and I looked up to see him smiling, "don't work yourself into a heart attack over it. And really man, I'm kinda hurt you'd think I'd sign the bullshit paperwork like this."

"I know, I'm sorry. But it didn't even occur to me that they forged signatures. I wonder how many of these are forged?" I wondered aloud.

"Probably a lot of them. Listen, they didn't fine you or write you a ticket right?"

"No," I admitted, "Not this time."

"Don't talk like that, man. Besides, I was here to see if you wanted to go to the Saginaw Civic Center with me?" Randy asked, his voice excited once again.

"I don't know man. It's Sunday and I still have a ton of work to do—"

"It's the big gun and knife show," Randy reminded me, probably not believing I'd forgotten about it.

The truth was, I had. It'd been a long week, and I'd been writing quotes and doing a ton of housing take offs in order to meet my weekly quota. More and more business had been going to Landry's Construction, so it time for me to generate more business or look at a new line of work.

"You know what? I totally forgot. Let me go inside and change real quick." I told him.

"Good deal, I'll drive if you want," he offered.

BOYD CRAVEN

☣ ☣ ☣

The gun and knife show took place once a year and, as long as you had your CCW, which I did, you could buy handguns there. I'd already gotten a couple of handguns, but with the recent shortage of AR-15s, there had been a surge in manufacturing. You could buy them almost cheaper than you could before Obama took office. People were worried about him taking their guns, and all he did was create a market where things were snatched up. Heck, ammunition was still hard to come by in Michigan.

Randy talked a mile a minute the entire way up I-75, his cube van much more comfortable than it looked and I just zoned out. I often did this when we took long trips. I wasn't ignoring him per se, but it allowed me to think about the situation that seemed to be getting worse with the HOA next to the farm. Obviously I knew Landry had to be behind it, but did he really just want to ruin my life? First his son, now his dad? Sitting on top of the hill in his four million dollar home…

"So, you going to get that AR?" Randy asked, instead of his rambling.

"If they have what I want, otherwise maybe I'll get some parts and build it out," I admitted.

Truth was, I was handy with things even though I never swung a hammer or cut a board for a living. I'd always done that part from the office, writing quotes and doing take offs from blue prints for a materials list. I came by my construction experience from my father and grandfather when I was a boy, and my dad's extensive collection of books and how-to's he collected over the years. It was an eclectic thing to do, but one whole wall of the old farmhouse was shelves full of my

14

father's books. Most of it was nonfiction, but I could always count on finding just about every Louis Lamoure or John D McDonald that was published up until about five years ago.

"How much of a build out are you going to do?" Randy asked, now interested that he'd gotten me engaged in the conversation.

"Nothing wild, a Rock River upper receiver and a longer, heavier barrel for accuracy."

"Shoot, you should be able to find something like that easily. Well, except for the barrel. You may have to buy one separate."

"Yeah buddy," I said, already warming to the idea, "and keep your eyes out for some of the little odd bits for me would you?"

"Sure thing."

☣ ☣ ☣

We paid for parking and walked inside. The amount of noise that thousands of people make just walking and talking was tremendous and I couldn't hear Randy even if I wanted to. I saw quite a few AR platforms, but nothing quite right yet. I was paying for some army surplus MOLLE gear when I felt a tug on my sleeve and Randy pointed towards a table behind me and to the left. I almost laughed. He'd obviously gotten food while I was buying my gear and had this enormous foot long he was inhaling at an alarming rate.

I got in line and was moving with the flow of the crowd when I saw it. It was everything I told Randy I wanted, right down to the Bushnell Optics and Laser sight on the bottom. It had a grip in front of the mag for extra control and the price was well within my budget.

A harried man walked up asking if he could help us, and I pointed to the AR and asked if I could check it out. He nodded and moved down the table to the next man.

I held the rifle up towards the ceiling and felt the heft of it, the grips. I aimed it at the floor and worked the bolt, to see how smooth it was. I bumped the laser sight when I was trying to right it, to return to the table and it went skittering off across the floor behind the stall. I started to apologize to the man, but the lady that was working with him had already grabbed it and was walking towards me with a hex key in her hand. With a start, I realized it was Kristen.

"I thought you had a lot of work to do today?" Kristen asked, smiling at me.

"I thought you were going to do the pot luck?" I replied, almost laughing.

Guns, seriously, the last place I expected to find her was at a gun show selling guns.

"My date ran out on me, so I decided to help my cousin out here and make some extra money. What's your excuse?" She raised an eyebrow, and I felt a stab of guilt.

I had planned on working, but with the cops being at the farm and Randy showing up reminding me about the gun show...

"Who's your date?" I asked, flubbing it and regretting it immediately.

"Apparently the guy who's breaking the merchandise," she teased and I handed her the AR.

I was surprised at how quickly she had the rest of the mount off and was putting on a different setup.

"This is an Inforce-Mil," she said by way of explanation, "Much better than the junk my cousin puts on here. You getting this one right?"

GOOD FENCES

"Yes ma'am," I said watching her hands move in a flash as she moved and stripped the red dot on top of the receiver, "wait, that's ok," I told her.

"Naw, no it isn't. I'm putting on an EOTech red dot for you."

"That's some expensive stuff man," Randy said over my shoulder.

He was right, it was almost $500 retail for one of those and I was hoping to get out of here with the gun and a bunch of Magpul magazines for less than $1300.

"Yeah, I'm not sure if I really—"

"This going to be your coyote rifle?" Kristen asked, never slowing or stopping.

"Well yeah, but I mean that's more than I was wanting to—"

"Charlie," Kristen yelled, "I'm giving this guy the family price."

"What's he got?" Charlie, the guy who had first gave him the rifle to hold yelled back over his shoulder.

"That custom job that never got picked up."

"I'm not discounting it for the heavy barrel!" He yelled and I had to smile. I wanted the heavy barrel, would have paid more for it, but those sights…

"Ok, so we'll set you up here," she said putting the finishing spin on the set screws, "how many mags and what type?"

"I want ten Magpul mags, and since I'm getting the family price, how much for ammo?" I asked her, noting the usual price had gone up all around the convention center in regards to ammunition.

Another shortage due to a mass shooting and suspected sniper shooting at cars alongside the highway.

"Ammo I don't have for you today. If you can give me about a week, I can bring you a few bricks if you can wait?"

17

"That's a few hundred rounds right?" I asked her, curious.

"Yeah, something like that," she admitted.

"How much per thousand?" I asked, wondering if the question would make her raise an eyebrow.

It didn't.

"The Freedom Munition's go for about $299 per thousand," she told me and I tried not to wince at the price, "but it's remanufactured. It's probably better than factory ammo, but if you are a reloading nut... You aren't a re-loader, are you?"

"No, just ready, aim, fire." I told her, starting to see her in a new light.

"Ok, then I can probably get you 5,000 without depleting the stocks by say, Thursday? Or do you want less? More?" Man, she was making this a hard sell.

"I'll take 4,000," I told her and she rang me up.

I had already pulled out my credit card, expecting to have to put up the $1200 extra for ammo on it but she came back, the price was much, much better.

"$1879.32, including gun, ammo and the upgraded sights," I almost fell over in shock. That was a lot better than I had been expecting. A lot!

I put the card back in my wallet and dug into my front pocket where I had put the larger wad of cash I had set aside and peeled off 19 bills. She changed me out and gave me a smile.

"So, you want me to drop the ammo off at your house when we get done doing inventory?"

"Inventory?"

"Yeah, I work at Chuck's gun shop in Flint on my off days."

"You're a gunsmith?" Randy asked, interrupting the very same pertinent question I was going to ask.

18

GOOD FENCES

"Gunsmith, saleswoman and 3 gun completive shooter," she snapped back.

"I think I'm in love," Randy said in a dreamy voice.

I punched him in the shoulder and threatened to tell his wife and that sobered him up quickly. Kristen laughed and boxed up the gun, taping it closed for 'safety' reasons. I knew what she meant.

"So, your place when I go visit McKayla after work on Thursday?"

"Yeah, that's fine, or give me a call and I'll meet you."

"Ok, we'll work it out," she stuck her hand out for me to shake, and feeling confused, I shook on it.

☣ ☣ ☣

"Dude, you didn't tell me she was a gun babe!" Randy gushed, "I can't believe you aren't into her."

I wasn't, but I was surprised at the whole gunsmith thing. For as long as we had talked on the phone and had our faux date, her work never had been brought up. Thinking back on it, I realized that she had deftly avoided the topic. I knew she lived downstate near Flint, so neither of us had really given the dating thing a chance, and more or less did it to shut up the pastor and his family. What we ended up with was an easy friendship, not romance. Maybe I was wrong? Randy seemed to be head over heels with her, but I didn't really feel that way even if she did give me the deal of a lifetime.

"So you catch the debate?" Randy asked me, interrupting my train of thought

"Which debate?" I asked, knowing that Randy loved all things politics.

It's what had gotten him interested in prepping to begin with. International politics, stability of the country's finances and the electrical power grid. They all worried him, and what could happen to his wife and daughters if he was as unprepared as some countries had been during the financial meltdown. Syria, Iran, Iraq, Greece even had issues. Every day there was talk on the news of half a million displaced immigrants fleeing countries that were war torn or thrown into chaos after services were cut.

"Trump's! Tell me you saw that," he ranted and I groaned.

Randy loved Donald Trump, he thinks he's the next coming of Christ the Savior, but I didn't have any political or party affiliation. I voted for whomever I thought had the same views as I did.

"It's on DVR, so don't ruin it for me," I said, smiling when Randy opened and closed his mouth several times, trying not to say something.

"Oh, ok. So… uh… I wanted to ask you a weird question," Randy said, suddenly shy and nervous.

I had noticed he hadn't purchased anything other than that greasy grimy hot dog, so I figured he was working himself up to asking me something, or just trying to get me out of my perpetual funk. Good friends are like that, I realized. I had a hard time coming to terms with the anger I'd felt at him earlier when I saw his forged signature.

"Go ahead."

"Well, if things get really hairy someday, do you think the girls and I could…"

I laughed, "Randy, we're neighbors and friends. Of course."

"Ok, now here's the hard part… Can you store two or three pallets for me in the barn? Brenda would shoot me if I put them in the garage."

GOOD FENCES

"That isn't a problem, want me to bring my truck over?" I asked him, knowing his cube van was usually full of tools and pipe.

"Well, Estes is going to deliver it. I was hoping you could pull it off the lift gate with your tractor?"

"Oh, well. That's no big deal. I was expecting to have to load boxes by hand and restack them!" I said warming to the idea, and I even had a good corner of the barn I could store them in that was completely dry and away from the animals.

It was by my dry goods storage. I built myself a processing station there and, although Randy had been in and out of the barn dozens of times, he hadn't noticed or at least commented on it. He'd seen the buckets and gamma lids, but that was just usual for me.

"Naw, this is some prepacked food I got a good deal on from Wal-Mart's website," he told me.

I jerked my head to the side and I must have had a funny expression on my face because he laughed and then looked back at the road before talking.

"It's Augason Farms. Most the stores around here don't carry it, but they will do site to store for free shipping, or if you get a bunch like I did, you get free home delivery."

"Augason Farms?" I asked, not believing it.

Wal-Mart of all places, buying prepper/survival food from Wal-Mart? Then again, that's exactly how I'd started. I'd buy bags of whatever I could afford and when I had enough to fill a bucket, I'd get out my stack of Mylar bags and jar of oxygen absorbers. I'd pour the rice, beans, wheat berries or whatever into the bag, toss in an O2 absorber and seal it with an impulse sealer I bought at a garage sale.

"Yeah, they had a full year's kit on sale for a grand

apiece!" Randy said excitedly.

"Dang, if I hadn't just blown all my money—"

"And gotten yourself a date? You didn't see the piles of ammo under the table, did you?" Randy said, and I realized my ears were burning.

"Come on man, that was Wolf ammo," I said, knowing I didn't want to shoot the cheap corrosive stuff if I didn't have to.

"I know, just messing with you. But for real, I'd be grateful if I could store those there. I'll rent the space if you need me to."

"No, we're good, but let's not make it four pallets now, four pallets next year, four pallets the year after that and—"

"Naw," Randy chuckled, his boisterous energy was infectious, "Just those first four. I have stuff at the house, but it's my backup plan."

I thought he originally said two or three? Oh well.

☣ ☣ ☣

Randy dropped me off and headed home. His wife had called, and instead of driving the short half mile around to his subdivision, he was headed into town to pick up pizzas. His penance for spending the afternoon with me at the gun show. Randy's wife, Brenda, was even more of a hardcore prepper than he was, which had surprised me. The four of them would have drills. Everything from suiting up in Chemical and Biological Warfare gear, to packing up and leaving the house at the drop of a hat. I'd been at the fence talking with one of his twins, Lindsey I think, when his whistle sounded and she dropped the handful of carrots she'd been feeding my goats and run to the house.

That had been the first hint at how seriously Randy took things.

3

Monday through Thursday flew by and my excitement over my ammo order grew. I'd talked to Kristen earlier in the day to give her my address and lit out of work early for the big moment. I'd done two material take offs and talked a couple through phase three of their build when the house was getting the interior finished.

I drove home a little above the speed limit and had a heart stopping moment when I ran through a speed trap heading out of town. The cop either let me go, or hadn't been watching the radar because I never got pulled over. Pulling into the driveway, I headed inside and got the gun out of my safe and laid it out on the kitchen table. I had an hour until I was supposed to meet Kristen, but I couldn't sit in that cramped office at work any longer.

Hearing somebody coming up my driveway, I headed out with the AR in my hands and smiled in anticipation. Sure, I could have gotten a quick box of ammunition, but I really wanted to rock out with this. I'd been saving for just such a gun for a couple of months now. My jaw dropped when it wasn't Kristen like I was expecting, but George Landry Sr. himself. I stood there stupefied with anger as he pulled up in his new Chevy, the dust cloud following him from the long gravel drive.

He pulled up next to my truck and got out, slamming the door and started to walk up to me. He stopped and blanched. "Hey, I just wanted to talk, there's no need for that!"

"What? This? Oh," I put the gun down on the window ledge and turned to him. "What's up, Landry?"

"I figured I'd come out and explain our position with regards to the complaint," George said, looking at me and then the window sill towards the gun.

I shifted my weight. "There's no position to explain, George. They found nothing wrong, except for making a false police report," I said. Tiny white lie, but whatever.

"Oh, what's that? False how?" My fiction had the desired effect; he started sweating.

"Some of those signatures from the HOA letter were forged. I know for a fact, as they left me a copy and since you built the subdivision and are head of the HOA—"

"Just wait a God damned minute—"he roared.

"George - don't. You know how I feel about that. You start screaming and yelling, I'm going to ask you to leave my property."

"Or what, you're going to shoot me with that?" George screamed, taking a step towards me.

"What? No, I have a friend stopping out with some ammo. We're going to sight this thing in and—"

"You can't shoot here, it's too close to the houses!" George was spitting and sweating; both were necessary for the nuclear meltdowns Landry was known for.

GOOD FENCES

"Actually George, I can. It's my property. The rule is three hundred yards set back from occupied houses. Look it up. I've got 240 acres here. There's national forest land on the northern edge of my property, so as far as the law goes, I'm perfectly legal."

George stuttered and stammered and I was enjoying the show and he was almost ready to blow his top when a red Acura rolled up the driveway. I recognized the car as Kristen's. I didn't want her in the middle of the ugliness, so I turned back to George, who was red in the face.

"I'd say you've got yourself about an hour to call whomever you're going to call when you get your panties in a wedgie, because I plan on doing some shooting."

"You can't, my son is back there!"

"Excuse me?" I left the porch and walked towards George.

"My son rides his mountain bike back there!" George pointed towards the north.

"What's he doing in my fields?" I demanded, my tone icy.

I knew it was pointless to hate his son, but he had got to be close to eighteen or nineteen... But he was trespassing and riding through the fields? Did he cut a fence? Unconsciously, I balled my hands into fists. Kristen got out of her car and pulled a Kimber from the small of her back, keeping the barrel pointed at the ground.

"Is everything OK?" Kristen asked, seeing my red face.

I looked down and relaxed my hands, trying to control my breathing and get my anger back in check. I figured it was a good thing I'd left my gun back close to the house and didn't have ammunition in it. Yet.

"Yeah. Mr. Landry here was just telling me his son

is riding through *my property* right now and telling me I cannot shoot my gun on *my property*…" I knew I was being an ass for putting heavy emphasis on 'my property', but of all people I'd hated to see move in next door, it was Landry Sr. and Jr., who had me grinding my teeth.

It was bad enough that when the subdivision had begun to spring up that Landry had tried to have the land on the road all re-zoned, including mine, but then he built his house basically across from the barn and immediately started to complain about the farm. Lord knows what he was going to do when Mr. Matthews showed up with his combine in fall and cut corn. The man had been leasing the eastern fields for as long as I could remember and his lease paid the taxes on the property. I'd never mentioned that to anybody else, but if George Landry knew about it, he'd try to do something.

The other reason I didn't want to mention him was I didn't want him to get caught up in my messes. Ben Matthews had been like an uncle or grandfather figure to me, where I didn't have one. He'd been a good friend of my father's and his grumpy nature even charmed my mother to pieces. He was what the kids now a days would have called 'old school', but a great man. He'd lived his entire life on the farm he was on now, born in the same room he now calls his own. I rather like the old codger and didn't want to cause him any more grief. Especially the kind George was dishing out.

"Why is your son trespassing on Brian's… Landry? George Landry?" Kristen's eyes went wide.

"Yes, and I'd appreciate it if you put your gun away. You don't need that here, I'm just trying to talk to Brian here and everyone is pulling out guns." George fumed.

"First things first Landry," I said, getting myself under control finally, "you came here on my property un-invited. I told you last time that you and yours aren't welcome here and I'd press charges if you trespassed again. Secondly, you coming here after making false allegations to the police sounds an awful lot like harassment to me, doesn't it to you?" I asked Kristen, who nodded, "And lastly, it's my land. You don't have any say about it, you are not buying it, you are not rezoning it and if you keep pushing me I'm going to move the pig paddock directly behind your house instead of into the barn!"

I wasn't joking, and somehow George could see it.

"Call your son, he's got less than an hour to get off my property." I told him, jabbing my finger at him to drive my point home.

"Or you're going to call the cops?" George asked incredulously, "Tell them my kid ducked your fence?"

"No, I'm going to start target shooting. Your son is an adult, if you don't want to give him the heads up, then that's on you. In case you want to call and complain to the cops, I already have a range set up that my family has used since my father was a boy. It's in the middle of the North West hay field with a dirt backstop. Make sure you give your buddies at the state police or the local yokels the right information, because I'm not going to be harassed like this."

"But, about the complaint, I came here to tell you we could all resolve this if you'd…"

"George," I cut him off, getting right in the old man's face. He'd been almost a father to me for many years. "I don't want things resolved. You and your son ruined my life." I emphasized the last three words.

"I came out here to regroup, and you bought up all the land you could on this road, and tried to buy mine out from under me. When your eminent domain attempt failed, you harassed me via the police. Five times now George, five times you've had the cops come out here. Now, I'm not a violent man, but I'm giving you less than thirty seconds to get your sorry ass in your truck and get off my land." I was nose to nose with him now and his eyes fluttered in indecision.

George stuttered, and then pulled a sheaf of papers out of his back pocket, throwing them on the ground at my feet. He stormed back to his truck, and I stood there, watching the dust cloud follow him out as he fishtailed back down the driveway.

"You know, you can relax now." Soft hands covered mine and slow, gentle fingers unclenched first one fist, and then the other.

"I'm sorry you had to see that." I stooped to pick up the papers George had dropped and turned to look at Kristen.

Sometime during my last tirade against George and all he stood for, she'd re-holstered her Kimber. She stepped back and gave me a nervous look and then glanced at her car. I got it; she'd seen the ugly side of me and she wanted to go. I didn't blame her. Eventually everyone saw the ugly side of me.

"No, I'm glad I showed up when I did; it looked like you were going to deck him."

"I was. I mean, I probably would have. Thank you." And I meant it.

"How about we get this ammo inside and we can have a coffee and talk about it?" She asked

I was surprised, but I smiled. "Sure,"

GOOD FENCES

Kristen knew the basics about my wife's death, but not who my new neighbors were. I'd largely ignored the fact myself until the harassment started. Every time I got a letter, I knew it all began with George. Or I'd have the cops show up like they did last Sunday...

"Are you going to call the police?" Kristen asked me after listening to me rant for a while.

"I don't know. I do want to ride the fence to make sure there's no cuts or breaks in it; I can't afford for one of the sows to get out and get hit by a car."

"So he went in through the pig enclosure?" Kristen asked me.

"I think so. Unless he went to the end of the subdivision, but that whole western fence needs to be checked now, especially if the goats get rotated into that pen this fall."

"Do you want a hand?" Kristen asked.

I considered it a moment and then nodded. The funny thing about anger and rage, is when it leaves your body, you are left feeling hollowed out and empty inside. Even after finding out that Kristen was a gun nut like I was, I still only thought of her as a friend, and by the look she gave me she felt the same. One friend helping another.

"Let me lock up the AR real quick," I said, walking away from my kitchen table.

I spun the combination lock to my father's old gun safe, and put the AR in the middle. I'd already stacked the boxes of Ammo on top of the safe, until I could get things organized.

"I see you like guns too," Kristen commented.

She smiled and reached out her hand out as if to caress one of the rifles. She was reaching for my father's deer gun, so I pulled it out and let her look it over. It was

29

an old Stevens .30-06 with Leopold scope mounts and my father's favorite scope, an old Leopold 4x. It wasn't the fanciest or nicest gun I owned, but it had been my father's. It was accurate to a half an inch at 100 yards, and had probably taken over a hundred deer on our farm alone.

She worked the bolt, held it up to the lights and then handed it back, making sure to engage the ambidextrous safety with her thumb. I smiled; of course she'd know this gun, and Savage Arms bought out Stevens. Kristen gave it back to me and I locked the safe.

"Ready?" I asked her.

She nodded.

"Let me make sure the critters have water and throw them a couple treats. It'll keep them from following us around."

"It's your show," Kristen told me, walking towards the door, "I'm just here to help."

We headed out, and when I got to the barn I opened the metal trash can I used to store my sweet feed. Usually the sound of the lid was enough of an incentive to bring the goats in in a rush, and this time was no exception. I gave my small herd two scoops, spread out on the inside of their barn enclosure and snuck out the back door where I'd shown the cops earlier.

Kristen didn't wrinkle her nose at the farm smell like the state trooper had, which surprised me. The other thing I noticed was that she wasn't fawning over the goats and the new kids that had been born recently. She did smile when one jumped on an adult and then bounded to the front of the line, but other than that she was pretty straight faced.

"Your fencing; three strand electric?" Kristen asked.

"Yeah, with a barbed wire topper. Goats and pigs are

GOOD FENCES

escape artists. At least, mine are. That's why I'm so worried about George Jr. cutting his way into the field,"

"Well, let's go check it out. You don't have all of the property fenced, do you?"

"No, just these two fields. Shouldn't take us long."

It didn't: we found a well-worn trail where a tree grew close to the fence at the back of the Landry's property. I took note of that and then followed the trail, which mirrored the fence line. Normally I would have overlooked something like that, figuring it was one of the animals just following the fence. They do that kind of thing all the time until a dirt path is created. The kid could have seen it, boosted his bike over the fence, and used the tree to avoid the wires.

"Up there," Kristen pointed up the field towards the North West end.

Coming out of the tall grass and crown vetch was George Jr. I immediately noticed his pale complexion and irregular gait, and he was pushing his bike. I started to go see if he was ok, when I was struck by the notion that I should instead call the cops and have him arrested. I discarded that and walked. I stuffed my hands into my pockets, lest they give away my feelings if I didn't want them to, like they had with his father. Kristen put her hand in the crook of my arm, and we walked like that until the boy could see us both.

He didn't hesitate at first, but when he got close enough to see it was me, he went even paler.

"Mr... Mr. Cartwright, I'm sorry I know I'm not supposed to be—"

"You ok? You're dragging your left leg pretty bad," I let him get closer to me rather than walking to him.

"I don't know. I crashed my bike and hit a rock," George Jr. said, wincing with every step.

31

"Let me look," Kristen said, forcing him to stop and pull up his pant leg.

The ankle was swollen up as fat as the kids calf muscle and the shoe was straining.

"Ok, tell you what, get on the bike, we're going to get you to your dad," Kristen said, a note of concern in her voice.

"I can't ride," George said, his voice betraying the pain he must have been feeling.

"You can't keep walking on a broken ankle either," I almost snarled, "Call your dad. He's been trying to get ahold of you."

George hopped on one foot and held onto his bike for balance. He pulled out the smashed remnants of a cell phone and tossed them to me.

I sighed. "What's his number?" I typed it into my own phone and George picked up on the third ring. "Hey George, this is Brian Cartwright

"What do you want?" The anger coming out of the phone almost matched what I felt deep inside.

"Meet us at the back fence, by the big willow tree."

"Why? You planning on threatening me again?" George Sr. asked.

"No, I decided to check the fences and found your son. He fell off his bike and –'

"What did you do to my boy?" George snarled, but in the background I could hear him moving and then the sound of wind making the speaker crackle.

"He fell off his bike. He's ok, but you're going to need to get him to the doctor. I think he broke his ankle."

"Let me talk to him," the demand was cold, the anger still there.

I handed the phone to a now sweating Jr. who had a quick terse conversation with his dad before hanging up and giving me back the phone.

"He thought you were going to shoot me?" George Jr. asked, looking at me funny.

"No kid, I was making sure you hadn't cut my fence to make your shortcut into the state land and trails back there," I told him, watching relief flood his face, "Get on the bike, Kristen will take one side, I'll take the other. Keep your bum foot off the pedals and let us roll you there."

It worked out well on the dirt path. Never since the accident had I been so close to the kid. Though he was closer to being a young man now. I'd had dark thoughts of throttling him on more than one occasion, but being this close to him, I felt torn. Confused. He was just a normal kid, not the reincarnation of Beelzebub like I loved to picture him in my mind's eye. We were about a hundred yards from the willow tree when I heard a siren light up.

Of course, he'd called the cops. As we got closer I saw I was wrong. Two EMTs stood at the fence line with George Sr., one of them rubbing his hand.

"Those wires are hot," I warned him, too late unfortunately.

"Found that out," the young EMT smiled back, showing me his palm.

"Georgie, are you ok?" Sr. asked, almost interrupting.

"It hurts, but not so much now that I'm off my foot. They pushed me back on the bike so it wasn't as bad as getting out of the woods," his son replied.

"Listen, Jr., slide off on your good foot, I'll get a grip under your arm and then Kristen will hand the bike to your dad."

"Got it," he said, groaning as he bumped his ankle

33

trying to dismount the bike.

"Want us to come around the fence with the ambulance?" the older of the two EMT's asked.

"Naw, he's still light," I scooped Jr. up, one hand under his knees, the other around his shoulders, and handed him over the fence to the three men.

Sr.'s face went white when I picked his son up; I knew the kid would be heavy but farming and getting back into living life had left me ample opportunity to get healthy again and the kid didn't weigh more than three sacks of feed.

"Thanks," Jr. said through gritted teeth, and I nodded in acknowledgement.

The EMTs immediately went to work, stabilizing the leg, then gave me a jaunty wave as they each got under an arm and helped him hobble towards the front of the McMansion and the awaiting ambulance.

"Is your life always this exciting?" Kirsten asked after we stood there in silence, listening to the motor's sound fade away.

"Sometimes, it gets even better," I told her deadpan.

"How's that?" Kristen asked me.

"Well, sometimes I get to shovel manure."

She smiled. "I wanted to let you know, McKayla and Pastor White won't be bugging you or I anymore, you know, matchmaking. I've started seeing someone. I wanted to tell you, I mean… You're a good friend. I figured I'd mention it since Randy—"

"Randy's an ass. He teased me the whole way home after the gun show," I admitted with a grin and walked back towards the barn next to Kristen.

"Oh, I mean, he's a nice guy but I wanted to tell you. In case, I mean, I didn't want you to get the wrong idea."

"Kristen, don't worry. There were some times I wondered, I'll admit, if I should have tried to make some sort of relationship happen because everyone says we're perfect, or we would be. I like you for a friend, and if anything ever happens in the world and you need a place… well, you get your stuff up here and bring your guy friend too. He'd have to be a nice enough guy to catch your attention, so I'm sure I'd like him."

That was a long speech for me, and I realized I meant every word of it.

"Thank you," Kristen said, putting her hand in my arm again, giving me a squeeze.

We finished the walk in silence, both of us smiling. The elephant in the corner had been identified, shown the light and was no longer an issue. I'd worried about trying to make it more than it already was, because if I screwed it up, I'd lose a friend. At that point, friends were what had brought me through Cathy's death to the point to where I didn't run around all day pissed off. Except, of course with regards to the Landry's. Maybe I could call Pastor White and schedule some time. He'd always been a good one to talk to about Cathy's death.

4

A week flew by in a flash. Pastor White had suggested that the reason why I suddenly wasn't angry with George Jr. was because maybe I was angrier at the father for his callous and illegal behavior. I admitted that could be true, but it wasn't his father driving. In the end, maybe it was because I was starting to forgive him and letting things go? I couldn't decide.

I'd fired off a certified letter from my lawyer, informing the Landrys that further trespass on my property would be met with charges from the cops. I didn't get an answer back, nor was I really expecting one. They'd moved on, and so would I, after I'd added another three feet of height and two more strings of barbed wire near the subdivision that butted up to the animal pens.

Work took forever it seemed, because I found that the custom AR I bought was a tack driver. I couldn't even tell how far I could sight the little beauty in for. Three hundred yards was good for me and the brushy portions of the property I walked. I still had my father's gun for long range hammering if the nails were far enough out.

The thing that had been swirling around my mind though, was security. The kid had scaled my fences and in a SHTF scenario, who else would? That question, as well as keeping the Landrys out, was my reasoning for upping the fences. So when Friday hit, I went to Family Farm & Home and picked up more posts, more staples and two huge rolls of barbed wire. They were loaded on my truck by a nervous kid on a fork lift, but the kid was well practiced and the load went in safely. I was headed home when my phone rang; a number I didn't recognize.

"Hello?" I asked.

"Hello, this is Bill. I drive for Estes and I have some pallets to be delivered?"

He rattled off my address and I smiled. It was Randy's gear, food or whatever.

"Yeah, you on your way?" I asked him.

"I should be there in an hour if you're going to be there?"

"Yeah, I'll be there a little before that. See you then."

I hung the phone up and smiled. I pulled over into a random parking lot and dialed Randy's cell before putting it on speaker and pulling out.

"Hello?"

"Randy, your stuff is coming today," I told him.

I expected a big bundle of excited happiness, but all I got was, "Oh, ok."

"Randy, bud, what's wrong man?" I asked him, confused at his lackadaisical answer.

"The HOA just served us papers. Apparently it's against the covenants to park a work truck in the driveway or on the road. My cube van won't fit in my garage."

37

"Landry," I fumed.

"Yeah, I think so. I think he blames me for telling you about the signatures."

"I'm sorry man, I didn't mean for my squabble to—"

"Brian, it's cool, I just have to figure this out. I'm self-employed and I am going to have to rent someplace to park it and then worry if my supplies and tools get stolen," he said glumly.

"Well, head to my place. Help me get this barbed wire I just bought unloaded and we'll see if we can figure something out," I already had an idea forming in my head.

☣ ☣ ☣

I used the fork attachments on my Kubota's front bucket to pull the pallet off my truck and then unloaded the five pallets from Estes. The driver had beaten me there, but Randy had showed him where to park so I could unload easily. Five pallets, not four. I didn't mind, but I was curious, because only four of the pallets were from Augason Farms, and the other one had Cyrillic writing on it and contained hard green boxes wrapped in shrink wrap.

We signed off on the shipment and, as the truck pulled away I shot Randy a questioning look, hooking my thumb in the direction of the fifth pallet.

He got a sheepish look on his face and smiled. "Dude, you're never going to believe what I got!"

He started to rip off the shrink wrap and open the green boxes one by one. Immediately I saw it was old radio gear, I knew that because my dad had an old set of it that was still in the farmhouse. That exact same setup. The green cases were metal on the outside, but foam inside, molded to keep the old electronics intact.

"You plan on going into broadcasting?" I asked him. Randy was still bent over, mumbling and opening boxes and making a big mess in general.

"Ah hah! Got it!" Randy exclaimed, holding up a smaller box in his hands.

"What is it?"

"It's an EMP hardened security setup. Cameras with built in microphones and a little monitor in this case right here," Randy's foot nudged an unopened case.

"So you got security and communications gear?" I asked him, wondering if he was starting to take this prepper stuff a bit too far.

"Well, yeah." Randy said, as if I was a kid asking a dumb question.

"Isn't that… I mean, it's cool to have. I have a set like that, but what would you use it for?" I asked him, trying not to let my doubt about his sanity bubble forth from my words.

"You got a radio rig like this?" he asked, excitedly.

"Yeah, it was my dad's. Old military surplus stuff he bought a long time ago. Used to have the antenna tower there hooked up," I said pointing to the old TV/radio tower that had been behind the house ever since I was a little kid.

"Yeah, I found this guy on eBay who was selling stuff. When I was out here last time your antenna is what got me thinking about communications and stuff if something ever happened. I wanted a way to reach out and talk to somebody with equipment that wouldn't get fried out in an EMP or CME."

I nodded then mimed putting a microphone up to my lips, "Red rover, red rover, would you send Randy right over!"

Randy laughed and restacked the boxes, leaving the security cameras and monitor on top of the pile.

"I can pack this stuff up in my van if it's too much for you to store…"

"Naw, it's not too much, but don't keep adding to it."

"Hey, what's… oh wow," Randy said noticing my dry goods station and the stack of buckets that normally was under a tarp.

"You aren't playing around," Randy said lovingly, running his hands across the buckets stacked up.

What I'd done was rip a 4x8 sheet of ¾" plywood in half and I used that between every layer of buckets. That helped keep the lids intact, which were the weakest part of the food storage. I'd lay the buckets two deep, eight feet across, then put another layer of plywood on top and start stacking. It spread the weight out and, since my floor was level, I was pretty confident that everything wouldn't collapse. Maybe. I had a ton of full buckets with piles of supplies to fill even more.

"No, I just remember doing something like this with my parents. My mom was into canning and my dad used to do the meats. We never stored grains like this though; I figured out a system that works for me by listening to the survival podcast and watching Southernprepper1 on YouTube." Most of the storage ideas were from the podcast, but Southernprepper1's channel on YouTube was just darn cool.

"You watch him too, huh? Good deal. We don't go for dry goods quite so much at my house," he said, inspecting buckets of rice, "but we have a ton of canned goods and freeze dried."

There would come a point where every prepper has to question his own sanity, or that of his best friend.

"Do you think we're overdoing it? This, I mean?" I

GOOD FENCES

motioned to the corner of the barn, where we literally had metric tons of food stored for ourselves.

"You know, I got a couple links to share with you. I know you don't care for Obama any more than I do, but what do you think will happen of a progressive liberal socialist gets elected, or a neurosurgeon?" Randy asked.

"Or what about if Donald Trump gets elected?" I asked, ready for him to go off on another tangent.

"See, that's exactly right."

"What is?" I asked.

"There's no good choices anymore. Trump's popular because he speaks his mind and he threw out the politically correct rhetoric. He might be the worst thing for America, actually, but he is fun to watch and listen to."

"I'll give you that, but I mean… Radio equipment? EMP proof security systems?"

"Tell ya what, when I get home tonight, I'm going to send you a bunch of links and a couple YouTube videos. Promise me to at least watch them, would you?" Randy asked, seriously.

"Sure, you know I like checking this stuff out. I mean, I was just wondering if we aren't maybe going a little too far." I was putting my concerns out in the open for the first time.

"Did your grandparents call stocking up food for the winter prepping?" Randy asked me.

"No, they just called it common sense."

"Is that root cellar behind the house up the hill still standing?"

"Well, yeah." I'd been storing my root veggies inside there all summer - and sometimes would take a nap in there as well.

"So is that just common sense?"

I thought about it, and I supposed I was starting

41

to see where he was going with all of this. The times and technology had changed. Would my grandpa and grandma have stored grains the way I was? Probably not, because the only safe way to store a ton of grains back then and keep it pest and vermin free wouldn't have been in plastic buckets, with Mylar and oxygen absorbers. It would have been in a drum, waxed shut or shut with a gasket. They didn't do that though, because the farm up the road usually stored all the grain in silos.

"I guess you're right." I conceded.

"Check out those videos and links. It's eye opening,"

"I will."

Randy began picking up the errant pieces of shrink wrap; he hadn't touched the Augason Farms stuff, so there wasn't much trash from those. I wanted to broach the subject of the truck, but I wanted to see if Randy was feeling the same way as I did about the senior Landry.

"Hey, before you go, what are you going to do about your truck?" I asked him after re-tarping the supplies and closing the barn door.

"I don't know what I'm going to do yet. I really hate that the HOA can kick us out of our house if I don't move my truck somewhere. I mean, I know I signed the covenant agreement, but I don't remember all these stupid rules they are throwing at me," Randy said, his voice moving in cadence as we both walked towards his parked cube van.

"When do you have to get the truck out of there?" I asked him.

"What do you mean?" He gave me a look.

"Do you have 30 days?" I asked, figuring that would be the default.

"Yeah, unless I want to fight it. Get signatures—"

"Randy, I have a kind of evil thought."

GOOD FENCES

"I'm good with evil thoughts," the smile lit up his face.

"So, having worked for Landry before I'm guessing the specific rule says you can't leave a work truck parked there overnight? Right?"

"Well yeah, actually," he said, the smile gone as he looked confused.

"So you park your truck at my house overnight and I park my truck at yours. In the morning one of us drives up and switch things out. On your off days, we leave your work truck parked there until night time. It'll drive Landry insane." I said, smiling.

"And here I thought you were a good Christian," he said solemnly and then broke out into laughter at my indignant expression.

"I am," I said, "I just think that it doesn't hurt to put the screws into a guy who enjoys doing it to others. Besides, I think I leave for work earlier than you, so your truck will be sitting there in the morning when Landry wakes up."

"Genius," he said smiling and climbed into the cab of his cube van.

"While E Coyote, super genius," I said holding a finger pointing at me.

"Just don't fall off any cliffs and you'll be fine Mister Coyote, and look at those links! I'll send them over to you in about ten minutes!" Randy said, yelling out the open window of his truck.

"Will do!" I yelled back and went inside.

"I need a beer," I muttered to myself, but fired up my laptop instead and looked at the pile of mail I had brought in.

Junk, junk more junk, bank statement and... I paused and ripped open the bank statement. It wasn't my credit union bank, but the one where I deposited the settlement money from Cathy's death. I fingered the envelope and then opened it up. The balance had gone up a small amount, despite being in a recession and the FED having everyone at a zero interest rate. I thought about all the toys I could buy with it, how much joy I could bring by giving it away to charity or church, using it for something somewhere. Not just sitting in an account, building interest.

Maybe I could buy that old 70 horse tractor from Mr. Mathews now that he got the new combine. I could really put in a survival garden… My email pinged on my cell phone and I looked. Sure enough it was Randy. I went to the computer where I had a bigger screen and sat down. I wasn't surprised to see direct links, but soon found his narrative in the text.

Hey man, there's this old show from the Twilight Zone (no sparkly vampires, I promise), you probably remember it. Called The Shelter - http://www.hulu.com/watch/440826 it gives a really good reason why you should keep your preps and shelter ideas to yourselves and why I think electronic security would be a good idea. I don't want to lose my stuff to the zombies!

As far as EMP and radios and security… Here it is right from the government - http://commdocs.house.gov/committees/security/has204000.000/has204000_0.HTM and then the actual EMP commission report from 2008 - http://www.empcommission.org/docs/A2473-EMP_Commission-7MB.pdf

Medicine; we all know how expensive things got once free healthcare that costs you money is…

GOOD FENCES

http://www.doomandbloom.net/ is a great blog, I think I shared it with you before already... but I did score a good find on antibiotics. There's this dude in Thailand that can buy you anything over the counter as long as it's for veterinary use. I'll have to dig his email address out to you, but you should really look it up. You can find that stuff on amazon and eBay also. It's crazy that human medicine costs twice to four times as much as veterinary medicine when it's the same thing in a lot of cases!

The radios are a no brainer, but the security stuff... here's another journal I read: http://theprepperproject.com/how-us-special-forces-would-secure-your-homes-perimeter-when-shtf/

I'm not saying it's going to happen Brian, but I'd rather be ready and raring to go if it does. If it doesn't I have a serious question for you.... Would you play walkie talkies with me? Hahahahahaha-hahahahhaha

I smiled. Randy had a way to cheer me up, and he was feeling pretty good. I figured I'd send him a copy of stuff I liked to watch in return, but I just gave him a list. We often did things like this, often re-sharing the same info over and over. Sometimes we gave each other new stuff to look at.

Randy,
https://www.youtube.com/user/southernprep-per1

http://www.clnf.org/ 7th day Adventist group. Oak Haven compound west side of the State. Where I buy all my bulk food to split up and put into buckets. All except for grains, rice, beans. Everything else comes from there and it's mostly organic. Get an ac-

count, it's free and worth it to buy in bulk and they ship!

http://www.amazon.com/60-Absorbers-De-hydrated-Storage-Survival/dp/B003X87CFW/ ref=sr_1_5?ie=UTF8&qid=1441821010&sr=8-5&keywords=oxygen+absorbers where I get my bags and absorbers to pack in the buckets. Open 1 bag, not expose the other 4 to the air.

http://www.amazon.com/Generic-Impulse-Machine-Sealing-Element/dp/B0077TDLNA/re f=sr_1_1?ie=UTF8&qid=1441821111&sr=8-1&keywords=impulse+sealer This is like the sealer I use. Mine is older and bigger, but it's got to be close. If you want in on packing stuff with me one day, I have an order coming a week from Friday I think.

Ps. I'll play walkie talkies with you, but if your wife gets up and hears you talking dirty to me, she's going to take away your crayons.

I hit send and went to the freezer to get out a bag of frozen veggies. It was my own blend of summer squash, pre chopped red potatoes, diced onions, and thin sliced peppers. I dumped the frozen glob out of the Ziploc freezer bag into a waiting skillet and turned the stove on. I got half a stick of butter from the fridge, dumped it in and grabbed a beer from the fridge. I did some mental math. The butter had probably cost me about .40, the squash, onion, potatoes and peppers came out of my garden and I'd probably put it all on a wrap with a handful of cheese. Some Fajita seasoning and I had a meal big enough for dinner and tomorrow for under two dollars.

Sometimes, living frugal gets addictive, but I doesn't have to be tasteless.

5

hadn't read the EMP commission report before, but it was sobering. I'd always taken at face value how horrible an EMP would be to our lives but this was worse, much worse. I knew I was sitting on a prepper's paradise of land, even though I only used a third of it. I had a house, wells, barn and livestock. I even had stored food and little money to play with, so I set about getting myself ready. The first thing I did was use my tractor after work to first dig deep post holes and set in new posts that were eight feet high. I did this for the entire length of the subdivision and then ended up needing one bigger roll of barbed wire to make sure Landry's kid didn't get back through.

I got a ton of curious visitors at the back fence, some I was meeting for the first time. One lady asked me about the reasoning for putting such a tall and preventative fence if all I was raising was sheep and alpacas. I had to laugh.

"Ma'am, it's goats, pigs and chickens," I told her with a smile.

She wasn't a bad looking woman and she had a cute kid on her hip who sucked his thumb and kept staring at me.

"Then why so high?" she asked, noticing I gave her the once over.

"The Landry's kid got hurt, so I'm putting up a bigger fence so kids don't climb it anymore. I got a lot of property here and if somebody got hurt and hurt bad, I may not run into them for a long time. I figure Robert Frost had it right; good fences do make good neighbors."

The boy had blonde hair and blue-green eyes. He pulled his thumb out of his mouth and gave me a wave, and small streamers of spittle flew with his chubby hand.

"Hey bud, my name's Brian, what's yours?" I asked him.

The kid suddenly got shy and buried his face under his mom's arm and I laughed.

"That's Spencer, he's named after his dad, and I'm Lucy."

"Well hello Miss Lucy, I'm Brian and I hope my tractor work hasn't disturbed you, and Mister Spencer, I hope you and your daddy don't get into this barbed wire here. It's ugly bad stuff, and these bottom wires are hot!"

"Hot?" The little boy asked, one eye now peeking out.

"Hot, like it will zap you." I told him.

He now was looking at me from five feet away with both eyes on me.

"It won't electrocute him, will it?" Lucy asked, sounding a bit nervous with some other emotion tugging at her.

"No, it'll give him a good zap though. My fence is

GOOD FENCES

about three feet from the edge of the property line, so if you're worried he'll touch it you can always build—"

"Spencer was the builder and tinkerer. Now I'm just…"

She started to cry. For all the things in the world to have happened, I didn't know what to make of this. If there were no fence there, I'd know what to do, what was expected, but I couldn't. The toddler who was probably two going on three looked up at her and touched her face with his clean hand.

"Mommy, you said someday we can see Daddy again when we go home to God. Don't be sad, Mommy."

I choked up and looked away. Apparently some dust blew into my eyes, because they watered when little Spencer said that. I wiped the moisture away and turned to look at her and reached through the barbed wire up top. She took my hand and little Spencer reached out and placed his little hand on to top of the pile.

"Have you found a church home since you moved here?" I asked her.

"No, not yet. We're one of the last houses on this side…"

I backed up and went to the tractor and found my notepad with my math and estimates on it and wrote down the address to my church. I scribbled some more down and walked back and slid the piece of paper through. She read it then looked at me funny.

"Your phone number?" she raised an eyebrow at me, her lip quivering in anger.

"Yeah. Listen, I didn't mean it like that. I'm a widower too. If you ever want to talk, I figure you might like to talk to somebody who went through the same thing. If you don't, hopefully I'll see you at church." I told her.

That calmed her and she took a deep cleansing

49

breath, re-adjusting Spencer to the other side and getting a better grip. She wiped the tears away with her free hand.

"How long?" she asked.

How long could have been a lot of things, but I was pretty sure I knew what she was asking. How long since Cathy had died? How long did it hurt, and how long will you still remember them?

"She died almost three years ago now." I told her.

"How long does it still hurt? Does it get better?"

"Lucy, when it quits hurting, I'll let you know."

I started to walk away because the dust was getting into my eyes again, making them water up. Spencer gave me a little wave as I got on the Kubota.

"I'll call you later on!" Lucy said and I had to smile at that. I nodded and waved back.

☣ ☣ ☣

I told the other neighbors who'd come out to ask what I was doing and why. I gave the example of the Landry kid breaking his ankle as an excuse, and no one really questioned that. They all knew my beef with the Landrys, or had to have guessed it based on the complaints that had come from their side of the fence. I got the rest of the barbed wire up that day and, by the time I was done, it was Friday, last day of work again. I was tired and the office wasn't busy. I didn't have any quotes to do that day so I went on Wal-Mart's website and looked up Augason Farms.

I know I shouldn't be dinking around on the internet while at work, but I was salary and never failed to put in long hours as needed. Come 3pm today I was out though. The boss didn't seem to care, even came over and told me to look up Azure Standard if I was looking for bulk stuff. That got me double taking and I looked them up. From what I could tell, it was a lot like Country Life, but they had a HUGE catalog. The problem I found was they didn't ship up by me, so I'd have to take a truck a few hours at a depot drop off. I bookmarked that for later and was about to pull my phone out and text Lucy when the boss came over again.

"So, Brian, in your spare time, you're a farmer, right?"

He knew this, and it made me wonder why he was asking.

"Well, yeah."

"Do you ever read, oh, blogs or websites out there that have to do with natural disasters and stuff like that?"

I was starting to get nervous. I normally don't look at stuff at work, but I'd brought an Emergency Essentials catalog in a few times. I claimed I got it because of the camping sections, but the website is beprepared.com so there was no doubt it also was a prepper's catalog. I just didn't buy food from there much. That's why I was looking at this other stuff, but I was suddenly worried that Mr. Chesil had caught on. It gave me an instant case of the nerves.

"Sure, when you live in Michigan you have to be ready for snow, ice, power outages. Be prepared for about anything," I winced inwardly for using the name of the website.

Mr. Chesil smiled, "Hey, I know it's slow here and I kind of put some things together the past year or two. No, no, don't worry. I just thought you'd appreciate this, especially if you like guns."

"What is it?"

"It's called armslist. It's like craigslist, but for firearms. There's a gun for sale I'm looking at, but I don't know anything about it or if it's a good deal?"

We spent over an hour looking it over, and looking up the specs on it. He even invited me into his office and put the phone on speaker. He talked to the guy and then set up a time to stop out later on before he hung up.

"I'm just getting started with the gun part of my preps. That gun was going to be a part of our group standardized equipment, but I'm not a hunter or shooter. My dad was a pacifist so I never learned them," he admitted.

"Group standard equipment? You're in a group?" I asked him, more than a little surprised.

"Yeah, three families. We've been working together to make sure we're all ready. I sort of got recruited in a couple years ago. I've got the food preps down pat, at least a year's worth for everyone, but what we've been lacking is firearms. My wife is all on board with prepping, but her parents were the same way mine."

I thought I was starting to see where he was going with this and why he was opening up. It shocked the hell out of me, I won't lie, and to go from thinking the other day that maybe Randy was going a little over the top to then somebody I never would have expected turning out to be a prepper…

"But what we don't have is practical knowledge on what to do when the beans, bullets and band aids run out. Our group members all live in the city, and we've started small gardens in raised beds, but none of that would be enough for us to eat from when things get tough."

"Ok?" I said, knowing the hook was coming.

"The group has been asking me for months now to approach you on this, and I've always thought you were probably a prepper, but you're also somebody who can teach us a lot. I don't know how you feel about things, but I'd love to hear your thoughts?"

It was what I thought that they wanted, not that they wanted me in or to teach them. I'd thought he was going to ask me to use the farm to teach them guns.

"I think the world is fast becoming a scary place. It's suddenly open season on Christians across the globe. Our constitution doesn't mean much anymore, and our money is in the toilet. I'm really scared of the Iran nuclear deal, and how suddenly our state is getting flooded with Middle Eastern immigrants that want to change our culture. I think it doesn't hurt to be ready for anything," I said, wondering if that's what he really wanted to hear.

Mr. Chesil smiled and patted me on the shoulder.

"You know, Brian, when you came to work here, you looked half dead. I know you were still mourning your wife, but over the course of two years you've slowly healed. I don't know if it's your prepping giving you confidence or your faith, but you don't look like you're ready to stand on the edge of the cliff anymore."

"I wouldn't do that, not even if I thought it, I couldn't do that," I stammered, a little startled because of how on target he was.

I knew he was right, which only disarmed me further.

"Are you looking for a group? A prepper group to train with, share knowledge and mutual support and aid?"

I had already made the offer to Randy and Kristen. I paused to answer for a minute or two, putting a finger up so he knew I'd heard him and I was thinking about it. Where I lived wasn't ideal, a farm in the middle of a big cluster of houses on the outskirts of a big city, but would a group be able to help in the mutual aid part? I was also shocked to find there were people who believed as I did, and part of me was lonely for company and friends. Randy was good people, and so was Kristen, but part of me had felt dead for so long that it sounded really appealing.

"I might be, I've got two couples I talked to already, but I'd have to speak with them first to see."

"Wait, you have a group too?" Mr. Chesil asked, surprise.

"Nothing organized like you do," I chuckled, "one is a friend and fellow prepper, and the other isn't really a prepper, just somebody I want to help if she ever needs it."

"She? You started to date again?"

I felt uncomfortable because all of a sudden this didn't feel like two guys talking, nor boss to worker, it felt like the strings of friendship and I wasn't sure if it was what I expected at all. Surprise!

"Well, the pastor's cousin set us up on a date and we met for dinner a couple of times. She's pretty awesome—"

"That's great!" Mr. Chesil boomed a little too loudly, making me wince.

"But… We're just friends. I found out though, she works at a gun store and knows more about guns than anybody I know," I admitted, trying not to laugh.

"You're both single, she loves guns and you're not marrying her immediately?" he joked.

"No chemistry. Though I thought about trying to fake a relationship to get the friends off my back, but it wouldn't work. I think she's the first woman I can say I'd only ever have a platonic friendship with."

"Well I'll be! I've never heard of one of those. You

GOOD FENCES

tell me how that works out when the lights go dark!"

"I'll be sure to, Mr. Chesil," I said, turning to put my hand on the doorknob to escape the conversation.

"Listen, you can call me Frank, and hey..." he said pointing towards my desk was, "I don't care so much you check things out at work, but you know..."

"Don't let it interfere with work when we have some?" I asked.

"Yeah, you got it," Frank said smiling.

"You got it boss. Hey, it's Friday, do you think...?"

"Go ahead, we're dead anyways."

☣ ☣ ☣

I was driving home when my cell phone rang. I hit the answer button, then the hands free.

"Hello?"

"Hey Brian, this is Lucy," her voice sounded nervous on the speaker, "I was wondering if you were busy later on today?"

"Naw, I'm done for the day. What can I help out with?" I asked, smiling.

Our first conversation on the phone had lasted three hours and we'd both had a good cry. It was something I'd never admit to Randy or any of the guys, but it felt good. I'd held my emotions in check for so long that the actual release was a bit overwhelming. It hurt, but when I was done I felt like I'd laid part of my pent up grief to rest.

"Actually, I was wondering if Spencer and I could stop out and bring you some dinner?"

My heart dropped down into my stomach. Was I ready for this? The first day I met Lucy and Spencer while working on the fence I had felt something. At the time I hadn't recognized it, and it took me a couple sleepless nights to realize that it was the stirrings of attraction. It took me several days longer to realize that it didn't make me an asshole for feeling that way. I still loved Cathy, but I didn't have to feel guilty about how I felt.

"You know, that sounds good to me. What time are you thinking?" I asked, wondering if I had time to go the store or do a quick cleanup of the house. Other than Kristen and the ladies from Church who had nursed my spirit back from the land of the lost, no single woman had been inside of my parents' homestead. Suddenly I worried about Spencer and if there were things close to the ground the little man could get himself into trouble with.

"Oh, any time. I switched my days off so I have today and tomorrow to putter around the house. I made a mean pizza yesterday and want to see if I can repeat my success. Oh, and wait…"

I heard mumblings of Spencer asking a question, something about goats and chickens.

"Oh, and Spencer wants to know if he can pet the goats and see if you have chickens. He's big into the farm stuff right now from watching his Baby Genius DVDs; it's all he talks about."

"Sure," I laughed, "How about 6 o'clock? I want to stop by the tractor store."

"Ok, sounds good! We'll see you then."

I smiled, excited. I won't lie and say I didn't have butterflies in my stomach, because I did. I turned into the driveway of Family Farm and Home and I think my grin was so big everyone smiled back at me when I walked in. I knew I needed more wire to fence in the back part of the property like I had the side that stood against the subdivision.

I put in an order for three big spools of wire, which

meant my old Chevy was going to be sitting on the fenders if I wasn't careful. I grinned and decided to let them load it and I'd go check the buck board / wanted ads. There was everything from house cleaning, to people selling rabbits, chickens, quail and farm equipment.

That got my attention and, although I had my new Kubota and a ton of implements, it didn't have the horsepower for what I really wanted to do with it. Again, I thought of Mr. Matthews old 70hp diesel, but I didn't have implements to go with that and it would be a huge pain to buy everything all over again.

"Mr. Cartwright, your truck's all set," said the same nervous kid from last time.

"Thanks, I'll probably be back for about 100 poles tomorrow," I told him.

"So that's about two bundles if it's like you got last time. You bringing a trailer?"

Last time, I hadn't gotten so many, but then again I hadn't also bought a third roll of wire either, I'd come back for it.

"Naw, I'll probably come back, half tomorrow when you open, half when I run out of those."

"I'll have them ready."

"Thanks Stan," I said, spying the nametag on his vest.

6

I was on the tractor when I saw a dust cloud bloom on my driveway. I'd gotten the last pallet on the forks when a car I didn't recognize pulled in. I waved and got a wave in return and spun the wheel and dropped the pallet in the barn. I turned the tractor around to drive towards the car to see it was who I'd thought. Lucy was holding Spencer in her arms and the little man was waving so hard I thought his arms were going to fall off. The other thing I noticed was the little black felt cowboy hat. I got a grin from that!

I drove up to them and killed the ignition, figuring the kid would get a kick out of it and pocketed the keys, just in case.

"Hey stranger," Lucy wore a nervous smile.

"Hi Brian!" Spencer said, then realized he'd spoken aloud, and hid his face in embarrassment like he had the day I'd met him a week ago.

"Hey guys, you want to come on in?" I asked, beating the dust off my jeans and walking towards the house.

"Sure, but I've got to get the supplies," Lucy said, handing Spencer over to me.

I almost panicked. I'd held kids before, but we'd only talked on the phone a couple of times and there she was handing me her pride and joy. Then I saw the look she was giving me and took him, swooping him from my knees up to my shoulders in a mock superman. Spencer shrieked in alarm and then laughter and put his arms around my neck as I held him. I shot Lucy a look and she was smiling.

"Don't do that too much, or you'll be wearing his chicken nuggets from earlier," Lucy admonished.

"Yes ma'am," I said and walked towards the front door.

Handing me Spencer had been a test of sorts. I knew lots of guys wouldn't even date a single mother, didn't want to deal with another man's kids. I may have joked about it, but I'd never had a chance to find out before, but I found it didn't bother me. Spencer smelled like baby shampoo and something sweet or sticky.

"Put your oven on for 400," Lucy called out.

"Oh, so who's doing the cooking?" I asked Spencer who was looking at me with wide eyes.

"Mommy is," Spencer said as I sat him down on the couch.

"Do you want to watch cartoons or something?" I asked him, fumbling for the remote and managing to put on the TV.

"SpongeBob?" Spencer asked hopefully, in a voice that sounded a lot like he said "bob bob."

"Yeah, let me see if I can find that…"

"Four then eight," Spencer said solemnly.

I had already hit the guide button, but I followed the

kid's instructions. Sure enough, that was Nickelodeon, and SpongeBob was on. I put it on and backed away, keeping an eye on him but going to the door to try to hold it open for Lucy who I promptly bumped into as she was walking in backwards with two rolled out pizza crusts and a bag of supplies.

We almost lost dinner before we could have it, but I grabbed the doughy crust as it was sliding off and Lucy saved the second one.

"Good catch," I said.

"Not bad yourself," Lucy told me, putting the pans and crusts down on the table. "Did you do the oven?"

"No ma'am. I was uh…" I looked towards the TV; some yellow sponge was making a "bwhahahahahaha-hahaha" sound, "making sure I could get the door by offering your son a distraction?" I said suddenly wondering if Lucy allowed her son TV.

"Oh, he talked you into SpongeBob?" Lucy's eyes sparkled and she was grinning.

"He even knew what channel it was on," I said somewhat defensively, holding my hands up.

"It's his favorite. Here, let me finish assembling the pizzas and toss them in the oven. I'll join you boys in a second," she smiled and gave me a one-armed hug.

It felt good having a woman so close. It felt right. Her smaller frame seemed to fit my tall lanky one perfectly; her head coming to just under my chest. I hesitated for a second then squeezed back, trying not to squish her but not wanting to be lame about our first physical contact. I suddenly realized how ridiculous that notion seemed and broke it off and headed to the couch. I sat next to Spencer who seemed entranced.

"So, who's the pink star guy?" I asked.

Without turning, Spencer mumbled, "Patrick Star."

GOOD FENCES

"Oh."

I heard the oven open and close and, in the time one episode finished, Lucy came over and joined us. She next to me, with Spencer at the other side. I never meant to set things up to be in the middle and didn't know if that was appropriate or…

My phone rang in my pocket and I hurriedly stood up to answer it. My ringtone was a joke, but it was a song I didn't want Spencer to hear. It was the Riff by Lordi, a Swedish band and the song was about zombies. I loved it, but didn't think there would kids around to hear it!

"Hello?" I answered, recognizing Kristen's number.

"Hey, I just left a gun auction. I was buying a ton of ammo for somebody but they backed out on the deal. You interested?"

"What is it?" I asked.

"It's 5.56, military version of the .223 stuff you bought last time. My cousin wants it gone, even if it's at cost because some of it's AP ammo. We don't want that at the shop, but we had to buy a ton of stuff to get what we wanted and that came with it."

"AP? Armor Piercing?" I asked, "Isn't that illegal?"

"This stuff is old enough to be grandfathered. I've got like 1500 rounds. I can give you a better deal than the remanufactured ammo?"

"Sure, sounds good!" I said, suddenly feeling like a man who'd won the lottery. I walked towards the kitchen where the smells of the pizza were making my mouth water. "When do you want me to come get it?" I asked.

"Oh, no worries, I'm actually in town. I thought I'd drop it off," she said, a hint of amusement in her voice.

At the same time, I heard the crunch of gravel and saw a car pulling up to the house. It was a red Acura, same as last time. I almost cursed aloud.

"I'll see you in a second," I said walking out the front of the house and pocketing my phone.

Kristen got out and walked up to give me a hug. I hugged her back, but it was awkward, because I didn't know where Lucy was, or if she was watching.

"Thought I'd surprise you, oh… Ohhh," Kristen held her hand up to her mouth and then a big grin came across her face and she slugged me in the shoulder repeatedly as she laughed.

"What? Owwwww, Dammit," I said confused.

"Um… Hi, I'm Lucy," I heard a voice say from behind me.

I was expecting the worst. I turned around ready to be killed by an evil glare, but Lucy was almost laughing, Spencer on her hip. I heard the car door open and turned back to Kristen, and a younger man, his hair cut short, wearing fatigues got out of the car.

"Howdy," I said, backing up a step so I could see the stranger and put some distance between me and Kristen.

"I'm Ken, how ya doing?" the man stuck his hand out across the hood of the little car.

"Great, I'm Brian. This is Lucy and little Spencer," I said as they joined my side, "Lucy, this is my friend Kristen."

"Nice to meet you," Lucy shook hands with both of them.

"This is my new friend Ken I was telling you about," Kristen said, "He wanted to come on an auction with me and it being a Friday and he's off duty for the next two weeks…"

"Oh, the pizza!" Lucy said, handing me Spencer and sprinting towards the house.

I held the little man, who immediately started to

talk about SpongeBob and trying to get me to go back inside.

Kristen's was laughing. "I gave you a hug and you acted like I was shocking you with electricity. I take it she isn't just a friend?"

I hadn't told her about Lucy. I mean, the date was impromptu and everything.

"First date," I said, "She lives on the other side of the fence, three doors south of Randy. Wait, I'm not sure if this is even a date or… She's a widower, like me," I stammered the words out.

"First dates always give me the jitters," Ken admitted, "Looks like you're doing fine."

"Here, you've got the kid, we'll carry the ammo in," Kristen said.

Back in the house, Spencer asked me to put him down and I wasn't surprised when he ran towards my couch and plopped himself back down, hugging a throw pillow close as the 'pineapple under the sea' song played.

"C'mon in," I said holding the door open.

I knew they must have been hit by the smell the same way I was, and it was heavenly. I turned to take a box from Kristen and saw the kitchen table had been set with five plates. I went with it, watching Lucy deftly cut the slices with a rolling cutter.

"Meat Lover's or Vegetarian?" she asked the room at large.

"Oh well, we were just going to drop off…" This time it was Kristen who stammered.

"I'd love a slice of that meat lover's, please ma'am," Ken walked in and looked around and then gave me a nod.

"One of each for me," I said.

"Vegetarian," Kristen said after hesitation, adding,

"Sorry, didn't mean to crash a first date on you," she patted me on the arm, "but that pizza smells awesome."

"That isn't DiGiorno!" Ken said, taking the place Lucy pointed to.

"Come and eat buddy," she called to Spencer who suddenly got busy and almost tripped himself running to the table.

"I uh, don't have a chair or booster seat." I admitted.

"I'm a big boy, I don't need a baby chair," Spender told me, matter of factly.

☣ ☣ ☣

It turned out that the crust was a sourdough pizza crust she'd been working on and the combination of that flavor plus the butter and garlic on the crust made it one of the best pizzas I'd ever eaten in my life. I had three large slices before I had to call it quits. The bag of supplies she brought had been pre-chopped toppings and cheeses. Regular mozzarella had been improved with feta and a sharp cheddar on the vegetarian. The slices were so thick, I ended up using a fork and knife, something I'd never do unless I was eating in public.

"Oh wow," Kristen said patting her stomach, "that was awesome."

And suddenly the girls started talking, lost to their own world of recipes and baking secrets that men weren't supposed to know about.

"You active duty?" I asked Ken.

He was a little younger than me, and looked like a short version of Arnold. He was all muscle, whereas I was lanky. He was darker skinned to my lighter. I could see how he would catch Kristen's eye. I hoped he was good enough for her, so I figured I'd needle him with questions to make sure he wasn't a creeper and then I wouldn't have to worry.

"Yeah, I've got two more years," he said between bites on his pizza crust, "how about you?"

"Never served," I said, "Thought about it, but got married right away."

"What happened?" Ken asked, his voice low.

"Car accident," I said as softly, but Kristen and Lucy both looked up at me.

I ignored them, and Ken made a pained expression. "Sorry man, I didn't—"

"No worries. Lucy, this pizza was probably the best thing I've ever had," I said, meaning it, but trying to change the subject all the same.

"Thanks, I love sourdough and wondered what would a pizza taste like with flavored sourdough crust; you're eating experiment number three!" She smiled at the compliment.

"I'm betting experiment #2 was just as good," Ken said, proving that the best way to a man's heart is his stomach, and the way to a woman's is genuine flattery.

"Number one was stinky," Spencer called, obviously standing on the couch so he could see over the back of it.

We all chuckled, and Ken asked me about the farm and the animals. I expected Spencer to perk up at that and remember that he was supposed to see them, but after he'd sat down, he'd remained silent. I hadn't seen him for a few minutes.

Kristen told Lucy how we'd found George Jr. limping home and how I'd tossed the kid over the fence to George Sr. I admitted I still felt conflicted and, when Ken started to ask, Kristen gave him a shushing motion. I appreciated that; I didn't want to spend the evening retelling my life story. Ken told us of the faraway places he'd been to; I'd expected him to have been in Iraq and Afghanistan, but he'd been in South Korea for a long spell and then began working at the recruiting station in Downtown.

He'd never married, had just a couple years left to retire - which put him a little older than I thought if he was doing the 20-and-out routine. Some of the stories he told made me wonder if I shouldn't make sure that Spencer wasn't listening in so, when I could, I sneaked over to the couch. The little man was laying on his side, his head resting on the arm rest. He had his thumb in his mouth and my throw pillow over the bulk of his body. Soft snores could be heard over some show about little mermaid people. I grinned.

I felt slender arms wrap around my chest and Lucy hugged me. After a moment, I hugged her back.

"If only he were so good for me when he's at home. He didn't tear one thing up this evening, or have a tantrum. I was worried he'd embarrass me."

We broke the hug and I grinned.

"He's a pretty good kid, I just can't believe he ate one whole slice by himself. That pizza was thick!" I said.

"Hey Brian, I got a favor to ask," Ken called over, looking shy for a moment.

"Sure?" I asked.

"Do you think I could sight in a rifle out here next weekend?"

"I don't mind, but why don't you use the range where Kristen works?" I asked.

"Well, they won't let me use something this big," he admitted sheepishly.

I sat back down at the table. "What do you have that the range won't let you use?" I asked him curiously, "a

.338?"

"Naw, it's a .50 cal. I got a Barrett finally, it's what's in that big hard case in the back of Kristen's car. Heard it was going to be at the auction and begged my girlfriend to let me tag along."

"A .50 Cal? Is it loud?" I asked, smiling.

"Sounds like a mortar going off." he admitted, looking nervous.

"The neighbors," Kristen reminded Ken, putting her hand on his arm.

"I'll be working on fencing all this weekend and next weekend. I have to down a couple trees, but other than that, I think it'd be a great plan. We could do a ton of shooting if you don't mind someone sitting out there watching." I said, smiling big

"Won't that make George Landry pissed?" Kristen asked.

"Exactly," I replied, smiling.

"I can make pizza again!" Lucy said, getting into the spirit of things.

"Oh, so you're… Got it!" Kristen said, finally smiling and getting what I'd been thinking, "How about I bring out my stuff and I can practice as well?"

"The more the merrier!"

We all agreed on the time. We'd start out Friday after work, and meet up again on Saturday. Ken would help me on Friday, and we'd spot the tree I was going to drop, the willow behind Landry's, and Saturday we'd shoot the crap out of some stuff.

7

Saturday and Sunday were spent with the Kubota and going back to the store to get the posts. I got the tractor work done during the coolest part of the mornings, then went out to pick up the wooden posts around lunch time. I'd drop those off near the front loader with the forks and then go inside to eat and nap. In the afternoons I set the poles in, leveling them out little by little. I was able to get 800' of poles set by myself that way, but I was a little discouraged by how slowly it went. I figured out that having to make a ton of trips into town to pick up supplies would be a pain.

Monday, things were still slow at work, so I did some math and figured out what I'd need to finish off the back of the property, then called the farm store. I wasn't surprised when they said they didn't deliver, but I was surprised when they said that Mr. Matthews, a neighbor, would for a fee. That almost knocked me over. I knew the old farmer had a ton of big equipment, but

GOOD FENCES

I hadn't realized that he also did this kind of stuff. I put my order in and paid over the phone with the account I'd not touched.

Improving the farm's fencing and making it safer for everyone would be something that Cathy would have approved of, but I still felt a little bit guilty about touching the account. I got over two dozen of the big rolls of barbed wire, as I didn't want to run hot wire that far from the house, and almost a whole flatbed worth of wooden poles. I winced when they read me the amount, but I knew I had way more than that.

"Ok, Mr. Cartwright, you are all set."

"Thanks, will Mr. Matthews be bringing me the receipt to sign?" I asked.

"If you can come in before closing tonight, we can get the order ready for you so it can go out tomorrow or Wednesday."

"That sounds like a plan." I said, "Thanks!"

A low whistle caught my attention and I turned to see my boss standing over my right shoulder. On it was my notebook with rough math calculating how much wire and posts I'd need.

"You building a fortress?" Frank asked, looking at the hand drawn perimeter where I figured out things.

The farm didn't have normal lots. Like anything else, some were irregular or zigzag depending on the trees. There was a big chunk on the south east side that was all woods, but the open fields were what I was planning on fencing off, maybe letting all the animals roam someday, in huge enclosures.

"Naw, a couple weekends back, a kid jumped my fence to go riding his mountain bike. He broke his ankle, so I'm just making sure nobody else tries." I said.

"Did you talk with your group?" Frank asked, and I

felt like a dolt.

"No, not yet."

I hadn't even talked to Randy, and had let his one phone call go to voice mail. I had either been talking to Lucy or working on the posts. That night I figured I'd start stringing more wire, but I made a note to call Randy and talk to him about groups and the benefits of them. I knew no man was an island and there was no way to stand alone if something happened, so I added that to the list of things to do that night, in addition to going sign the credit card receipt.

"Ok, I was just wondering... Have you seen what's going on in Syria right now? The Russian troop build-up?"

"No, actually I haven't," I said, straightening up.

"Both Russia and China have warships in the coastal waters. Just makes me nervous. I don't like to talk about stuff like this here, but it's got me worried."

"Sorry, I uh... had a date on Friday and sort of watched cartoons when I wasn't setting fencing."

"Cartoons?" Frank Chesil said with a raised eyebrow, "A date?"

"Not the girl I told you about. It was a neighbor. She's pretty cool, has a 2 year old who loves SpongeBob. Figured I'd watch it for research purposes."

"Ahhh, one of the guys in our group has twins who love watching SpongeBob," Frank said. "Hey, is there any way I can talk to you outside of work about this? I'm getting worried, and maybe I can give you some info to talk to your friends about the group?"

"Sure," I said, "Want to come out to my place?" I asked.

"Sure, how does Thursday sound?"

"Actually, that's perfect."

GOOD FENCES

"Good, I'll be in touch," Frank said, clapping my shoulder and going back to his office, shutting the door softly.

"That was weird," I thought to myself, but I was happy to have somebody to talk to about things, other than just Randy.

☣ ☣ ☣

I signed the credit card slip and then checked the wanted boards on the way out, and noticed something that never before would have caught my attention. The old trailer park had some old single wide's they were selling for $400 each. I considered how much time that would save me building a raised ground blind, having something already 4-5 feet off the ground. It didn't even have to have anything in it, just a shell…. But something that big, I could paint it camo and sit in it, going window to window until I found a target. Lazy hunting, but it would put meat on the table. I pulled a tab off the ad and headed out.

Mr. Matthews showed up on Wednesday as planned, and gave me a weird look when he saw all the new work that was visible across the western field. The new poles still stood out as they hadn't weathered yet.

"Good fences keep neighbors good," he grunted.

"Yes sir," I said with a smile and then asked, "Hey, how hard is it to move a mobile home?"

"You thinking of putting a trailer park up in here?" he asked with a raised eyebrow.

"No, I was thinking of putting one up the hill about 100 yards from the cornfield."

He grinned, showing teeth, "A big fancy hunting blind?"

"Yeah, you got me," I admitted.

"I can do it. Is it one of the ones from the trailer park?"

"Yeah, I uh… Yeah?"

"I just got me one of them for the same thing," he smiled.

"How much would it cost to move it?" I asked.

"Well, let's get it here and we'll talk. You want me to bring it Friday or so?"

"I haven't even bought it yet."

"Go to the park Manager, Melinda, and hand her 4 C-notes and tell her I'll be by shortly to pick it up. I'll bring you the best of the lot."

We shook on it, and he got into the cab of his truck and made an expert U-turn in the wide driveway.

I smiled, knowing this was going to be fun. I fished the slip of paper out of my pocket and promised to drop off money on my way to work in the morning. Melinda thanked me and told me she had several ready and if I could put in a good word with Mr. Matthews for her she'd appreciate it.

I had to smile at that. Old man Matthews was probably 70 or 100 years old, depending on who you were talking to, but even the ladies at church seemed to line up to talk to the cranky old dog every chance they got. He reminded me of the Sgt. from Platoon myself, but that was just the way he was. Very gruff exterior and one of the best men and friends, a family could ever have.

"I have so much to do this week," I griped aloud and then got back on the tractor, stretching wire and grabbing the hammer and staples to nail them in place.

"So much to do."

GOOD FENCES

Frank whistled when he saw the pile of wire in front of my barn and the half dozen large bundles of poles stacked haphazardly.

"Wow, when you said you had a farm, I thought what you showed me on paper was it. That was big enough but…" his words trailed off as he looked to the east.

"Yeah, I don't farm all of it, but there's 240 acres left after my parents sold some off for taxes."

"Damn those taxes, they get worse every year," Frank muttered.

"Yeah, and I think it's going to get worse now that damned subdivision has gone up," I said hooking my thumb in the direction of the finished fencing.

"Yeah, it'll probably go up in the next five years or so. Listen I was wondering—"

He broke off speaking as I turned to see who was driving down the driveway. More than once in the past two weeks I'd considered buying a gate and intercom system to slow things down, but I didn't want to seem unneighborly. Friends, as well as the Landrys, would drop in unannounced all the time, and usually when I was arm deep in animal manure or working on a big project like the fence. Still, I had to smile when I saw who it was.

"Oh good, Randy is coming," Frank said.

I turned to him, surprised. "Wait, how do you know Randy?!"

"Hold on a sec," Frank said, walking towards the truck and smiling big as Randy came bounding out, pumping his hand and smacking him on his shoulder.

"Hey, I didn't know you two knew each other?" I asked Randy, looking first to my boss and my buddy.

"Yeah, well. Remember when I said we had a group?" Frank asked.

Oh, wow.

73

BOYD CRAVEN

☣ ☣ ☣

Turned out Randy had been talking and prepping with Frank, for a few years. Because of OPSEC (operational security) Frank was never mentioned and Frank never mentioned Randy.

"I always thought you looked at me like I was borderline kooky when I first brought this stuff up to you," Randy admitted.

"I did, but then I looked at things… Wow. So… was this whole thing set up in advance?"

I had to know. Had Randy gotten me interested in prepping in order to recruit me later on? I was dying to know the motivations, but I also felt a little hurt that my friend had been holding back; or was the friendship simply an effort to recruit me also?

"No, not really. I just can't keep my mouth shut entirely, and I figured if you were interested in it you'd tell me and if you weren't you weren't." Randy shrugged.

"I'm the one who brought up recruiting you one night as we were having a couple of beers," Frank said, "You guys were already friends and you'd already started prepping. I joked to him that the group should go find a big farm and buy it for a bug out location and Randy said he already had a spot at his neighbors."

"You do," I confirmed, "Speaking of beers, I'll be right back," I said, knowing I should have connected the dots when Frank was talking about twins and Sponge-Bob; he'd been dropping me a hint and I missed it!

I headed into the house, leaving them sitting on the chairs on the front porch talking. I figured this would be a long one, so I grabbed a twelve pack of Coors out of the fridge and went outside. I took the chair opposite of them, pulled the box open and handed the beer out.

74

GOOD FENCES

"So you guys want to bug out here?" I asked Frank

"I hope I never have to bug out," Frank took a long pull and looked at the bottle in disgust, "I thought I paid you better than this!"

"It's been a slow month," I said, grinning.

We all clinked our bottles and started to talk again. It wasn't just current affairs they wanted to talk about, it was also their other group member team. One was a Veterinarian who married a nurse practitioner, the Simons'. They both were well to do, but didn't have much practical knowledge other than doctoring. To me, it sounded great in theory but I didn't think things like that would happen, still…

"You know what, guys?" I asked, pulling the last beer out of the box another hour later, "I like the idea of it. Tomorrow I'm dropping a big tree back there, and then I'm going to have a bunch of folks come out on Saturday and shoot some guns, why don't you and the Simons' come out. I'll call Lucy up and we'll do a big potluck on Saturday."

Frank and Randy were all smiles and agreed. It was going to be quite a bit of fun, and if it tweaked Landry's nose a bit, even better. I almost hoped the cops showed up. Nothing to see here boys, move along. For once, it'd be a riot and not the normal grind of all work and no fun.

We finished our beers and Randy and Frank said goodbye, promising to bring their families out. Apparently Frank lived in the older subdivision further down the road near where it split off the highway. All these preppers, all within a 5 mile radius. I made a note to self to text Lucy to let her know more folks were coming. I smiled and enjoyed the beer buzz, my feet up on the porch. I knew I had to go do animal chores before I fell asleep, but sitting in the fading sunlight felt good.

I reluctantly got up and did them, collecting eggs, making sure the critters had water and put in the day's ration of hay in for the goats, along with a few scoops of grain. The pasture was good this year, so they didn't need much, but I liked to check out the animals and make sure the water troughs weren't full of mosquito larva. That done I headed out of the barn, locking up and thumbed a quick message to Lucy on my phone. I got one in return and smiled.

"I can't wait to see you again. Someday we'll have to go on a real date. I'll get a sitter and we can go somewhere fancy like McDonalds or something!"

I snorted and headed in.

☣ ☣ ☣

I wouldn't normally drink four beers at a sitting, and I felt it the next morning. It was becoming a habit that Fridays were slow and slack. Frank pointed at me and gestured to the door, so I got while the going was good. I'd forgotten to pay the park, and I'd just pulled in when I saw Mr. Matthews on his tractor, hitched up to a single wide. I pulled in shame-facedly and waved as I cranked my window down.

"You forgot to pay," he called, grumpy.

"I just came here to do it."

"I gave her money; follow me to your place and you can pay me there," he said and put the old 70 horse in gear.

I gulped and turned the truck around to follow him. I was almost out when a bottle caught my peripheral vision and it smashed into the side of the truck right behind the driver's window. I put it in park and got out, careful of the glass underfoot. I could smell it; it was some sort of cheap tequila. I looked around to see three guys standing there, another one pulling his arm back to make another throw. They were all about 20 or 50 depending on how the shadows played across their features; one wore a white wife beater and the other two had sagging jeans, barely covering their privates. Mr. Wife beater let go of the bottle he was holding and I jumped as it impacted at my feet, showering my legs with booze and glass.

"What the ever loving fuck?" I shouted, walking towards them.

I knew three-on-one odds weren't good, but I wasn't planning on fighting them. Only a fool would take those odds, but I was pissed. I looked back and saw the small dent on the side of the truck where the first bottle had smashed, and I got up close to the men. I vaguely recognized the one in the wife beater; I'd seen him around town begging for cigarettes and generally being an ass. He was usually drunk, and now I knew where he hung around.

"That's my momma's trailer," he slurred.

"Why are you throwing shit at me and my truck?" I yelled, hearing the door to the manager's office open somewhere behind me.

"You took my Momma's trailer," he repeated.

"Yeah, uh huh," the other two agreed.

I looked them over from about five feet away. The one had sores on his arms and neck and was scratching at them, and the other guy was in even rougher shape. They had the look of drug users, tweakers to be exact. Crystal meth had become the drug of choice for many drug users in the area. It was supposed to be cheap to make and give an irresistible high when smoked. But it also turned users into slobbering idiots, like the ones in front of me.

I knew a lot of the folks in the park from church, and they were probably as horrified at these men living there as I was having to deal with them. I knew they weren't an indication of how folks who live in modular or mobile homes are, but these three were prime examples of the types breaking the laws and getting news coverage. In short, they represented the stupid minority who were making it worse for everyone else.

"Don't throw shit at my truck. You do that again, we're going to have problems!" I threatened, pushing a finger into Mr. Wife beater's face.

He swiped at my hand and then swung a lazy fist at me. I stepped back, pulling his arm from the telegraphed haymaker, and he tumbled to the ground, too drunk to right himself.

"That was my momma's trailer. I know who you are, motherfucker." The man child slurred.

"And I know who you are." I said, pushing the one tweaker who started to get too close. He stumbled backwards over the drunk. "Now knock it off, or I'll call the cops on you guys," I snarled, and the last of them backed up.

"We're cool," he said with his hands up.

It was hard to hear him because the drunk in the wife beater was staring to swear up a storm and the tweaker I pushed was making vile threats. I didn't care, as long as they didn't do anything else. I stormed up to the truck, looked at the minor dent and decided to just let it go. It wasn't that big of a deal, and if the dent really bugged me, I could pop it and repaint that section.

"Everything all right? Melinda asked, standing on the other side of my truck by the passenger side fender.

GOOD FENCES

"Apparently that's his momma's trailer," I said, pointing to the guy who was only now gaining his feet.

"Yeah, it was."

"Did they cook meth in it?" I asked her.

Her eyes opened wide and a shocked expression covered her face.

"No, of course not why would you…" her voice trailed off as she looked at the other two and then stomped back towards the office.

"Don't forget to put a good word in for me," she yelled over her shoulder and slammed the office door, most likely to call the police.

☣ ☣ ☣

The old farmer was nowhere to be seen. I caught up with him just before he turned in my driveway and put my flashers on, something I should have been doing instead of dealing with the three guys. Traffic was very light for a Friday, but it was still early, not quite 4pm. I followed him all the way up to the house and the barn and I jumped out of my truck to open the big gates to let him into the back field.

In horror, as the single wide was passing through the gate, I realized that I hadn't set up a spot for it. I shut the gate so the pigs wouldn't escape and waved to get his attention. He slowed down to a stop before the hill and then idled down his tractor. I climbed up the right side so he could hear me.

"I don't have a slab poured for it!" I yelled.

Mr. Matthews shrugged, "It's got two axels. Go get me some bricks."

I ran back to the barn and hopped into the Kubota and drove it out, locking things back up again. On the north side of the barn was a ton of old cinder block and stones from various projects. I quickly filled my front end loader with the most perfect blocks I could find and drove up the hill. I must admit, the whole thing was exciting and worrying. I climbed the hill out behind the house and looked up to see that he already had the trailer in position. I'd given him a vague idea on where I wanted it, but he had it exactly where I'd had thought to place it in my mind's eye.

I pulled up beside him and he looked at me on the tractor and smiled. The grouch gave me a smile?!

"Put a couple under the tongue and we'll jack it up and get it off my tractor," he yelled. I hurried off to comply.

With some sweating and grunting I got everything into place and, with the hand crank, it lifted off the hitch easily.

He motioned me to go towards the gate and I raced down there with a now empty bucket, leaving the rest by the trailer to use to jack up the corners and middle at a later date. I beat him there first with my little tractor and got the gate open. He pulled out and parked his tractor next to the barn, beside the piles of fence posts. He turned the key and hopped off.

"Hey, thanks Mr. Matthews," I said, a little louder than I'd intended. Standing beside the tractor had been noisy and I'd underestimated the silence.

"No problem." He took the keys out of the ignition of the tractor and started towards me.

I pulled out my wallet and pulled out $400 from earlier and gave him that.

"What do I owe you for transport?" I asked, remembering to be a little quieter.

"A ride back to my place," he said, nodding at my

truck.

"Is your tractor getting too hot?" I asked.

"Naw, it's not hot. Runs rough but she's a good girl."

"So, what do I owe you for transport?" I asked again totally confused.

"A ride back. I don't use that beast much anymore and I seen you looking at it with lustful eyes. Truth is, this is probably my last year farming. Going to just enjoy writing my letters and reading books till Jesus takes me home. I figure you can get some use out of it."

The enormity of what he was saying had me stunned, and I tried to talk a couple times.

"Listen boy, I don't have no family left. Me and my wife never had kids. It was wonderful that your parents always included me and Greta in family stuff. I'd always intended to leave your father the farm, but he was taken home too early. Something happens to me, it's already set up to go to the heirs of your parents."

"Is there something wrong? Are you sick?"

I certainly felt sick; I'd had no idea and I was floored.

"No, but I'm 84 years old this year. Farming and watching you grow up are about the two things I loved the most. I'm sorry your Cathy died so young like she did, I was hoping to see you two with some little rug rats, but the Lord took my Greta the same year he took your Cathy. I figure you have enough sense to run things or sell it when I'm gone."

"I don't know what to say., I said lamely.

He opened the passenger door and climbed in, slamming it behind him.

He yelled through the open window, "You say 'yes sir, thank you sir,' or ya get cuffed. Now get yer ass in here before I get ornery. General Hospital is coming on and my DVR is on the fritz."

"Yes sir, thank you sir," I repeated, trying to swallow a lump in my throat.

The ride back to his farm was very short, we were practically neighbors through the fields. I didn't want to talk about it, I was still overwhelmed, but he told me that if anything ever happened to him he had a copy of his will in the credenza of the house and another in the safety deposit box at the bank. It was already signed and notarized.

I just never knew the cranky old farmer thought of us as family. I always knew he liked hanging around, but after my parents died I'd not seen much of him, figuring he was dealing with his grief the same way I was. I thanked him profusely until he turned pink and swore and then he gave me half a hug, barely making contact with me. I was touched.

Driving home, my phone buzzed and I answered, recognizing Kristen's number.

"Hey," I said.

"Hey, we're here now. Did you know there's tire tracks going up the field behind your house?"

"Yeah, just dropping off Mr. Matthews then I'll be right there."

"So I see you bought the tractor you've been lusting after, huh?" her voice betrayed her amusement.

"Naw, I practically stole it," I told her and let her know I'd be less than five minutes.

We hung up and I shook my head not knowing what to think. I was pulling in my driveway as my phone buzzed again. It was Kristen, but she must have seen me and ended the call. Parked beside her Acura and the tractor was a box truck, about twice the size of Randy's cube van. Country Life. I kicked myself, I'd put that order in two weeks before and I'd forgotten. Good thing I had company, but I didn't know if I wanted them to see where I was going to put it. I decided I'd just unload it all to the bench and call it good.

"Oh, hey," I said, shaking hands with the driver who was already opening the back of his truck.

"Howdy. Ms. Kristen there introduced herself and told me you were seconds away," he said, trying not to stare at my friend, but failing.

"Hey Kristen, Ken," I said waving.

I signed for the pallet, counted the number of items instead of doing a hard check through every box and unlocked the barn door so I could start carrying stuff. The driver gave me a quick wave, and shot a look at Kristen again before he climbed back into his cab and made an awkward reverse and then tried to make a three point turn.

"So, how you two doing?" I asked, picking up a big bag of oats and carrying it into the barn.

"Pretty good, looks like you had a busy day," Kristen said.

"You have no idea," I said.

I filled them in. From the trailer park, to Mr. Matthews to the punks and the order and all the work that needed to be done.

"If you're too busy to shoot tomorrow, that's ok." Ken said.

"Oh no, sorry for complaining, it just seems like there's never enough hours in the day and I forget appointments like the Country Life order!"

"You going Amish?" Kristen teased.

"Naw, it's just—"

"He's a survivalist, Kris," Ken said.

I laughed. "Naw, I'm not a survivalist. Timothy McVeigh was a survivalist. I'm just a farmer, or a prepper if you want to use a label."

"Well, it's smart," Kristen said. "I've always wanted to get into it, just never did."

"I've got a storage unit all set up," Ken said surprising both of us.

"A storage unit?"

"It's a unit full of food, cot, composting toilet and some of my extra toys I can't keep in my apartment." Ken smiled.

"Things that make you go boom?" I asked, meaning his guns.

"Guns and my reloading gear mainly."

"Damn. Is everyone in this world a secret prepper?" I asked him.

"No, the zombies are the neighbors who never prepped! Those are the ones you gotta worry about. The rest of us go along to get along."

"What about lone wolves and mutant zombie bikers or whatever?" I asked, referring to my favorite post-apocalyptic fiction.

"Don't worry about them none, if you have a group—"

The gravel crunched and I groaned. I was so getting that gate and I was going to do it right away. Coming down the driveway was a state police cruiser, its lights flashing but no siren. I sighed and walked out.

"Don't pull your gun on this one," I said sweetly to Kristen.

"I didn't pull a gun on the Landry man, though he deserved it, I was just making sure if it came to a fight, it would be a fair one," she grinned.

The trooper pulled in and parked in a cloud of dust.

"I'm so putting a gate across my driveway," I said to them both.

GOOD FENCES

"True that," Ken said with a grin.

"Good afternoon Mr. Cartwright. I'm sorry to bug you again."

"Afternoon, Sir," I replied, not remembering his name from his first visit.

"I got a complaint that you are putting mobile homes in on your property and that you're building fences without a permit."

"I'm what?" I asked.

"I'm just here to field the complaint and write the report."

"A mobile home park?" Kristen asked.

"A hunting blind," I told her.

"Damn," Ken said, "I've got to stick around if it's always this fun here."

8

For the second time in three weeks, I led the cop around my property. I could have told him to go fly a kite or come back with a warrant, but I wanted to get this done and over with. I also wanted to move the pigs again and cut the tree down so Landry could see it. Instead I showed Officer Crabtree (no kidding!) the newly installed posts.

"See, I'm not adding a new fence, I'm making it taller. That idiot's son," I pointed and the back of the Landry's McMansion, "Fell off his bike and broke his ankle. He says he was just using my field for a shortcut to get to the state land back there, but I have no clue where he fell."

"So you're just adding posts between posts to string the wire higher?" He asked.

"Yes sir," I said.

"That Landry is really starting to piss me off," the cop muttered. "What about the mobile home thing?"

GOOD FENCES

"I did buy one and it's up the hill over there. I was going to camo it and use it as a hunting blind."

"Well, let's go see," he said and we walked up the hill, both of us annoyed at George.

"You should have brought me out here before now," Ken told Kristen, "All the fun shit happens around this guy," he laughed and Kristen playfully swatted his arm.

We walked for about ten minutes, getting the cop's pretty blue uniform pants messy from the tall grass and mud, and he looked at the single wide and laughed.

"What is it?" I asked him.

"That's perfect. He can't say shit, even if he wanted to push the issue more," the cop said and then coughed, "I mean, you still have both axels on it, and it's got the tongue attached. As far as I'm concerned, that's a camper/trailer. That can't be more than forty feet."

"I didn't measure it," I said.

"Tell you what, Mr. Cartwright. I've fielded three other complaints from that guy and this is the only one that seemed worth checking on, besides, I live at the sub and the end of the road. I'm off after this. I'll write my report from home and I have the weekend off." He grinned as we turned to walk back.

"Well, your office might get one more call then."

"How's that?" he asked me.

"See that big pile of dirt and the wood and hay bales?"

"Yeah? Your shooting stop, right?"

"Yeah. Tomorrow we're going to light up a ton of ammo."

"Nothing wrong with that," he said, looking at the grins the three of us were now sporting.

"I've got a .50 Cal Barret I'm going to sight in," Ken said smiling broadly.

"I'd like to see that," Officer Crabtree said as I noticed his name tag finally.

He was grinning broadly as he got it.

"In fact, you mind if I come out here with a toy or two and 'practice," he said using his fingers to air quote.

"I don't mind. Fun starts at noon. Bring your own beer but we'll have food and a cookout later on."

"Good, that'll put me here when that jackass tries to interrupt my weekend off. Of course they'll call me, because I live right by you," he smiled.

This worked in my favor, especially as he seemed annoyed with Landry as well. It would be good to have the cop on my side and I regretted how I talked to him and the township cop in my frustration the last time.

"I'll see you then," he said as we finally got to the gate.

"Bring all you want tomorrow, I want it to sound like World War III," I told the pair of them.

"We going to cut that tree down tonight still?" Ken asked.

"How about we just feed the critters and have a few beers? Lucy will be out of work later on."

"You really want to piss that Landry guy off, don't you?" Ken said smiling.

"Yeah, I kind of do. Did Kristen tell you..?" I said not wanting to have to tell it.

"Yeah, no worries bud. I think the fact you didn't kill the kid when he broke his ankle says a lot about you. You seem to be a pretty good guy."

"So, how did you meet Kristen?" I asked him, embarrassed and trying to change the subject.

"Gun show, she talked me into buying a sweet AR Rig," Ken said and I burst out laughing.

Kristen looked a little put off, so I led them inside

and opened my gun safe. I pulled out my new baby and held it up to him, so he could get a better look at it. Ken took it and worked the bolt, then held it up, pointing towards the ceiling to feel the balance.

"Little heavier in the front than I'm used to, but you got a nice barrel on here. Chromed?" Ken asked me.

"Yes," Kristen said, "Some guy wanted an AR for prairie dog hunting. I put this one together myself. My cousin was pissed that I didn't get a deposit when I started the build, but if Brian here hadn't bought it," Kristen pointed at me with a sour face, "I was going to give myself the family discount on it after the gun show. When I saw his eyes light up when he asked for a peculiar mix, I knew I'd have to build another one for myself."

I was still laughing but I had to know, "So you have a matching one yet?"

"No, but come Monday I will."

Ken looked to me and then to the darkening sky outside.

"You know, it's supposed to rain tomorrow," he said.

"I had a job where I was wrong more than half the time like the weatherman does, I'd never have a worry in my life. Besides, I think we're supposed to have a break about noon or so, then it picks back up in the afternoon. I won't be putting much fence in this weekend," I tried to sound disappointed, but it had been a rough week and I was already sore.

"Yeah, after you worrying about it so much, I bet it hurts your feelings," Ken grinned.

I liked the guy. He was on the level and seemed to understand my dry sense of humor.

We shared some beers, though not as much as I'd had earlier in the week, and they headed home. I threw a little extra in for the chickens in their hanging feeder, and did one last check for eggs before checking on the goats and pigs. If it rained hard, most of the animals except for the pigs would head inside to get out of the weather. Just nature of the beast. Some of the pigs did too, but my big old sow loved the rain; she'd stay out in the pen until she was almost completely washed off.

I headed to the bedroom, noticed I'd left the AR out, and took it with me, putting it on the dresser by the bed. I usually locked up everything but my Glock, which I slid into the drawer, but I was tired, worn out and feeling like I needed some sleep.

My dreams that night were about what I was used to. Horrible memories. The crash, then the realization that Cathy was dead. Most times I woke up sweating, sometimes my eyes were wet.

I woke up to my alarm blaring. I fumbled around until I found the button to smack. 4:30 am. I pulled myself out of bed and walked towards the kitchen and turned on the coffee pot. While that was percolating, I headed into the bathroom and took a quick shower.

The dreams usually made it hard for me to pop up, and I usually needed several minutes to get my breathing under control, but not that morning. I chalked it up as a victory and washed the night sweat off myself. I was turning off the water when I heard my old coffeepot gurgle, the sound it made when the last of the water went through the filter. Dressing quickly, I grabbed my laptop for the twenty minutes of catch up time that I gave myself to caffeinate my bloodstream.

The news was full of the Russian troops building up in Syria, and they confirmed that they had "technical advisers" in the country already. Great, another war. I checked out the far right wing stuff that MSNBC loved to demonize but I loved their slant. *Fox, The Blaze* and then *The Drudge Report*. I scrolled through with things quickly, only pausing to get more caffeine. The news was pretty bleak. Things were moving along at a scary rate in the world. China had devalued their currency, which had an effect on our stock market, which caused Europe's stock market to have a bad week as well.

I knew a little bit about the economy, but not enough to know the how's and why's. I did know the Chinese were the largest purchaser of our bonds, which was how the government was keeping our currency afloat, instead of printing more and more money. For all I knew, they were probably doing that as well but, like I said, I only knew the basics. I expected things to get real scary like they did back in 2008 when the housing market crashed and many people lost jobs.

Thankfully I had a cushion I could use if something tragic were to happen to me or my job, but if the currency was no good, what good was it to have it sitting there in the bank, drawing 5/8s of a percent interest? I looked up the prices of gold and silver, something preppers always claim you can't have too much of, and waited for the sun to come up. It finally did and I trudged outside to start my morning chores.

The rooster was already crowing, and the girls were awake and softly clucking at me. I made sure their hanging feeder was topped off, and that the automatic water-er was working, before checking out the goats. Most of them were already outside so I dumped a couple scoops of sweet feed into the bin for them and checked on the pigs. I had to smile. My big old sow Ruby, who I expected to play in the rain, was inside the barn and laying on her side. Her breathing was a little labored. Like a dolt, I checked the calendar I had tacked on the wall and realized I'd forgotten something else as well.

Ruby was due the next day. It looked like she was coming a day early, so I opened the gate to get into the inner pen quietly so I wouldn't attract the others from rushing back inside. Pigs are smart, at least as much so as a dog, and I should have remembered to separate her last night but hadn't. Too much too quick and my brain was scrambled.

"Here, Ruby," I said, walking up and rubbing her head between her ears the way she loved.

She grunted, lifting her head to look at me. A pink face poked its head through the doorway to their outdoor enclosure, and I ran over to slide the inner door shut, leaving me alone with the big sow. Ruby was close to 450 pounds, and the one who I bred every heat. If there was ever an animal that was safe on the farm, it was her. All the rest could go to freezer camp for all I cared, but not Miss Ruby.

"Come on girl, let's get you into your own hotel room," I said, rubbing her side, which was distended and swollen from her pregnancy.

She grunted at me again, then rolled over and got her small feet underneath her and lifted herself up inelegantly. I opened the door and she followed me out. The holding pen and crate were the next stall over, but she wouldn't go in there on her own. I ran to the far door and made sure it was closed, then got my secret weapon out that I kept on the bench: a handful of dried apple chips from Country Life. They weren't hard or brittle, more like leathery. I found out by accident that the pigs loved them even more than the fresh ones.

"Hey pretty lady, you want some of these?" I asked her.

GOOD FENCES

She used her snout to push my leg, almost knocking me over.

"Hey now!" I said, dropping a few on the ground in front of her and walking to the farrowing crate.

She grunted, ate the offered treat and waddled over to me, her eyes begging for more. I tossed them into the back of the pen and she walked in reluctantly, like I was holding a gun to her head. I'd come out in a little while and check on her, but with that taken care of, she was good. I reopened the inner door of the pig pen and walked back towards the house, feeling good about the morning. For two days in a row, I'd forgotten things, missed things. I knew I still had a ton of bulk food on my bench waiting to be packed, but I didn't have it in me yet; I needed one more jolt of caffeine.

I took care of that and checked out some of the info Randy had been sending me. A couple of facts stuck out: at any given point over the United States, there's approximately 5,000 airplanes and jets in the air. It only took 2 jets into the twin towers in New York to kill thousands of people. If an EMP hit, 5,000 jets falling from the sky... I shuddered at the thought and considered what I had here that would survive an EMP and if they were already shielded from something like that...

The windmill, the woodstove. I wouldn't have to worry about the septic system, but I had no way to pump it when it got full. None of my home electronics would work, unless you counted the old radio that was still set up in my dad's den. Randy said it was tubes and crystals, so all it'd need was 12 volts of power. I'd never had any interest in it, but in an EMP event, it would be a great communication device. I got a notepad out of the kitchen junk drawer and a nub of pencil and sketched a want list.

I wanted a small, portable solar panel. I could probably get one from Harbor Freight in town. I wanted some sort of solar setup for the house. Not only because of what could happen following an EMP, but it'd be a great backup alongside the generator in the inevitable power outage that seemed to happen every winter. Ice would build up on tree limbs and cause them to snap and fall on the lines. Even with all the extra time put in by the power companies to troubleshoot problem areas, two or three power outages every winter were still the norm.

So, solar panels. I knew the Saginaw Home Depot had them, wasn't sure if they still did, but I figured I could place an order over the phone and have them delivered. What else? I was all set for food, good on water - if I didn't mind going to the barn for it - and pretty well set for firewood. But I could always use more propane. The only thing it ran was the water heater and stove, but I knew I could use it for supplemental heat in the winter time with a high efficiency ventless wall heater. Those didn't take any power to run, so I added that to the list to buy from home depot someday.

My phone rang as I was draining the dregs of the pot and I got up to answer it. I fumbled around the bedroom, almost knocking the AR off the dresser when I pulled my cellphone off the charger.

"Hey Brian, whatcha doing?" Randy asked, excited.

"Having a cup of coffee, reading the news."

"Oh, so you saw then?" he asked.

"Yeah, and I did some reading on a couple articles you sent me. Pretty spooky stuff my man."

"It is, but don't let the spook bog you down. The key is to be ready for whatever it is and not worry about it when it happens."

94

GOOD FENCES

"Easy for you to say," I said, smiling at his 100% excitement for everything in life. "Hey, if an EMP happens, would solar panels still work?" I asked him, curious because I didn't really know what went into them.

"Yeah, at least during the daytime. You'd have to unhook them at night though."

"Why's that?" I asked, interested.

"They have a blocking diode, kind of like a check valve in plumbing. They let power go down to the charge controller, then off to the batteries, but if the blocking diode is fried, the saved charge can go back and discharge at nighttime."

"So what's the answer, keep extra diodes in a microwave somewhere?" I asked, knowing microwaves were sometimes used as small faraday cages by some of the tinfoil hat brigade I'd come to read more and more of.

"That's one way to do it, but you'd still have charge controllers and all the other stuff to replace too. Faraday cage... I dunno, I think we could build one pretty easily inside the barn."

"Wait, what?" I asked, both excited and confused.

"I mean, I sort of know the theory from when I was in the Navy and we could probably set it up over that concrete slab the buckets were sitting on. Everything inside it should be safe."

"How do..."

"Hey, I'll show you. Do you have any re-rod and old metal sheeting?" Randy asked.

"It's a farm; what do you think?!"

"Ok, I'll head out a little earlier. Is it ok if the Brenda and girls stop out later on?"

"They're always welcome, you know that." I said, remembering the last time the twins were out and how excited they were to pet the goats.

"That sounds great, I'll let Brenda know."

"Oh, Ruby is due anytime now, so we might have some piglets popping out. I bet you the girls would love that."

"What, bacon bits?" Randy chuckled and so did I.

"You head over whenever you want to buddy," I told Randy and then said my goodbyes.

I stretched, my shoulders and back popping. It wasn't much past 7am, but I was ready to tackle my day off. I'd been lazy enough already, so I got my boots back on and headed to the garage where I had my chainsaw.

I'd planned on waiting for Ken, but I could drop the tree and start cutting limbs until folks started to arrive. I took one of my two older quads and a small black plastic dump trailer to haul my gear. Chainsaw, my bucket that held bar oil, files, extra chains and of course a gas can. I worked slowly and let the kinks of the week unwind themselves.

☣ ☣ ☣

Sometimes, there's something magical about cutting firewood and dropping trees. You look at the tree and see the way it leans, how it's connected to the land. Then you look and see where the wind is pushing it. Some people have the knack for dropping trees and some people have a knack for dropping trees on fences and cars. I hoped I was a still part of the former camp, and that Murphy had slept in late that morning.

The willow wasn't as big as some that lined the property, probably only three feet diameter at the trunk. It grew somewhat crookedly, pointing northeast away from Landry's fence. It would be an easy drop, and I wouldn't have to worry about the kid using it to scale my fence any more. Two more reasons I wanted to drop the tree was that Willows are known for dying and getting hollow, dropping limbs and damaging property. I'd avoided dropping this one because it shielded me from George, but it was time to go. The second reason, was it was 7 a.m. on a Saturday and the tree would give George a perfect view onto the back field of the farm I would never sell him.

Maybe he could buy front row seats to the target practice today if the weather held out.

I fired up the saw and started with the lower branches I could reach. I pulled on heavy leather gloves and cut them into smaller chunks before moving the quad and getting ready to do the main trunk and the limbs that were too high for me to reach. I was almost ready to pull the starting cord on the Stihl when I heard George call out.

"Hey!" he called angrily from the other side of the fence.

"Hey George," I said, putting the saw down.

"What are you doing? Do you know what time it is?"

I smiled inwardly, checking off one goal for the day.

"Well, it looks like it's between seven or eight o'clock judging by the sun, not wearing a watch. Safety first you know."

I smiled sweetly at him.

"It's seven thirty in the morning. You woke me up."

"I'm sorry George, I've been up since 4:30, I figured waiting three hours so you could sleep in was neighborly of me, wasn't it?"

"You can't cut down this tree," George said, seething in anger.

"Sure I can. My side of the fence."

George ground his teeth together and I noticed that he was in a fuzzy blue bathrobe and a pair of slip on sketchers. His legs were bare under the robe and his hair was flying all over, no longer in a poised coif he was known for.

"Half of it is on my side, and I don't want to see the trailer park you're putting in back there."

"Oh, yeah, I forgot to thank you for that. The police checked everything out and they agreed that it's a camper and I can park one of those wherever I want. It's agricultural land here still and, unless you try to rezone me, for which I can get an exemption, you've got no leg to stand on."

"The HOA policy about trees states—"

"George, I'm not part of your home owner's association. This is my family's home and land. We've lived and farmed here for 3 generations," I said, leaving out the part about how I had been led to come home because of his son, "and you built a subdivision next to a farm. I'm sorry, but farmers' farm and you are complaining about farm stuff. So, too bad George." I said, firing up the chainsaw.

I made two or three small cuts to make a wedge, then started to cut from the back side of the trunk. I got most of the way through when I heard the snapping and popping. I killed the saw once I'd pulled it free and backed off in case the base of the trunk kicked back at a bad angle. The tree fell exactly where I wanted it to and I swear I felt the ground shake a little. I heard a ton of cussing and swearing and smiled when I looked over at George.

"This is unacceptable! I'm going to call the police!" He shook his fist at me through the fence. I noticed his free hand was on the fourth wire, the first string of

GOOD FENCES

barbed. Too bad he was one too high, or it might have been funny.

"Go ahead. I don't need a permit to drop a tree on my land, nor do I need your permission, George. You don't own everything around here. For all your money and power you've been trying to get me to change ever since you put that house in. Why? Why here, why by me?"

I was genuinely curious about it, and since he seemed to be a captive audience…

"Because the land was cheap, because it was zoned perfectly. I didn't know your family farm was here, when I first looked at building this goddamn subdivision, you weren't even living there. You and Cathy were living in a condo in town and…" he trailed off.

"Yes, Cathy and I were living uptown in a condo. Once she died, I never went back there. I couldn't. Too many memories, but you wouldn't care, would you? You screwed me every chance you got and you're trying to do it all over again." My voice was growing loud, and I heard a couple of doors open as people peeked out.

Great, I was attracting even more attention. I thought it'd be fun to piss off George, but all I was doing was getting angry myself. That wasn't what I'd intended.

"Listen," I said quieter, "There isn't much you can do about any of this. Why don't you just be a good neighbor and leave me the hell alone? Besides, you're standing on my property. I'd like you to step back."

He looked at me in confusion. "What are you talking about?"

"See those stakes with the white paint on them? Those are my property boundaries. I left a three foot buffer in my electric fence so I can weed whip the back side so the weeds don't short out the…"

99

Instead of backing up, George walked forward, red in the face. He grabbed the wire and stuck a meaty hand through, a finger already pointing in my face. What he did differently that time, however, was grab the third wire, the smooth wire. The electrical wire. He jerked his hand in shock and tried to pull back through the barbed wire, digging a long furrow in his arm that immediately started to bleed. He cursed again, shaking his arm around.

"Sorry George, but if you weren't messing with my fence and trespassing, you wouldn't have gotten hurt. I asked you to back up, but I guess your son got his common sense from you, huh?" I asked, needling him.

I know it was a horrible thing to say, to take a poke at his kid like that, but he needed to understand the world didn't revolve around him. I pulled the starting cord on the Stihl and cut the willow stump down some more. I'd come back in a couple of days and drill deep holes and fill them with kerosene before lighting it, hopefully killing the tenacious tree. Otherwise I'd be back out in a couple years redoing things as it grew back from a sucker.

By the time I made my last cut on the stump George was gone, but two neighbors north of him were outside and waiting at the fence line.

"Mister, it's really kind of early for that," a young man in a suit and tie said.

"I've been up for a few hours now," I said, "I waited to do this but I don't want to wait until it gets hot around lunchtime."

The man considered that thoughtfully, "I suppose I see your point. Is that why you're always up and about so early?"

"Well, yeah, I mean… this is a farm so there's always

a ton of stuff to do and I try to get the worst of it done when the heat isn't so bad."

"I'm a lawyer, we tend to stay indoors... I was already up this morning, going over a brief for Monday. It didn't wake me up, but it did my wife. She wanted to come out here herself..."

"Sorry about that, this is really the last big project next to the subdivision's side of the fence for the season. The only other noise you're likely to hear is when I use the rifle range out back."

"Rifle Range? I thought you were a fireworks guy. You shoot guns here?" The man looked scared.

"Well yeah, and I hunt with them, use my bow and arrows... you know?" I said, not understand how a guy from Michigan seemed horrified.

"There's really no need to hunt for meat if you're already raising it, is there?" he asked, staying clear of the fence. Good, he must have learned by George's example.

"It adds variety, different health considerations," I said not wanting to add that it was also a sport; some people don't get that part.

"I just don't think anybody should ever need guns. I'm going to check into the zoning, you shouldn't be shooting this close to the houses," the lawyer said, a bit perturbed.

"Sorry you feel that way, but the law says 300 feet from any occupied dwelling. I am over 600 feet away from them so there's nothing I'm doing that's illegal. I've even had the cops come out and verify the legality of it," I said, not mentioning that the cops had been called on me, not that I invited them.

"Well, zoning and laws can change," he said, before turning and walking towards his house.

"Good luck with that," I called after him.

"Hey Brian," I heard a familiar voice call a ways off.

I walked down the fence line and saw Lucy with little Spencer sitting on his place near her hip.

"Hey Lucy, good morning."

"You had to go and poke the bear, didn't you?" she asked, smiling.

"Yeah, and I realized it wasn't as much fun as I thought it would be. I'm going to chop the rest of the limbs up and work on taking it to the wood pile later on today or tomorrow."

"What if it rains today?"

"Well, I suppose we'll still have a bit of a party, especially if you promise to make some pizzas like last time!" I grinned and Spencer grinned back at me, before Lucy smiled too.

"Sounds good. I forgot to set my alarm, so your saw was a godsend. I've got to get the dough mixed so it'll rise by noon.

"Ok, but it doesn't have to be ready by noon, that's when folks are showing up." I told her.

"Looks like you've got company," Lucy said, and I turned to see the shape of a cube van coming down my driveway.

"Randy's up early too. Hey, you're welcome to come out whenever you want, you don't have to wait until noon."

"We'll see. Both Spence and I need a bath first. I'll be over soon enough, Farmer Brian," she gave me a warm smile.

"Bye," I said, my face already hurting from the stupid grin on my face.

9

The weatherman was only half wrong. Randy and Lucy came early, and everyone else showed up at noon, and we all set out to go shoot up some targets. I set up a line of steel targets for the regular guns, and a couple paper targets for the .50 cal. Ken and I got our guns zeroed in and were grinning like fools when Officer Ben Crabtree stopped in, bringing what looked like a genuine M16. He laid it out on the table and Randy and Ken talked with him about it nonstop.

I sat back at the picnic bench as Ben started to shoot. He was pretty good, and he ran it with three shot bursts and then on full auto. Kristen and Lucy were smiling, and Spencer, who was wearing a spare set of ear protection I had from when I was a kid, was looking at everything and clapping and cheering. The kid was really into it, and the only thing that bothered him was the boom of the .50.

We all traded and I got a chance to try out the M16,

the trooper tried the .50 and then we switched again. The clouds were starting to darken and the wind picked up, so I packed up my stuff. We headed back to the house to put our guns up and get the pizzas started in the oven. We were headed in my front door when Liz pulled in with the twins and I walked into the house and put the TV on SpongeBob.

Ben's cell phone rang, and he laughed when he saw the caller ID. He answered it, and it was his Sargent calling in, to ask him to check on shots fired at the farm by Ben's house. He told the Sarge that he was here, and had in fact been target shooting with friends. Said the range was safe and he'd take cell phone photos if proof was needed. The Sarge had nothing else to say so he hung up and that was it. George was neutered. We all joked and laughing about the incident and I told them about the tree earlier, and how I kind of felt bad he got cut up. They all agreed it was instant karma for George.

None of us thought that George would have called both police departments, but the local cops showed up just as the sky let loose and thunder boomed, rattling the old storm window frames. I smiled and welcomed both of them inside, to get out of the rain. Immediately they saw my new buddy Ben Crabtree of the Michigan State Police and all of the hard sided gun cases lined up on one wall.

"Kick your shoes off boys, come grab a plate," Lucy said, starting to cut the first pizza that had come out of the oven, already switching it out to put the second one in.

"I don't know ma'am, we're just here to see about—"

"Is that pepperoni?" the younger cop asked.

"Here you go hun," Lucy almost pushed the plate into his hands.

GOOD FENCES

He looked at his partner, shrugged then kicked his shoes off and sat at the table. His first bite had him rolling his eyes up into the back of his head in pure cheesy pleasure. I can't say I blame him, I was almost dying from anticipation and the smell was heavenly!

"Oh my ghhwehsh. Thwis is wsoooo good," he mush mouthed around the big bite.

We all laughed and I went over to Lucy, putting my arms around her and pulling her to me in a hug. I needed it, and she didn't resist at all, so she must have too. The older cop's professionalism was put to the test, but he reluctantly kicked his shoes off and grabbed a plate from Ken as he handed slices out.

"I don't want to eat up all of—" the younger one protested weakly as he finished his first slice and was offered another.

"Oh don't worry about that," Lucy said, "I've got one more in the oven with two more to go in. I heard Randy's girls were going to be here and I know my little monster has been asking for pizza all week. So eat up, and tell us what we can do for you today?"

"Well, we got a phone call about shots fired, but it looks like you all were doing some target practice. Besides, the state boys already beat us here it looks like," he said nodding to Ben, who was eating a slice himself.

"Yeah, we fired off a couple thousand rounds until it looked like we were going to get rained out. I don't know, maybe more?" I answered.

"I'm guessing that nobody fired off a bazooka?" the older cop asked with a straight face, "or maybe pipe bombs?"

We all looked at each other, and a pregnant silence ensued until we heard from the TV "bwhahahahahaha-hahahhahahahaha" as SpongeBob busted up laughing

105

in an annoying voice. That set us all off laughing, and the cop who asked turned a little red in the face.

"Look in that big pelican case there," Ken said.

"Naw, just tell me," the younger guy replied from his seat at the table.

"I got a Barrett .50, needed someplace to sight it in."

That did it, the two cops were suddenly all smiles and after they had finished two slices apiece they went out to the covered front porch so Ken could get it out and show it to them. I finally had a slice from the second pizza and sat down next to the twins. Spencer was sitting in the middle, leaning into Ashlyn… or was it Lindsey? He looked half asleep.

"Looks like we may have a sleep casualty here. Want me to bring him over for a slice?" I asked Lucy.

"No, if he's hungry, he'll tell me when he wakes up." Lucy came over and sat on my leg, leaning back into me.

I had to put my arm around her so she wouldn't fall and we suffered through an entire episode where SpongeBob lost his identity, or name tag. Still, I was mildly amused and some of the humor seemed above the kid's heads the same way that the old Loony Tunes did when I was a kid. Things seemed to be moving fast and I was a little worried. When Lucy and I hadn't been spending time together lately, we'd been talking on the phone. It wasn't much, but we both fell into a comfortable closeness that had never turned more intimate than a hug.

"Awwww, look at em," Kristen said and Lucy stood up quickly, a flush already coloring her cheeks.

Kristen was looking at the twins with a now sleeping Spencer leaning into them.

"Randy, your girls are stealing from the cradle," I said over the back of the couch and both Kristen and Lucy slapped my shoulder.

GOOD FENCES

"Abuse, Police!" I said, but not too loud; I didn't want to wake the little man up.

☣ ☣ ☣

The cops left and we all got to talking. Lucy and Kristen were the only non-preppers in the group, but Randy's wife Brenda was working on that. At some point, somebody produced a deck of cards and we paired off into Euchre teams and spent the entire afternoon and evening eating leftover pizza, playing cards and having fun. I couldn't remember ever having a house full like this. A lot of new friendships were made, a lot more friendships got closer. As the kids got more food and the twins tried to teach Spencer how to play the board game 'Life', the grownups talked about scenarios why preppers prep.

I admitted how ill-prepared I felt and how I thought things were a bit kooky at first, but lately it had been making more and more sense. I talked about my list and Randy popped up from his seat to run to his truck. The faraday cage! I told him to sit down, I had no plans to go out in the rain until I had to, and that was mainly to check on Ruby girl.

"What's wrong with Miss Ruby?" Ashlynn asked, concern in her little voice.

"Oh, she's due to have some babies today or tomorrow. I've got her in the separate pen now."

The kids all started talking at once. "I want to go see!" "I want to go too!" "I like piggies!"

We all shared a smile and, for the first time, the rain let up. It didn't stop but it wasn't pounding so hard. I know when God's listening, because everyone turned to look at me smiling.

"Ok, let's go."

☣ ☣ ☣

Six pink piglets were rolling around in the hay near Ruby. I wasn't sure if she was done or not, so I didn't let anybody in or near her. I warned the kids that pigs could be dangerous if they got a mind to be. Instead, I let the twins throw apples to her as long as they were careful not to hit her or the babies. Ruby ignored them, which told me she was either just done having birth, or had one or two more.

"Goat babies!" one of the twins yelled and the whole party moved over to the goat pen, where all the goats were standing together, some of the baby Nubians jumping on the backs of the adults to see the humans that came to play with them.

Those guys took every offered apple and begged for more, causing such a ruckus I was worried it'd disturb Ruby. I finally convinced the twins to stop when I suggested that they could go and collect eggs from the hen house. It was one of their favorite things to do, and I should probably have asked Randy first, but he just nodded and shrugged his shoulders. They both darted in, alarming the chickens and making feathers fly, but they came out all smiles, holding half a dozen eggs each. I made sure everyone had water and we walked back to the house.

It was one of the most memorable days I'd had, and I felt bad I hadn't seen Frank. I thought I'd invited him, but my memory has been sucking lately. Maybe he just got busy and couldn't make it.

"You guys want to do this again next Saturday?" I asked hopefully.

Everyone did, and I made a note to self, and mentioned it to Randy to have Frank come out. It was almost nine when everyone finally left, leaving Lucy, Spencer and I alone in the house. I suddenly felt a little nervous. We'd had a first date, we'd shared hugs and it was the first time we'd really been alone together, unless you counted the times we'd stood at the fence talking, or a quick visit. I decided to check on the kiddo, and he had fallen asleep again after consuming his weight in pizza, his hand on a car still on the Life board game. I smiled and picked him up, putting him on the couch.

"Here, I'll help," Lucy said kneeling down to help me get the board game put back up.

Our heads bonked and we both stood up laughing and rubbing them. My eyes locked with hers and she leaned in. Our first kiss didn't end the world, nor blow my mind, it just made me forget everything. I finally opened my eyes and stepped back a step. She smiled and then turned away and went to the kitchen, tears showing in her eyes.

"I'm sorry, I didn't mean to…" I said.

"Just, give me a second."

I tried to. I finished picking up the board game and put it up. When I turned, Lucy was sitting at the kitchen table and was patting the chair next to her.

"Don't take this the wrong way Brian, but I can't do that again. Not so soon."

I knew what she meant. "Yeah that was wonderful… But… does it feel like it's moving too fast?"

Lucy nodded.

"It's ok, I totally understand." I told her, and I did, I was feeling the pangs of guilt myself.

"You do?"

"It feels like a betrayal. I don't know. Maybe I'm being stupid," I said walking away from the table a minute.

"You know, I really like you, Brian. I know that

109

seems fast, but let's take this slow."

I turned back to her, smiling. "I'm not going anywhere. Let's be friends first," I said, "Until we're both comfortable."

"Sounds good. Give me a hand with the little man so I can pack up and get out of here?" Lucy asked me, smiling.

"Yeah, that's no problem!" I went over to the couch, and turned off the TV before picking up Spencer.

We got him buckled in for the short drive and I confirmed that she was going to follow me to church the next day, and we'd talk in-between as needed.

The kiss had been unexpected, in that it had awakened emotions in both of us that we hadn't expected to feel. Maybe we weren't ready to feel them, but I knew would feel better about things when we could figure it out.

I watched her tail lights fade as she drove off, and wished I hadn't put the fence in along her stretch. It'd be nicer to just walk her home. I thought about checking on Ruby, but decided to wait till the morning. I'd do the dishes up and head to bed early. No conspiracy theories, no news... Just contented sleep.

I grabbed the AR and laid its case on top of my dresser in the bedroom and put the Glock on my nightstand.

"Groovy," I mumbled, crawling into bed.

☣ ☣ ☣

That night, I dreamt of something different. It wasn't a guilt dream at all, it was more of a continuation of what the day could have been if it hadn't rained. We were all outside, all the families playing, working and laughing.

GOOD FENCES

I was confused as to why this moved me so, but then I realized it was the sense of family I had been missing all this time.

☣ ☣ ☣

Church was good and, as I was trying to sneak out of there quickly, the pastor stopped me when we were shaking hands.

"Is this Miss Lucy and Mister Spencer with you?" he asked.

"Yes sir." I admitted, smiling.

"Kristen finally saw fit to fill me in," he dropped me a wink, "but I have an unrelated question for you. The Sandersons are having a bit of a hard time and the father just lost his job. They were asking me if anybody needed any construction work done and I know you do construction…"

I didn't, not really, but something clicked. The mountains of work that wasn't getting done, the pile of money that only grew even if it became worthless. Projects and prepping I really wanted help with. Non mission-critical stuff.

"Have them give me a call. I probably have enough work for him and his three sons for about a week while I work on my boss," I said.

"Wonderful! I'll let him know."

Lucy and I headed out with Spencer, who insisting on walking by himself. Lucy almost had to bend her knees to hold his hand, but she made it to the doors I held open for them and I walked them to their car.

"What are you doing this afternoon?" she asked.

"More fencing. How about you?"

"Thinking about Lasagna and a movie. Interested?"

Was I?

"What time?" I asked.

"Dinner's at 6. Give you some time to get farm work done."

I agreed and we headed our separate ways. I was just pulling into my driveway when an unknown number rang my cell. I answered.

"Hey Mr. Cartwright, this is Brandon Sanderson. Pastor said you might have some work for me and the boys?"

"Hi! Hey, yeah I do actually. You any good at putting in a fence?" I asked.

"I've put in a ton; chain link, wrought iron, you know... Pretty much anything. Must be a pretty big fence if it's a week's worth of work though."

"It's an eight foot tall barbed wire. I already have post holes dug, just need some strong arms, backs and a good crew chief to do it. I've been at it for two weeks by myself and I'm about whipped."

We talked a bit more, and soon he was out at the farm with his three kids. They started that afternoon, which suddenly freed up my day. I dug out my list and decided to head towards Saginaw to hit my favorite store. Home Depot. I could get there, buy some toys and get back home in time to unload, clean up and go to Lucy's house.

10

The next week flew by in a hurry. Not only did the Sanderson's finish the section of fence I wanted, I had them put in fencing all the way around the Farm. Brandon Sanderson asked if there was more they could do, and I know what it feels like to be broke, and there was one more project I wanted done so I told him yes. If he'd go to Family Farm and Home and buy two of the biggest heaviest gates and opener he could, I could probably keep him busy through Friday. Sure enough, as I was leaving a little late on Friday I got a text saying they were done.

I'd already pulled money out of the bank to pay the Sandersons in cash, so I didn't have to declare it if they didn't want me to. They'd worked very long hours to get things done and I'd gone through a surprising amount of materials. Still, it was worth it for my peace of mind.

"Hey Frank," I said, opening his office door.

"Hey Brian, come on in," he said with a smile.

"A bunch of us are going to meet up tomorrow at the farm and shoot some guns and stuff. It's BYOB and potluck style. Interested?" I asked him knowing that we'd already broken through the boss/employee barrier somewhat.

"Sure, what time?"

"If the weather holds out, how about noon-ish?"

"I'd love to! Thanks for the invite."

"Great, I'll see you then!"

"Have a good Friday!"

I left and headed to the farm store to sign my credit card slip for the day. I'd had the Sandersons pick up the materials but I had to go in and sign for it. It'd been a habit as a ton of projects were finished, including a little 10x10 room in the barn on the other side of the far-rowing pen. It was a small faraday cage built to Randy's specs, and I planned on storing stuff in there. I signed my tab and headed home to find my way blocked by two big industrial sized gates that looked heavy enough to stop a rampaging Ruby. A chromed chain wrapped around it, with a Krieg padlock holding things together.

"They didn't have an opener big enough," Brandon said from the other side of the fence.

I was grinning and grinning big. This was awesome. The tubing on the fence was easily two to three inches thick, powder coated in a blue color. The wooden posts next to the steel ones were eight feet tall and the gates were easily six foot tall.

"I don't think that pig of yours can escape from this," Brandon said.

I blamed a rampaging Ruby for my wanting such heavy gates, but in truth, it would be fun to have an afternoon not interrupted by George's antics. Speaking of which, I hadn't heard from him or about him or anything to do with him for some time. They handed me the keys and I unlocked the gate. I pushed one side open and it swung smoothly, level.

I saw that they had used my Kubota to regrade the road so the gate was a close fit to the ground. The balance and level was perfect, so what was probably 300lbs of steel swung as smoothly as a car door.

"The propane company stopped out today, you have a new tank and a second truck filled it. They said you didn't want this one hooked up yet?" Brandon asked.

"Yeah, I'll do that when I figure out how I want to use it. I'm thinking about a propane back-up generator someday, but honestly, with the prices of propane going up, I figured since I'm spending some of Cathy's money, I might use part of it as an investment against inflation," I told him, testing the swing of the gate again. "This is awesome," I tried not to jump up and down in excitement. I told them I'd be right back, and went to the safe in the house and got the cash to pay them - with a big tip each.

Their eyes were huge as I counted out the week's wages to each of them, and promised to call them when I had more work, or if they were interested in firewood cutting and splitting. They were.

"But, tomorrow I'm going to talk to my boss. He's heading out this way and I can show him your work in person."

"Really? That'd be great, and the boys here?"

"They look pretty good to me. I just do quotes, I don't swing hammers for a living, so it'd be to a different boss or crew, nothing I know much about actually."

"Thanks Mr. Cartwright," I heard from four different voices.

We all shook hands and the boys whooped and

laughed in happiness as their old pickup truck left. I locked my new gates and headed in. I'd have to get a sign. Something snappy like... Call first... or do you have an appointment? With all the new fencing up, I was definitely going to put up no hunting and no trespassing signs. Even my section of woods was fenced off, though eight foot of fencing wasn't going to stop a whitetail deer. Still, it felt good, secure.

I headed inside and grabbed a beer and sat down on the front porch. Gone were the piles of fence poles, the 400lb rolls of wire, and I was able to fit both tractors inside the barn. I was sitting comfortably until I remembered that I had a half a pallet of solar stuff and two wall heaters I'd bought the past Sunday that I wanted to put in there until I figured out where I wanted to set things up, and while I was up, I might as well go check on Ruby.

She'd ended up having 7 piglets and they sure were growing fast. With her new brood and the 4 grow outs, I was soon going to be over crowded. I knew it was time to call the abattoir, but I hadn't gotten a ton of people pre-purchasing the pork. It'd all sell eventually, but I might have to pay the abattoir some freezer space. I finished my beer as I looked at the pile of dry goods I still hadn't done, and the new faraday cage. It was a simple enough affair, a metal double insulated room that was grounded to the floor. According to Randy, it'd work no matter what. I believed him, and moved the cardboard boxes of solar panels inside it.

I'd got a charge controller and some other do dads that Randy said I needed, and I put those in there also. While I was at it, I considered the impulse sealer but decided I'd better use it first. I reluctantly un-tarped my supplies and did my least favorite part of prepping. The mind numbing process of putting away food.

GOOD FENCES

I tore open the bag of rolled oats and got a bucket and 6 gallon liner out and filled the bucket. When it was done, I sealed the top, put a lid on and kept going. Each 50lb bag of oats was 2 ½ buckets, so I ended up storing five in all. Then it was time to split up the nuts, which were basically shelf stable. I used 1lb bags and filled a bunch of them up. I'd drop in an oxygen absorber and then seal it quickly until I finished a box. Then I'd put those nuts into buckets. I'd layer them in a fun way. One layer was peanuts, pecans, cashews, almonds, pistachios etc. Then I'd make the same layer on top of that until the bucket was full.

My phone chirped, alerting me to an email or text message, but I kept going. I was just about finished when it rang with Lucy's distinctive ring tone that I'd assigned to her after Sunday. I wiped my hands clean and answered.

"Hello there," I said.

"I was going to stop in and surprise you with a salad and some company, but there's this big ugly gate blocking you off from the road."

"Isn't it a thing of beauty?" I asked, already moving towards my Chevy.

"Men," she said with a giggle, and hung up.

I knew she was expecting me to go let her in and I didn't plan on disappointing her. I shut and locked the gate behind her and she followed me back to the barn.

"I just have to finish a few things up in here before we eat," I told her, returning to my bench with the bags and sealer.

"What's that?" Spencer asked, seeing the stacks and stacks of buckets.

"Just some rainy day supplies," I told him.

I walked over and found a miscellaneous bucket

that I'd never put a lid on and found the foil pack that I was looking for right away. I ripped it open and handed it to him.

"What's that?" Lucy asked me suspiciously.

"Ice cream," I told her with a grin.

Lucy pushed me aside and grabbed the foil packet, "Never get between a woman and ice cream," she instructed, and took a bite of the freeze dried treat.

"Oh wow, this is pretty good," she said, handing the packet back to Spencer.

I'd made those small foil packs with kids in mind, and apparently it wasn't a bad idea because the kiddo put one in his mouth cautiously to test it out. He then began to devour it and I had to laugh. I had about ten more minutes' worth of work to do and I knocked it out while Spencer and Lucy checked out all of the animals.

"Babies," Spencer told me solemnly as I was putting things away, brushing off the desk and throwing away empty bags.

"Yeah, we got quite a few of them here at the farm, don't we buddy?" I asked him.

"I want to be a farmer too!" Spencer said, all grins and smiles.

"Yeah, well farming doesn't make you a lot of money, you know," I told the little man.

"I want to be a farmer," he insisted.

Lucy petted his head. "So you shall be. Come on, looks like Brian is done. Let's go eat before the salad goes bad."

We headed in and, after washing my hands I sat down. Spencer was eyeing the salad with a face of skepticism and I had to laugh. I never used to like eating it either, so I could understand.

"I don't want this," he complained.

I knew it! "Hey buddy. Looks like mom put some chicken nuggets in yours," I said, pointing to the chopped chicken.

"Yup," Lucy said, shooting me a grateful smile, "and it even has branch on it," she said putting the sauce over his salad in his kid size bowl.

I assumed branch was Ranch, because that's the dressing we were using.

"It's yucky."

"If you don't want to eat it, I will," I said stabbing another forkful and taking a big bite.

The kid looked at me skeptically. Then he got ahold of his fork in his little fist and stabbed a piece of chicken. The salad wouldn't fly off, so he shoved it in his mouth, leaving a white streak of dressing on his cheek. His eyes went wide and he smiled, almost showing me his food.

"Good?" Lucy asked.

"Umm huh," he said, stabbing another forkful again.

"Listen Brian, I wanted to ask you about tomorrow..." she began, referring to our get together.

"Sure?"

"A couple of the ladies I met at church were wanting to take me to the mall. I don't really have any other lady friends around here being new. Would you mind if..."

"Hey, that's understandable. If you want, leave the little man with me and go have a girls' day. We'll have a lot of fun, maybe rope Kristen and Brenda to go with you too?"

"Wait, I wasn't asking you to watch Spencer," she said, looking concerned.

"Oh, sorry." I hoped I didn't just cross a line or push a boundary, I was trying to go slow... uuber slow.

"Well, I was going to ask if you didn't mind if I went with them. I'm not big into guns, really. I'd be home in time for food, and…"

"I don't mind, Lucy," I said, putting my hand over hers, and then took another bite to eat.

"I want to stay with Brian if you go," Spencer spoke up between bites, "He doesn't put a timer on Sponge-Bob!"

My eyes went wide and Lucy flushed in embarrassment. It took me a second to understand, but then it was me who felt it. I wasn't not used to kids. I'd never had any, and I was an only child. I just treated Spencer like he was a people. Not a little kid, nor a grown up. He walked and talked very well for his age, and I sometimes forgot he was only 2.

"I'm sorry, I didn't know you limit TV time," I said after a moment of silence.

"It's ok. I just don't want to be that single mom who uses the TV to babysit her kid. I don't mind when he's here, it's a treat and he knows it. I think he's turning out to be a little manipulator actually," she said, poking at his nose.

He pretended to bite at her hand and she laughed, pulling it back in play and making sure all her digits were still there.

"Truly though, I don't mind. He's potty trained and the place is in top shape after the Sandersons helped me get caught up on a ton of projects."

"I noticed that. Is that new fencing?"

"No, just reinforced the old stuff that was there, making it taller. I originally only wanted to do the North fence," I admitted, "but they are out of work. The factory the four of them worked at just closed down and Mrs. Sanderson has been sick. They're without insurance and the bills are racking up…"

"You're a good man," Lucy said smiling at me, then

turned to her son who had almost flipped his bowl up-side down.

I busted up laughing. I had seen what he was doing; he was tipping the bowl to lick the rest of the Ranch dressing out, and he'd lost his grip. He grinned with a white smeared face and Lucy sputtered as she fumbled with the bowl before it could fall and break.

"Rawr!" Spencer growled, almost startling his mom into dropping the bowl.

I lost it and laughed hard until I was almost falling off the end of the chair. A very red faced Lucy was threating vile deeds like no Legos and no coloring books... I got up and got a clean wash cloth out of the hall closet and wetted it. I walked back in and wiped the little man's face clean and what had slopped onto the table by him. I was about to toss it into the sink when I heard a gunshot go off, then another.

"Is somebody back there shooting at the range?" Lucy asked.

"No," I said pulling my Glock out from the small of my back and making sure it was primed. "That was from the direction of the front gate. You two stick inside, just in case." I said.

"Ok, be safe. You've got your phone?" She asked me.

"Yeah, right here," I showed her with my free hand.

I left the house without letting the screen door slam and I held the .45 loosely in my hand while I walked down the grass beside the driveway. The shot sounded like it was by the front gate, but it could be just as easily as a kid or some drunks popping off a shot at street signs. In Michigan, anything is possible, but I wanted to be safer than sorry, especially with Lucy and Spencer in the house.

As I got within sight of the front gate, I saw the flash

of tail lights and an old white Ford pickup left the end
of my driveway. I didn't see anybody, but still walked
up carefully, watching everywhere. I reached through
the gate to check the lock when I got cut. A sharp sliver
from the lock got me and I sucked at the wound. I pulled
the lock through to my side and saw two slugs flattened
and embedded in the lock.

"Great," I said.

I pulled out my keys and tried to open it. I couldn't
even turn the key in the lock. Just my luck. Get the best
lock money can buy and it doesn't pass the test of the
locks on TV. They can take a bullet and... Wait, they
wouldn't open if they were shot. This one didn't either,
but now I was stuck inside of the fortress I called a
home. Too bad I hadn't got the license plate of the truck.
It looked familiar to me, but I couldn't place it.

My first call was to Ben, to let him know somebody
had tried to shoot out my locked gate. He asked if it was
an emergency or could he come by later on today or tomorrow and do his thing. I told him it could wait and
then called Randy.

"Hey bro, what's going on?"

"Hey man. Remember about when I was talking to
you about padlocks and you told me Krieg's were the
best?"

"Yeah man, you can't break into those things. You
can't cut them off and they're bulletproof—"

"Funny you should say that, it didn't unlock but it's
now jammed closed."

"What?" Randy asked.

"I had a front gate put on today. I haven't been home
two hours and somebody tried to shoot the lock off and
now I'm stuck inside. I don't want to wrestle the gates off
the hinge pins. It'd take 4 boys to do it," I told him truth-

fully, because it had taken everything the four of them had to do it according to Brandon.

"Hmmm. I'll be by in a while. You don't need to run out somewhere do you?"

"No, I'm a captive audience," I said with a trace of irony in my voice.

"Ok, no problem. Let me finish dinner and I'll call you when I get to the gate."

"Thanks buddy," I told him.

"See ya soon bro."

We hung up and I walked back to the house, making a fist to slow down the bleeding. I walked in and Lucy saw the red on my fist and ran over.

"I'm fine, just a cut," I said, holding the Glock in my left hand because I'd cut my gun hand examining it.

"Put that up, would you?" Lucy asked me sweetly.

"I can't reach my holster with my left hand. Here, I'll put it up on the high shelf for a minute."

I turned the water on and then held my hand under it. The cut was right into the meat of my right hand and the water had me wincing in pain. Lucy got my first aid kit out of the bathroom cabinet and gave me a wad of gauze to hold onto while she dried my hand and got supplies out. She got me fixed up right away, but told me I probably should go get it looked at.

"Do I need stitches, do you think?" I asked her, a little weirded out at how protective she was being.

"Maybe, I don't know. I'd just feel better if you got it looked at."

"I don't think I'm going to be shooting tomorrow. I'll probably rip it back open." I said.

Then I sat there for a moment and watched Spencer who'd been eyeing my hand with a look of concern.

"It's ok buddy, I got cut, that's all."

123

"You were bleeding. I fell down once and my leg bleeded right here," he pointed to his knee.

"Did Mommy fix you up good?" I asked him.

He nodded and I heard the approach of a vehicle. Randy's truck stopped next to the house. How did he get through if the lock was uncuttable?

"I'll be right back," I said.

I walked out to a happy Randy who stepped out of the cube van holding a pair of bolt cutters.

"I thought those locks couldn't be cut!" I protested.

"I didn't cut the lock, I cut one link in the chain."

The stupidity of the moment wasn't lost on Randy as I muttered and growled a 'thanks' out. He just laughed and accused me of having no lateral thinking.

"What took me so long was finding you a generic lock. Here, this one's got four keys," he said handing me a still sealed package.

"You went shopping?"

"No, I use those for locking up the back doors when somebody messes with my truck. Last time I bought two. Figured you needed to relock it."

"I do, thanks." I said, pulling the package open and getting the keys out. I handed one to a very confused Randy.

"What's this for?" he asked.

"We have to do the car swap thing here soon so you'll be in compliance of the HOA," I replied, grinning.

"Duh… Thanks. I see Lucy's here so I'll just…" he gestured back down the driveway.

"Thanks a million, buddy."

He left and I headed back in. Lucy was doing my dishes so I tried to bump her out of the way but she told me to knock it off and not to get my hand wet till I'd had it checked. That made sense so I just put the dishes away as they came out of the sink. Spencer must have brought a couple matchbox cars, because he was rolling them across the table making little motor sounds. It all felt a little… Domestic. Weird. If we were taking it slow, how did it feel so right, yet make me feel guilty?

I shrugged it off and, when it was time to tell them goodnight, I followed them to the gate and locked it behind them. Ben never showed up, but I figured I'd see him the next day. I walked back to the house, my hand smarting, but I was still excited for Sunday, even though I wasn't going to be shooting. It would be fun!

11

"Crap, my phone is dead," I muttered, looking at it stupidly and unplugging it from the charger.

I looked at the soft morning sunlight coming in my bedroom window and realized that I'd overslept somehow. I padded out of the bedroom and towards the kitchen to hit start on the coffee maker. Like a ritual, I'd set it up for the morning. I flipped the button and then headed into the bathroom. I did my business and, as I was brushing my teeth, I noticed the water pressure starting to drop. Confused, my brain muddled, I flipped the bathroom light switch up to see what was going on.

"Great, the power's out. No wonder," I said grumpily.

My well pump ran on 110v so I knew I could hook up the generator if the power was going to be out for a while, but then it hit me. My coffee machine wasn't going to work either if the power was out. I sulked for a moment because that meant no internet, no computer time, and no coffee unless I wanted to cook it on the stove in my dad's old percolator.

I'd have to find it, but it was probably way past time to do animal chores, so I got dressed, grabbed a basket and headed to the barn. I collected eggs after refilling the hanging feeder to make sure the little velociraptors didn't attack me, begging for treats. It was a good ploy, so I could sneak the eggs out before some broody hen went all ape on me, or the rooster tried to flog me. I made sure everyone's water was filled. I'd been spoiling the goats lately with sweet feed and fully expected the twins and Spencer to do so again that day, so I just threw in a handful to let them know that I still loved them.

The pigs were happy, but it was Ruby who seemed to be smiling. Her 7 little ones that weren't very little any more were wiggling all around. I noticed that I should change the bedding later on, then I went into the little faraday cage where the little portable Harbor Freight solar panel was. I could set it up on the kitchen table and charge my phone, in case anybody was trying to call.

In the modern day and age, everyone uses a cell phone it seemed, and I'd long ago gotten frustrated by only telemarketers calling the land line, so I'd had it disconnected. I wanted to call Lucy to apologize for not being up on time, but the phone was dead. Instead, I unboxed the panel and set it up on the kitchen table, and plugged my phone in.

I grabbed my keys and walked towards the front gate. If Lucy couldn't call me because I overslept from lack of alarm, I'd have no way of knowing if she'd tried to stop in already. Maybe the gate was a bad idea. In any case, I walked instead of driving my old truck because the morning was a little colder than usual and I wanted to get my blood flowing. There was no way I was going to chance a shower with such low water pressure and I kicked myself for not replacing the pressure tank in the house. A better tank would have at least given me the chance to have a two minute shower, but I doubted I'd get more than a drip the way it was acting.

I unlocked the gate with a little difficulty, my hand still stinging every time I gripped the key and tried to turn it. I got it open and pushed both gate panels to the sides. The walk back to the house had me almost feeling human and I remembered where I'd last seen my dad's Percolator; it was in their bedroom with his hunting gear.

See, when my parents died, I pretty much left everything alone. The room I slept in was my bedroom as a kid and, although the pictures of pinups and baseball stars changed out for more serious pictures, it was still my room. I rarely went into my parents' room because of all the picture frames that my mom had on the dresser, but I did so about once every other week to dust and make sure that the rodents hadn't gotten into anything.

In the distance, I could hear a quad already going where I assumed the state land to be, hopefully having a blast. The ATV trails went for miles and miles. I was almost to the house when I realized the sound was coming up behind me. The gravel crunched and I turned to see Randy flying up the driveway on his old Honda.

"Dude," he choked out, "We've got a problem."

"What's that?"

"I went to bed early last night and I woke up to no power," Randy told me, his face pale.

"Yeah, mine's out too. You worried about keeping the food cold today?" I asked.

"Brian, my cell phone is dead," he pulled his Android out and showed me.

128

"Yeah, mine died too. I had it on the charger, but the battery must have been low when the power went out."

"Brian, my car won't start, neither will my wife's."

I pondered that a moment and then walked to my truck and dug behind the seat until I found my jumper cables and reached in and turned the ignition on, letting the truck warm up a second.

"I can come give you two a jump if you need it."

"Dude, you're not getting it. Kill the truck man."

"What?" I asked, starting to get agitated.

It was too early on a morning I'd overslept and had no coffee, and my normally excited best friend was being the biggest Debbie Downer in the world.

"It happened."

"What happened?" I asked, not getting it, wanting coffee.

"Turn the truck off man, let's go inside." Randy got off the ATV and rushed me towards the house.

I moved the box the portable panel came in and checked my phone to see if there was enough charge to turn it on. If I couldn't call out from a low battery, I wanted to shoot Lucy a text apologizing for oversleeping and leaving her out there without a way to get Spencer to me. I grunted and un-plugged and re-plugged in my cell phone, then looked at the red light of the charger and saw it was still on, but my phone was dead.

"Did you have this in the faraday cage?" Randy asked, pointing to the solar panel and cell phone adapter.

"Yeah, I pulled it out after checking on the bacon bits," I said, playing with the cord and plugging it in again.

"Did you miss the smoke on the horizon, towards both Flint and Saginaw?"

Suddenly I felt my stomach drop and I walked towards the window and looked out. In the horizon there was smoke coming from the Northeast and the Southeast. Now that Randy had mentioned smoke, I realized I'd also been smelling it for some time but had written it off. The interior of the house always had a faint campfire smell from all the logs we'd burned over the years in the flat top wood stove. Smelling it outside hadn't really triggered any realization but when my un-caffeinated brain put it all together, I could see why Randy had a terrified look on his face.

"You think it happened?" I asked, my voice coming out in a hoarse whisper.

"Do you still have your dad's radio hooked up?" Randy asked, his voice worried.

"No, my truck battery will run it," I said reaching into the junk drawer and pulling out some pliers and headed outside.

I popped the hood and then had a thought. Even though I'd restored the '68 step-side, I'd put in a modern radio and replaced the speakers. Classic car and truck owners all over the country would vilify me if they knew, but I liked more than AM stations when I drove. I turned the truck on, and reached out to the radio, my fingers trembling. I hit the power button and nothing lit up on it. I killed the truck and opened the hood and had the battery out in a matter of minutes.

I carried it in while Randy paced nervously, trying to wear a hole in my linoleum floor. He followed me into my parents' bedroom where my dad had a desk setup with his old radio equipment. I put the battery on the back of the desk and then hooked the alligator style clips up to the posts. I didn't know much about my dad's rig, but when I turned it on and all I got was static I went looking for the antenna wire. I found it, and put the wires into the two terminals and tightened the wing nuts. I still got static, but there were other things in the background as well.

I turned the dial, changing frequencies and found an emergency broadcast.

"........ *all people are advised to stay at home. FEMA has been alerted and is mobilizing. If the instances of looting and rioting as in Flint, Michigan, Atlanta, Georgia and St. Louis, Missouri continue, the vice president will have no choice but to declare Martial Law. I repeat....."* The transmission cut out for a moment, *"........ This message will repeat once every hour until new information is learned. Thank you."*

"They didn't say if it was an EMP," I told Randy after turning it off.

"No, they wouldn't,"

"You bringing the family over?" I asked him, scared.

"Yes. No. I don't know. Only if things get bad, maybe? I don't know, maybe it just knocked out some substations. What was it, back in 2005 we were out of power for a couple of weeks?"

"I remember," I said.

"People didn't go nuts back then, it'll be good,"

"People also had running cars. Don't go driving that thing around too much, or you're going to be a target if it really is an EMP event."

"Or a CME," Randy muttered.

"I doubt it's that. It would have fried the power lines, wouldn't it? Something's burning out there," I pointed to the smoke columns.

"Airplanes," Randy said, his face pinched.

"Planes?" Then it hit me. "Oh shit. Depending on the time of day, there's something like 5,000 airplanes and jets in the air."

Randy gave a look that said he felt just as sick as I did. We both walked to the windows and watched the smoke for a moment.

"You know, whenever you don't feel safe there..."

"I know, man. I just wanted to make sure you knew. We have no way of knowing if this is the first, the last or... I'd put your solar stuff back up for today, just in case it isn't over."

"Ok," I said, "Can you tell Lucy that I'll be by in a little bit?"

"I will, just don't drive in, OK? I have a feeling that working vehicles are going to become a hot commodity."

"I hope you're wrong."

"I hope I'm wrong too. I'll see you buddy, I'm going to check on my girls."

"Can you lock my gate on your way out?" I asked, and Randy nodded.

☣ ☣ ☣

I put the battery back in the truck and, for the first time in a long while, I made room for it in the garage, backed it in and closed the door. I thought about stripping the battery, but I didn't. The fictional prepper books I'd read claimed that people didn't turn into ravenous zombie hordes for at least two weeks, but it didn't seem to be something to worry about right then. I walked across the fields, hoping that the pigs and goats were now accustomed to not hitting the fence, because without power and without it coming back, the little escape artists would drive me crazy hunting them all down.

The sun was starting to warm the air finally, and I had several goats follow me to the fence line so I made like I had an apple and chucked it. When they turned to go hunt down the tasty morsel I didn't actually have, I slipped between the two upper hot wires and into Lucy's backyard. I walked around to the front and rang her doorbell.

Or I tried to. Nothing sounded and I could smack myself in the forehead as an idiot, but I knocked instead of knocking myself out. I heard footsteps and then in the side pane of the door I saw the curtain pull back and Lucy smiled at me through the glass.

"My parents said not to talk to strangers," she said smiling, but her voice betrayed how nervous she felt.

"Avon lady," I called back.

She grinned wider and opened the door for me. Her house was technically a McMansion, but it had been bought and paid for when Spencer Sr. was alive and they'd had dreams of filling the space full of children. That had been mine and Cathy's goal someday in an unspoken future, but it was too late for that now. Instead, I had a farm and some animals. Some people have cats.

"You doing ok?" I asked her.

"Yeah, power's out. Why?" Lucy asked.

"Randy didn't tell you?"

"No, he said you'd be by in a little bit. My car won't start by the way, I don't know what's wrong with it. I was going to call you this morning and see if you could give me a jump, but I forgot to plug in my phone last night or something."

"It's or something," I told her, wondering if Spencer was still sleeping.

I explained what I thought had happened and Lucy held her hand to her mouth in horror. Of everyone who'd come out last weekend, Lucy was the one who didn't believe that much of what we were prepping for would ever happen. She was happy enough to hang out with us and shoot and enjoy the company of the women folk, and us guys who didn't snort like Ruby. She was obviously going to need some time to wrap her mind around it.

Somebody knocked at the front door and Lucy stood to go answer. I reached to feel for my Glock and came up empty. Damn, I was getting twitchy already and the lack of routine had me off today. My Glock was still on my night stand and my house was unlocked.

"Can you check on Spence for me? He's in his room," Lucy asked.

"Sure thing," I said, and headed down the hallway.

The little man was rubbing his eyes and standing up in his crib. He grinned when he saw me and held his arms up. I recognized that, so I swooped him up and pulled him in for a quick Spencer Squeeze Specialty hug. His Mom's words, not mine.

"Where's Mommy?" he asked in a sing song voice.

"She's at the door talking to somebody, let's go see."

I walked out to see the door open and Lucy looking absolutely pissed. George Landry Sr. was in there, with a notepad in his hand.

"… I don't care what you think. Brian isn't doing anything with the power." Lucy spat.

"What's the problem?" I asked, stepping behind her.

You'd have thought I'd just stabbed George in the heart and kicked him in the sack in the same instance, because the color left his face and he made a gagging sound in surprise.

"George here is trying to get me to sign a petition to have you and your farm… What is it? An Injunction to stop operations?"

I handed Spencer to Lucy.

"Wow, you know what George, if I hadn't seen this

in person," I snagged the clipboard from his hands, "I wouldn't have believed it."

George sputtered and I read my supposed infractions. I wasn't surprised to see this hand written with the power being out. Apparently my attempts at turning my property into a multi-family mobile home park and running illegal power feeds back to it had caused the power outage. I was being asked to cease and desist all operations that didn't involve anything more than mowing the lawn. Even the animals were being asked to go. If it wasn't the morning after the apocalypse, I probably would have been angrier than I was. Instead, I ripped the page off the notepad and handed it back to George, planning on reading it again later.

"Give me…"

"No, go make another one," I said, swatting at his bandaged arm, "and trust me George, pray. I had nothing to do with this power outage. If I were you, I'd fill all your water jugs up and see if your four fancy fireplaces can actually hold a flame this winter," I said, trying to be helpful but the hatred came out anyways.

"Oh, and why is that?" he asked in a patronizing tone.

"Because," I whispered to him, "it gets cold in the winter time."

I slammed the door in his face, and he knocked again. I stood there, ready for him to reach for the knob but he cursed and walked away after half a minutes wait.

"He has no idea, does he?" Lucy asked.

"No, he probably really believes this power outage is my fault. I don't know what he's going to do when his Escalade won't start."

"He drives a BMW actually," Lucy said, and I did a double take.

"Anyways, I wanted to walk over here and tell you that you and Spencer are welcome to come to my place. It's going to take some work, but I've got running water and food and…"

"You really believe this is it?"

"Yes, yes I do." I told her truthfully

"Wait, how did you get here, I don't see your truck?"

"With the power out, the fences aren't hot anymore. I'm not advertising that fact, but you can slip through and shortcut to my place whenever you want."

"The fence is hot," Spencer told me.

"Yeah, it sure was buddy. Not right now though, it's a secret."

"I don't know. Let me figure things out here first. What are you going to do?" Lucy asked me.

"Go talk to Randy, see if he can help me run some pipe from the barn to the house sometime this week."

"Ok, you be careful," Lucy stood on her tip toes and kissed me quickly before turning and heading back into the darkened rooms.

I let myself out and walked across the street to see Brenda watching me from a second story window. The sunlight flashed off something and with a start, I realized it was a scope. She must be sitting up in her office looking at everything near and far. She gave me a wave and yelled over her shoulder. I couldn't hear anything, but it was probably in response to one of their drills. I'd just gotten to the sidewalk when Randy came out, his usual excitement now tempered with worry.

"Hey man, is everything ok?" He asked me.

"Yeah, yeah. Thanks for the wakeup call this morning man. Uh… I have a favor to ask you."

"Sure, anything," he said quickly.

GOOD FENCES

"I want to run a waterline from the cistern tank from the barn to the house. The barn is gravity fed, so I don't know how to figure things for the pressure drop and…"

"I can do it a little later on. The girls are packing things up and I've got the little trailer hooked onto the quad in the garage."

"You guys coming out already?" I asked him.

"I talked it over with Brenda and we think it's best to do it now instead of a week from now. Drive the quad out there once with the bulk of the stuff and move the rest in the middle of the night?"

The enormity of the situation was flooring me, but it made sense. Then again, I did have the new camper trailer out back… I didn't actually have to hunt in it, and it was cheap and easy…

"Is that ok?"

"Sure, sure, I was just curious. I figured you had materials and…"

"Here comes trouble," Brenda yelled.

Walking down their side of the street was George. The front step to the front door was bumped in for some architectural reason and the bricks had sheltered me from the gentle breeze, but it had also blocked George's sight.

"Not again," I muttered.

"Come on in, I'll get rid of him." Randy said.

I stepped in and off to the right behind some curtains. The twins were in the living room there, laying on the floor in pink pajamas, with coloring books in the sunlight that came in from the windows to the south side of the house.

"Hi, Uncle Brian," they chorused.

"Hi, shhhh…" I whispered and they nodded and

137

went back to coloring. They were always great kids, and this was just one more example of what a good job Randy and Brenda were doing.

I strained to listen.

"……..your work truck is still in violation of the covenant agreement you signed—"

"I don't know what kind of bug crawled up your ass, but you better go somewhere and pull it out. The van isn't working. The power is out and I have 30 days." Randy's voice rose and for the first time I was seeing him almost losing his cool.

I almost wanted to see him punch the shit out of George, but that wouldn't have been very Christian of me and I didn't want to chance Randy getting hurt.

"If the van isn't working, then that violates—"

"Call a tow truck on me then," Randy slammed the door in his face and stomped towards me.

He held up a hand as if asking for a moment then he paced and mumbled to himself.

"The apocalypse happens and he's worried about HOA conventions?" I almost laughed.

"It isn't funny," Randy snapped back.

"It's what I've been dealing with ever since they put in your neighborhood man. George has sent what, six or seven complaints out now? Look at this," I said handing him the note.

"The man is crazy," Randy said after reading the note and handing it back to me.

"Yeah. Anyways, I just wanted to see about running water. If you need a hand moving, I can bring my truck out and we can do a bigger load." I told him.

"Naw, there's bound to be a ton of quads and scooters, motorcycles that still run. An old truck in perfect shape that runs? You'll be the talk of the town by the end of the week. Stash it for now man, stash it."

"I already did," I assured him. "Come out whenever you're ready. Here," I pulled one of the keys off the keychain, "it's for the front gate. We can always sneak in under the hotwire now the power's out, but I don't want the other neighbors to see it, you know what I mean?" I asked him.

"You already gave me a key, man," Randy reminded me and I smacked my forehead in a DUH motion. "Yeah, let me talk to Brenda and I'm going to go back to packing. Thanks, man."

"See you soon,"

12

The first full day of the apocalypse didn't bring Zombies or angry mutant bikers of any sort or flavor. Instead, it left me wondering how to handle the mundane. What to do with what was in the fridge? The freezer? Should I open it to cook and eat things up first or should I let it slowly warm up on its own? I didn't know, but I figured that soon it wouldn't matter much and that my buddy and his family would probably be bringing their own food and supplies from their fridge.

I was a little worried, but I knew I was somewhat prepared for just this. I'd war gamed in my head what would happen in this very scenario, but it still seemed surreal. I needed to figure out what to do with everyone, and decide where they would go. Maybe the two empty bedrooms upstairs? When my parents were hopeful about having more kids, they'd started to refurbish the upstairs from when my dad was a kid, but no siblings ever showed up, stork or no.

GOOD FENCES

So I had my parents' room, my room and two small 8x10 rooms upstairs. Plenty of room and enough basics in furniture. I looked at the TV, and DVD Player and wondered what Spencer was going to be like without SpongeBob, and then figured it didn't matter. Probably sooner rather than later I would be taking the useless electronic equipment out and discarding it, as space would become a premium.

I headed into the bathroom and looked at myself in the mirror. I needed a wash and a shave - I'd gone out in public looking like I just came off a bender that had landed me in jail. I considered how to get the water going before everyone arrived, to make myself feel more human, and then it hit me. I could use the same trick I'd used to prime the house well pump the one time it lost its prime!

I disconnected the washing machine hose, which had two female ends. I walked outside and connected that to the end of the hose that ran from the house, which was mostly used for watering my mom's old rosebush. I uncoiled that as far as I could, and it reached halfway to the barn. Inside the barn, the animals didn't know or didn't care that there was no power. It was just another lazy day for them. The old school backup system my grandparents had installed was going to save me a lot of trouble.

I stretched the hose from inside the barn to outside, until I met the hose from the house. With the washing machine hose, both were able to be joined perfectly. I went back and turned on the water from the barn, then went to the house and opened the tap from there. I crossed my fingers and went inside. I could hear the toilet filling up, albeit a little slowly, and I decided to wait a bit and see how it was going to go.

141

While that was running, I went into my parents' room and found the percolator. I turned on the kitchen faucet and was rewarded with running water, although it didn't have the same pressure as it had had before. I filled the percolator and turned on the propane stove. When it got warm I was going to add the coffee grounds and make what my dad called cowboy coffee. I grinned at the memory and walked into the bathroom and tried the tub faucet. It sputtered violently and then water shot out. There must have been quite a bit of air in the line, so I let it run on hot for a minute and was soon rewarded with steamy water.

Never before had I been so thankful to have a propane water heater. I'd threatened myself with replacing that and the stove a dozen times as the prices of propane had sky rocketed. But I sure was thankful I had it still, and I had about one and three quarters of a tank full, probably close to nine hundred gallons if the new tank was topped off. I quickly showered and shaved, praying the pressure didn't drop too much at the critical moments when the soap was in my hair and in my eyes, but it didn't.

Feeling refreshed, I dressed and added the coffee to the now hot water on the stove. Now what? So much of my day was go here, do this. Look at my phone. React to what somebody says who called. Emailing links back and forth to Randy. YouTube. Watching Television. Listening to the radio… I smacked my hand on my forehead went to my parents' room. I knew the old battery my dad had was probably toast, but it'd been kept inside. I pulled it out from under the small desk his radio gear was on and took it to the kitchen table where I hooked it up to the little folding Harbor Freight charger.

I found the little charge controller attachment and

hooked that into the solar panel, then added the alligator clips and watched. The lights on the cheap charge controller that came with the briefcase folding panel lit up and I waited to see the battery indicator's charge status.

"You know, I'm going to feel stupid if this is full," I mumbled.

It wasn't full, but it was definitely close to being dead. I decided to leave that battery alone and spent some time in the garage, pulling the battery back out from the truck, then hooked it up and sat down. The emergency broadcast I heard while having my first cup of coffee was a repeat of the earlier one, with not a lot of new information. The reception wasn't great, but hearing another human voice was a small comfort.

Flipping through the channels, I found one where people were talking and mostly speculating on what was happening. I decided to try the CB band and found someone from downstate who was talking about the riots that had begun almost immediately in Flint and, from what the talker had said, also Ann Arbor and Dearborn. That confused me, until somebody on there got on and starting ranting about Muslims, Islam and ISIS in general. At first I was mortified that the guy's bigotry was out in the open for everybody to hear, but I realized that it didn't make what I was hearing untrue.

At some point the previous night when the power went out, immigrant and guest students had started banding up. They weren't a majority, but when a mob of ten to fifteen decided to, say, beat down a Christian because of his faith, most of the bystanders stepped aside knowing they didn't have enough numbers. Also, several planes had fallen, and a good chunk of Flint by the Bristol road area was on fire, with the flames marching east.

I took all that in and felt sick to my stomach. I knew that area well, and had friends who used to live there. I turned the radio down low and laid down on my parents' bed and listened to the radio until my eyelids got heavy. It wasn't long and I was out cold.

☣ ☣ ☣

Naps in the daytime, even mornings, left me groggy and fuzzy headed when I woke up. I was woken by a loud knock at my door, and I bolted upright, confused by the unfamiliar surroundings. I turned off the radio and grabbed the Glock from my bedroom and put it in the small of my back.

I opened the door and rubbed my eyes. It was Frank.

"Hey boss. How you doing?" I asked lamely.

"Not good. Hey, nice gate man! I'm sorry you haven't met the other couple before, but I was wondering if I could bring the doctors here at some point in the next week or two?"

"Doctors?" I knew I should know what he was talking about, but my sleepy brain wasn't yet putting the words into a cohesive pattern that I could recognize as speech. I struggled a second and then realized he meant the other members of Randy and Frank's group.

"Yeah, I'd like to meet them. Hey, did you have to climb the gate?"

"Yeah, no way I wanted to tangle with that barbed wire. Now that things have happened, you might want to consider wrapping your gate in it or something."

"Or something," I said thinking about it. What good was a gate if people could just climb it? For that matter, who was in the white truck and what would have happened if they had climbed the it instead of trying to shoot the lock off?

"Ok, I just wanted to check in. I didn't see your truck here so I figured you were out and about but I'm glad I knocked."

"Me too, boss," I said, shaking his hand.

"I'm going to take my quad and head over to Randy's. I don't want to leave it parked out by the road for very long. I covered it but still..."

"Randy and Brenda are packing up to come on out this way. Hey, how long do you think it'll take until things get scary?" I asked, knowing that Randy and Frank had been preparing for this a lot longer than I had.

"It's hard to say. By the sound of it, Islamic students in the cities started rioting last night. Summer of rage, and all of that. Out here on the edge of the boondocks..." Frank made the iffy gesture with his hand. I knew the feeling. Maybe yes, maybe no.

"Ok. Hopefully next time you stop out I'll have the gate reinforced. If not, come in from Lucy's house through the hot wire," I told him, pointing across the field to the pale yellow house.

"Will do, and I'll see you soon," Frank Chesil said and began to walk back down the driveway towards the gate.

I went to my safe and got my AR out and started loading all the magazines. "Just in case there really are zombies," I told the empty room.

Never before had I felt so alone in a quiet house. I decided to either listen to the radio again, read a book or wait for Randy and his family or Lucy to show up. They both knew they had open invitations.

☣ ☣ ☣

I spent the rest of the day reading, doing animal chores and waiting. I knew I should be doing something far more productive, like putting in more food, or figuring out how to make the food in my freezers last longer, but I didn't. My garden was full of long season crops and, other than squash and tomatoes that I picked daily, there wasn't much else. I'd already pulled my green beans and peas, and planted a few pumpkins, but none of that needed immediate care, and, if I was going to start living off of that stuff, I needed to do more, but the shock of the situation had me sitting in disbelief.

"I want a beer," I told the darkening house.

I got one out of the fridge, picked up my AR and headed to the front porch to sit in the shade. Even though it was summer, it was pleasant outside and the mostly dry weather had kept the mosquito populations under control. Either the buggers were vying for the nomination to move from pest to state bird, or there were only three or four around, usually to bite you when you're asleep. For the first time, I realized I couldn't hear any traffic. You never know what that's like until you go so far out into the woods or country that there really isn't anybody else.

Sipping my Coors, I watched the smoke fill, and wondered what was burning and, more importantly, why. One idea I'd been tossing around for a while was getting a big dog, but I never had, telling myself that I'd be gone at work too much, or working outside here on the farm to spend time playing with and training it. Now I found myself talking to myself and waiting for something to happen.

I knew Randy would probably be coming that night, so I watched the sun go down. It was the most peaceful sunset I'd ever watched, despite the fact that thousands of people may have lost their lives. Probably going to be many more by the week's end and, within a month, I feared that whomever had done this to us would have probably killed close to 40-50 percent of the country. Some reports were talking about numbers close to 90 percent. I didn't want to quibble over statistics, because none of them were pleasant to think about. With the sun tucked behind the horizon, I grabbed one more beer and sat on the porch and waited in the dark, forgoing a candle or lantern so I could keep my night vision.

One hour passed, then two. Roughly sometime after 1am I heard a motor fire up in the distance. I sat up, trying to get a fix on the sound. If it was Randy, he'd have a key to the gate. If it was somebody else, they were going to need to be careful with their vehicle and gasoline. Those things were going to be as valuable as food, bullets and medical supplies soon.

As soon as I thought that, I thought of Mr. Matthews and his pacemaker. We had just talked about that two weeks before, after he gave me the tractor. I hadn't gone back out to his place because I was still trying to swallow the fact that he was literally leaving me his farm when he passed. It was part surprise, part embarrassment. The half a hug had left me shocked, confused and touched. I needed to check on him, and soon.

The sound of the motor rose and fell, turning off. I heard a clanging and then the motor fire back up. I left my beer and got off the porch, moving towards the big tree on the left of the driveway near the woods. It was dark out, but I was hidden in an even darker patch of blackness, shadowing the shadows. I got my AR into a comfortable position and waited, pretty sure it was Randy and not the dumbass who'd shot my lock.

Soon, I heard the motor approach and stood up,

smiling. Laboring under the weight, Randy was pulling a four foot by eight foot trailer with his twins riding on the edge of it. He had a mountain of stuff under a tarp and he looked around as best he could with the headlights knocking out both of our night vision. He hadn't seen me, so I stepped out and waved.

He killed the motor and waved back before turning and making a shushing motion towards the girls.

"You make it out ok?" I asked him.

"Oh yeah. I got a few curious stares as I left, but that's all. What we couldn't put in the trailer was locked into the garage," Randy told me, seemingly wide awake and full of energy and enthusiasm.

"Where's Brenda?" I asked him, a little worried.

"She was helping Lucy, and they're going to come in under the fence. I figure I can go get more stuff in the morning in a few hours, or at least show up so people don't think I really left and abandoned my house to get broke into," Randy said.

"You girls want to head in?" I asked them.

"Is it dark?" one of them asked and, in the gloom, I couldn't tell one twin from the other.

"Yeah, but I want to talk to your Dad a minute," I said, wanting some privacy.

"Go ahead girls, sit at the table, I'll be in a moment or two."

"Yes, Daddy," they chorused and headed in.

"Did you get any rest today?" Randy asked.

"Yeah, about all I got done actually." I said, somewhat grumpily, "What's it like over there?" I asked him.

"You know that lawyer guy down the road from me?" Randy asked, and I struggled to remember who the neighbors where and then the lightbulb went on.

"Yeah, the guy who doesn't think people should

GOOD FENCES

own guns. Lives right by Landry." I said.

"Yeah, that's the man. He had a wind up radio in his basement that somehow survived. He cranked it up and half the block listened to the emergency broadcast a few times. Right in the middle of the damned street. I couldn't believe it."

"That doesn't sound so bad," I told him, wondering why that would count as unusual in light of what was going on.

"Yeah, but everyone basically had a block party. Landry said since the freezers were going to die soon, he fired up his monster grill in the driveway and everybody is working on getting drunk." Randy said disgustedly.

"Yeah, that sounds like a little bit of a waste, food wise."

"That's the thing, I don't think anybody there realizes how bad this could get. Probably will get." Randy was starting to work himself up, and I needed to stop that, otherwise I'd be sitting up all night with him.

"You said Brenda and Lucy are coming through tonight?" I asked him, curious but keen to steer the conversation back to less excitable things.

"Yeah, Lucy came and talked to Brenda after you left. At first I thought they were arguing upstairs when they got loud, but it was Lucy and my wife having a good cry. Lucy's going to come out here, but since she lives so close to the fence she'll get her stuff as needed and make appearances around her place so people don't just..." Randy's words tapered off.

"Kick in her door, take her stuff?"

"Yeah. She's worried about her late husband's stuff. She's packing the necessities, all food and clothing she can, but she wanted to go through some old trunks just in case. So Spencer could know who his dad was if things are as truly fucked as I think they are."

"Thanks Randy. How about you and the girls hold down the fort and I'll head over to the fence and wait for the girls?" I told him.

"I can go—"

"Your twins are sitting in my house in the dark. I think it would be less strange for them if it was you sitting in there with them," I interrupted.

"Ok, hey, we never talked about this, but if I put them down before you get back, where do you want us all to sleep?"

I thought about it a moment and decided I didn't care, even though I'd rather Lucy and Spencer were downstairs by me, "You know which room is mine, just pick one and we'll hash it all out in the morning."

"Ok, see you soon. Fire some shots if you have any trouble, we'll come running."

"If you hear shots fired, I've already found the trouble," I said, punching him on the shoulder and walking towards the gate to the fields that bordered the subdivision.

13

I made my way slowly to the fence in the darkness, picking my path carefully so I didn't trip. I made it without incident, but was startled by a pig who was out late in the adjoining pen. I almost pissed myself and made sure to find out which one it was to be made into bacon strips and Thanksgiving dinner.

"Hey," Lucy said, standing on her side of the fence, a sleeping Spencer in her arms.

"Hey," I replied, full of rich conversation tonight, "you OK?"

"Yeah, I'm just worried, Brenda will be right back, and she's grabbing the last bag."

I looked around at a couple of suitcases sitting by the fence, along with what looked like a diaper bag. I knew Spencer was mostly potty trained, but figured it was just another vessel to transport things.

"Those suitcases have rollers," Brenda said, huffing as she dragged out a duffel bag.

"It'll leave a trail from the fence to the farmhouse," I said.

"Everyone out there is getting so stupid drunk right now, I doubt anybody will notice," Brenda told me, true disgust in her voice.

I listened and could hear voices, laughter and the quieter murmur of people talking in the distance. I couldn't hear that from my house and part of it was comforting, part of it was disturbing. It was after 1am, and those folks were probably doing the exact opposite of what they should have been doing: gathering resources, taking stock of their situation. I understood the want for a party, to make things feel normal, but I'd heard the same broadcasts they had. All I did was have a couple of beers and some leftovers I could eat without heating up.

"Is it getting ugly?" I asked, Lucy handing me the little man through the top hot wires, being careful to avoid the barbed wire.

"Not yet, but it will soon enough," Brenda predicted grimly.

Once I had Spencer, Lucy ducked under the fence herself. Brenda passed bags through the gap and, despite the weight, I took the two heaviest suitcases and carried them, not using the wheels. I didn't want to advertise that half my fence had been rendered worthless. I had half a roll of barbed wire in the barn, and it was probably enough to run one strand down the middle of the Western fence line, but that was about it.

The walk back, I wasn't as graceful as the walk in. The suitcases I held to about shoulder level, and they kept banging into the AR slung across my back, hitting me in the kidneys. Getting to a worn path, I set them down, drenched in sweat.

"Don't overdo it. We still have to build a solar shower," Brenda told me grinning.

"Why? I have hot water?"

The girls looked at each other, then back at me with wide eyes.

"I might kiss you." Lucy threatened, "I feel so gross."

"How did you manage that?" Brenda asked, "I thought you needed Randy to hook something up?"

"I'll show you in the morning," I promised.

I rolled my shoulders, cracked my neck and then grabbed the handles of the suitcases and started walking again.

"This I want to see," Lucy said, "But I've got dibs on the first shower."

☣ ☣ ☣

Lucy picked my parents' room to sleep in. She went in to get her shower done and Spencer fell asleep on the couch with the twins. Randy and Brenda ended up upstairs. I grabbed blankets for the kids and covered them up, not wanting to disturb them. Randy had lit a 24 hour emergency candle, and that was the only illumination downstairs. Brenda and Randy were going to grab showers in the morning and then we'd unload everything and figure out where we wanted to put all their stuff.

I put my AR in the safe, and was pulling my shirt off to slide into my bed when I felt warm hands brush across my back. I spun around, and it was Lucy, in a soft-looking bath robe, a towel in her hair. There was just enough candlelight that I saw her smile before she stepped in close and wrapped her arms around me in a hug. I could smell the shampoo she used and I felt my body reacting, but I just hugged her back and let her rest her head on my chest.

153

"Thank you," she whispered.

"No problem," I whispered back, "all three kids fell asleep in a tangle on the couch. Do you want me to get Spencer out for you?"

"No, he'll be ok. I'll leave the bedroom door open," she said, her fingernails grazing my skin, driving me slowly crazy.

"Yeah, I'm going to do the same," I stepped back, breaking the contact and pulling my holster out of the small of my back and putting it in the top drawer of my tallboy style dresser.

I made a mental note to figure out a safer way of storing guns when there are kids in the house without making them inaccessible if an emergency should ever arise.

"Thank you, I mean it. Goodnight,"

"Goodnight," I muttered, my skin breaking out into goose bumps.

I put on an old pair of shorts, and slid into the sheets. With no air and fans running, it was a little hot, but not too bad. Every once in a while a cool breeze would come in through the open window. Sleep didn't find me right away, but when it did I dreamed of happy times. Spencer in a graduation cap and gown, Lucy by my side. In my dreams she held me tight, comforting me with her presence. I didn't remember anything more after that.

☣ ☣ ☣

The crowing of the rooster woke me up. It was the loudest thing. Strange, because I barely noticed it before.

"Brian!" a panicked Lucy was shouting from her doorway and, when I started to bolt upright, I found the comforting presence from my dream was still there.

"Oh my God, he scared me," Lucy said as Spencer stirred.

At some point in the night, he'd gone in search of his mother, but had found me instead. I'd slept on my side, but the little man was laying under my arm, arms and legs hanging down either side of me. Lucy lifted him off and I gave her a shrug.

"First time for everything," I said, stretching after getting up.

"Uh huh," Lucy said, giving me a quick look.

I got ready fast and was greeted by the smell of bacon, eggs and hash browns. I marveled at Lucy's ability to whip up food, but when I got to the kitchen I was pleasantly surprised. Randy stood there, a pink bathrobe that probably belonged to Brenda wrapped around his upper torso, and everyone was sitting around the kitchen table. Lucy was telling Brenda about her scare and little Spencer was waking up in his mother's arms. Somehow, though usually an early riser, I'd been beaten up by everyone.

"Did you all sleep good?" I asked everyone.

Turns out, no. Strange house, strange house noises and no electronic comforts like the soft glow of lights that they'd all become used to.

"Uh Randy, I think Brenda might want that back," I told him, tugging on the elbows of the pink bathrobe.

"Not until he's finished with breakfast," Brenda said, smiling.

Randy looked down and started laughing, "I thought I'd grabbed mine."

"It was dark, I'm sure deep down in your subconscious, you love wearing pink frilly things," I teased and his daughters snickered.

The girls asked and got permission to run to the

barn for more eggs and we all ate well that morning. With not much else to do after cleanup, we all drifted outside to unload Randy's trailer. Most of the food went into the kitchen, but their personal belongings went upstairs. Lucy didn't have as much as they did, but said she grabbed probably 2-3 weeks' worth of clothing, and was planning on going back for more of the food.

"What about the stuff in the fridges?" I asked.

"We'll be eating real good for the next week or so, but I think unless we figure out some way to save ice, we're going to be having warm beers for a while," Randy joked.

"You know, of all the things to prep or figure out how to make... What do we do when the beer runs out?" I asked, being serious.

Brenda punched me on the shoulder playfully and I was about ready to call abuse when Ashlynn pointed to the driveway and said, "Strangers!"

I was caught flat footed on the front porch without my Glock. It was still on the dresser so I ran in and spun the dial on the gun safe on the way back out. Randy gave me a nod and grabbed my AR and took a position by the kitchen table inside where the sunlight wouldn't shine off the optics and he'd be hidden from view. I'd originally saw one figure, but it turned out to be four now that they were closer. Brenda and Lucy herded the kids inside.

"There's four of them, all male," I said through the open window.

"Recognize any of them?"

I strained my eyes. One looked familiar, but I couldn't place him. "No," I told Randy.

"I'm coming out. Brenda, leave the girls with Lucy. I need you here in my spot,"

"No problem," I heard Brenda say from behind me.

GOOD FENCES

One of the figures was holding a pistol, I realized with a start. It was held low, by his leg. None of them were really looking at me, but they were walking straight at the house as if they owned the place. My door opened and closed. I didn't look back, but I heard Randy's heavy footfalls. I finally spared him a look and he had the AR, probably leaving Brenda his 1911... Shoot, she probably had her own gun now that I thought about it.

"You want to talk to them?" Randy asked me.

"Naw, I will," I said, stepping off the porch.

I took a few steps out into the sunshine, feeling the warmth on my skin. I reached my hand back and pulled the Glock, holding it at my side loosely, in as much as a guy holding a gun can do in a non-threatening manner. Then it hit me; I recognized the guy on the right middle. It was Mr. Wife beater from the trailer park. He wasn't kidding when he said he knew where I was. I made sure they saw me, and they changed direction slightly, heading my way.

"Morning," I called to them, and they stopped about twenty feet away.

"Morning, Brian. Seems like you stole something from me."

"Oh? What's that?" I asked, noting that he seemed pretty sober.

His other friends on the other hand... nope. Two of them were the same ones who were there when I knocked down the shithead who was talking. Both had glassy eyes and vacant expressions.

"You took my momma's trailer," he said.

"You mean I bought your momma's trailer," I told him, not understanding how a $400 singlewide elicited such a response.

The fourth man I'd somewhat ignored, moved his

157

hand from behind his back. He was holding a large hunting knife. None of them looked like they were ready to spring, but then again they probably didn't know what to expect either.

"That don't matter, it's my mom's. She bought it brand new when I was a kid. You can't just take people's stuff like that,"

"Hey, it's all legal, I even got a title." I told him, feeling my hands start to sweat.

"Wait," Randy's voice boomed, almost scaring me in the tone he was using, "you're telling me that you all are willing to get shot over an empty single wide? Isn't that going to be your hunting shack?" Randy asked.

"Pretty much," I said and Randy busted up laughing.

I looked to my side to see if he'd lost it. The laughter came out of his mouth sounded genuine, but he used it to bring his gun up to face the sky as he appeared to hold himself back from bursting forth.

"Shack? That's my home, I grew up there. You're going to give it back," he said, cocking the revolver, but not lifting it yet.

"First one moves, will get shot. I'd advise you to drop your gun and walk away," I told him.

"You aren't getting it man. I'm leaving with it, today," he said, his hand starting to move.

The man on the far left with the knife tensed and, as he was starting to make a run, a single gunshot from my left sounded. I didn't see a hit, but he crumpled, screaming in pain, one hand holding a spot above his knee. I drew my gun up and centered it on the idiot's head. He had been as startled as I was at the shot, but I'd recovered faster, had mentally prepared myself. He looked at me with hate-filled eyes.

"Toby!" he shouted and then turned to stare at me

again, "I'm going to put this down and check on my brother," he said, moving slowly.

He put the revolver on the ground and then knelt next to the writhing form on the ground. The tweakers just stared at us with slack-jawed confusion at the sudden escalation of violence. They probably just came along with Mr. Wife beater as a show of force, potential extra muscle to intimidate. They probably weren't expecting as many people to be here.

The kid knew a little first aid at least. He looked at me, and then Randy, calculating his chances then dove for the gun. Both Randy and I fired and the dirt kicked up around the revolver, both of us somehow electing not to kill the trash that was littering my lawn.

Mr. Wife beater rolled away and put his hands up before standing.

"Don't try something so stupid again, get him up," I said to the tweakers, motioning with my gun.

One of them seemed transfixed on the bore of the .45 but the other one pulled his arm, breaking his concentration. They both struggled but got Toby stood up, one of them under his arm so he didn't have to put weight on the leg.

"What's your name kid?" I asked him.

"Scott," he spit out.

"Well Scott, it's going to take more than four rednecks, a knife and a cheap gun to come busting in here. I don't know what you really hoped to accomplish, nothing works anymore. Cars, trucks, cell phones. Even if I wanted to give you the trailer back, there'd be no way to tow it," I tried reasoning with him to prevent more bloodshed.

"My truck still works, best damn truck in the world," Scott bragged, "I coulda towed it with that, still might if you let me and don't give no more hassle."

"That's not going to happen. I haven't even checked out the insides, but if you're dead set on getting it back no matter what, you're going to die and die a hard death. You see that locked gate?" I pointed down the driveway.

To their credit, they all turned and looked, "You come over somebody's locked gate, armed and wanting to take away their property or lives, well in Michigan we have something called the 'Castle Doctrine', and I could have shot all of you dead already. Once when your dumb fuck of a brother tried to rush us, and again when you went for your gun. Your tweaker buddies don't worry me, but I figure they are here for your moral support, so they would have caught lead as well. Now, leave the knife and gun and get the fuck off my property."

The last bit was delivered aggressively, and the tweakers almost dropped Toby. Scott flinched, realizing I wasn't some pushover. In truth, I'd used language and anger to make myself sound more intimidating than the happy go lucky widower I usually was. Not so happy, not so lucky. Now I wanted to show them what their death could look like, what they would be facing if they ever came back. I had no doubt that it was them who shot the lock. Hopefully this would be the last time I ever saw them.

"You boys start walking now, and me and my buddy are going to escort you to the fence," Randy said, motioning with the AR.

Scott tried staring us down, first Randy and then me. I just gave him a wicked grin and took a step forward.

One of the tweakers tried to take a step backwards but tripped over his own foot, pulling Toby and the other guy down on top of him. They struggled and wrestled with each other until they were done cussing and swearing and got to their feet. As they walked towards the gate, I knelt down briefly to pick up the pistol and then watched Randy's back as he got the knife. He stuck it in his belt. I really hoped he didn't fall, but I couldn't blame him for taking it.

The walk back was full of vile threats from both sides, ours and theirs. Lots of cursing and lots of supposed butt hurt by the brothers. Since I didn't feel bad, it didn't bother me much and I was starting to feel like going through with my threats if they didn't quit running their mouths.

"Then I'm going to come back here and kill everyone," Toby said, his eyes glassy in pain as they tried to climb the fence.

"One of you get over the other two toss that garbage out of my yard, then follow him over," I snarled at the half-baked attempts.

"Just unlock it," Scott whined, no longer sounding cocky and confident.

"Naw, you didn't give me any time to get my keys. You came in over the bars, the only way you are ever going through them is if you're being carried by six," I knew I was laying it on thick, but I really didn't want to have to kill the young men.

Whether it was the drugs or the booze or being born stupid, it seemed the four had the survival instincts of a lemming. Finally, they got Toby over, who didn't fall like I thought he would, and then the tweakers scaled the fence as quick as they could.

"I'll be back," Scott told me before walking to the white ford pickup truck I'd seen before.

I don't know if he meant to use a phrase from the Terminator, but he was a weasel-dicked version of Arnold, and it wasn't scary at all.

"If you are, point out a spot by the fence here for me," Randy said, speaking up.

"Why's that?"

"So I can tell your buddies where to dig your grave," Randy replied.

We were flipped the bird and watched as the old truck started up, missed a little bit and then took off down the road, leaving behind a plume of white smoke.

"That was weird," I told Randy who stood beside me still.

"Let's head back to the house. We're going to have to post a guard by the gate, you know?" Randy asked and I nodded. "So next time four guys walk up and they are armed or you think they are, stop them further away than you did. OK?"

I looked to Randy, confused and started walking to keep up with him. "Why further away?"

"The guy with the knife… If I hadn't been expecting that rush and had the gun more or less ready, I never could have fired on him before he buried that knife in my guts. There's been studies that say a reasonably quick on his feet guy can close 21 feet worth of distance before a cop can take his gun out of his holster and shoot."

I thought about that a moment and then nodded in understanding, "You saw that on *Mythbusters* last week, didn't you?"

Randy gave me a pained look and then busted up laughing, "Yeah, but it stuck with me," he said, "when the guy was working himself up to spring I kept thinking of that episode. That's why I was cracking the bad jokes and letting you pretend you're all badass."

I knew he meant it in jest, but I figured I'd explain myself a little bit. "I didn't think anything else would have scared them off. I don't know. Try to speak their language? Know what I mean?"

"What's that, booze, meth and stupidity?"

This time I cracked a smile, "Naw, no fear, violence, anger, no remorse. I don't know how to get through to somebody that stupid. I think they were asking for a bullet."

"True that."

❀ ❀ ❀

The ladies and kids were relieved to see us return. Brenda had gotten my father's long gun out of the safe and had a pretty good rest set up. I realized she'd had us covered all the way to the gate with the big gun. I'd been wondering why the screen had been removed from the storm window, but it suddenly made sense. Up close, it wouldn't have mattered. For a long shot, it would have been enough to throw off the gun's trajectory.

"You scared the bad men away?" Spencer asked.

"Yeah, buddy. Everything is A-OK. Nothing to worry about, but one of us is probably going to have to sit outside so we can watch the gate for people climbing over." The first was for Spencer and the last was spoken to the room at large.

Brenda nodded and Lucy went to the safe and picked up one of my .22s. I smiled.

"I can't touch those, so don't bring it by me. I don't want Brian mad at me." Spencer told his Mom, and I chuckled.

"Do we get to learn how to shoot all of those?" Lindsey, the quieter of the twins, asked.

"Probably someday, honey bear." Randy said, messing up her hair.

163

"Daddy…"

I smiled. It wasn't the same as we'd had a week ago, but it was definitely comfortable feeling in a world gone crazy. But trying to steal a house trailer back? I had to shake my head at that.

"You know, we probably can't let the girls run to the bar for eggs on their own anymore. Not until we do something with the gate, and get the security system I bought set up," Randy said.

"Yeah, I think that's a priority. I don't know what else to do other than that. Ok, let's work on that this morning, rest up and then we'll move the rest of yours and Lucy's stuff later on, when it gets dark. Unless… you don't think they're going to have another subdivision party, do you?"

"I don't know, but they're stupid if they do. We can get stuff pretty easy now the trailer is empty, if I can pull it up to the fence with the quad. We stashed the rest of our stuff in Lucy's garage," Brenda said.

"Can we move the trailer by hand to the fence?"

"You're worried about the sound?" Lucy asked.

"Yeah, when you fired it up last night, I could hear it for a ways. I don't know how we missed hearing those rednecks pulling up to the gate."

"They probably came sometime last night and tried to get in," Lucy interjected, "when they couldn't see in the dark they probably went back to the truck to wait for the morning.

"That's a scary thought," Brenda said, her eyes going wide.

"Brian, can I play a board game?" Spencer interrupted.

I nodded and the twins and Spencer took off towards my stash of them on the shelf.

GOOD FENCES

"Well, if they come back, they're going to have a long nap," I said.

"In the dirt," Randy finished.

The girls gave him a sour look and I smiled, pushing him towards the front door. We had a gate to reinforce. I had an idea of how to do it, but it'd take the tractor, some fence pliers and the roll of barbed wire.

"Come on Randy, give me a hand."

"What do you need me to do?" Lucy asked.

I felt bad, because she was going to get stuck with the kids and food, because Brenda had already grabbed two boxes of .30/06 and was readying a small backpack she had brought with her. It already contained some lightweight camo clothing and bottles of water.

"I'm going to find a spot in the barn where I can see all around," Brenda said.

"You a good shot?" I asked her.

"Randy dear, I'm a little older than you are, no don't look surprised. I'll bet you dishes for a week I've killed more deer than you have." Brenda told me.

"More deer than me? A week's worth of dishes? You know I grew up on a farm right?" I asked her, incredulous.

"If you can beat 43 bucks and 20 does then I've got dish duty."

"63... but... but I didn't bet!" I waffled.

"I always filled tags for my dad and mom. Dad's eyesight was so bad he could only just hit the broadside of the barn, as long as you led him into the middle of it first and shut the doors."

Lucy busted up laughing as I looked at the sink, pouting manner.

"About that gate," Randy reminded me.

Oh yeah. The gate.

165

BOYD CRAVEN

☣ ☣ ☣

We used the bucket to carry the big role of barbed wire to the fence. I started out by weaving it between the bars up and down. I was scratching the hell out of the pretty blue paint, but if it meant no more cretins climbed the fence, then it was worth it. Once a strand was weaved up, it was pulled tight with two pair of fence pliers, twisted together so it pulled taught, and then cut off with bolt cutters. Once both sections of gate had wire going up and down we weaved the barbed wire side to side in the same manner. We had spaced everything about four inches apart, not really enough to get a hand or foot-hold. The heat started to kick up and Randy headed back to the house to grab some water.

I kept going, a little slower so I didn't hurt myself. My leather gloves not only protected my hands, but also kept my bandage from getting dirty. I'd have to clean it out after sweating and working with the rusty wire, bandaged and gloved or not! I paused to look up and saw where the sun's position was in the sky. So much for getting the security systems up today; it looked like it was already past lunchtime.

Randy returned after a few minutes, his hands full. I smiled and kept going. Just a few more wires to pull through the left gate and then we'd be done. I'd feel secure and safe. A few minutes later, Randy and I were breaking, sitting on the edge of the bucket. Lucy had made us both stacked ham and cold cut sandwiches.

"You know, we have to figure out a way to dry out meat. When I shoot a deer this fall, what am I going to do, can it?" I asked him.

"I thought you were wanting to build a smoke house?" Randy asked.

166

GOOD FENCES

Build something…. I could totally do that, right after everything else we were going to do. But I had an idea of how to do it cheap and easy. I didn't know if it would work, but something had to be better than nothing. We finished off the fence and Randy sat on the back of the tractor to watch our backs as I put it back in the barn. The day had started out bad, but after wiring the gate, I was feeling pretty confident.

"Brenda, you in here?" Randy called.

"No hun, I'm in the house," she called back.

"Last couple times we've gotten together, Lucy has ended up doing the food and kids," I told Randy before we left the barn, "I'd like start teaching her some stuff. You, Brenda and I, taking turns,"

"Yeah," Randy said, wiping sweat off his brow, "I was thinking that too. More she knows, the more she can help. What'd really help though, is having Ken and Kristen and Frank and the Docs…"

"I know you're right, but it's all still a little hard to swallow, you know?" I asked.

"I know, and it's just day one. Nothing really bad has happened yet," he told me, starting to walk to the house.

"You shot somebody on day one," I pointed out.

"Naw, I just grazed him. I aimed for the left side of his leg. I didn't want to hit the bone and have it deflect and take out his femoral artery."

"You're that good?" I asked him, not sure if he was pulling my leg or not.

"My wife's the one who taught me. 63 deer Mr. Farmer, don't you forget it,"

That shut me up. Knowing my luck, there'd be dishes to do!

14

I can clean it out," I told a belligerent Lucy who was looking at the wet dirty bandage on my right hand.

"No, sit down and let me look at it. I should have known better than to have let you…"

"Young kids in love," Randy said to Brenda with a smile.

"Shut up!" we chorused, and started laughing.

I relented and sat at the table. The kids were still involved in a board game, but it didn't sound like the normal game of life I grew up playing. The twins were showing Spencer a new way and none of it sounded like it was geared towards him winning. I worried about that, but then realized that any contact with kids, especially girls who weren't his mother… Well, the little guy was basking in the attention he was getting.

"Ouch! Are you trying to cut me open more?" I griped as she ripped the tape off holding the gauze pad in place.

GOOD FENCES

"Don't be such a baby," she snapped back.

"Yesterday you wanted me to get stiches, how is that being a baby?"

"Told you so," Brenda said to Randy.

"Told him what?" I asked.

"That it wouldn't be long and you two would be acting like an old married couple. You're both in the five to ten years of marriage range. Give it another ten or so and you'll be able to read each other's minds without wanting to strangle them," Brenda said.

I flushed and I'm sure Lucy did too, but I couldn't tell as she was sitting beside me, her hair obscuring her face as she worked on my right hand. She did, however, mutter some very un-lady like, un-Christian things that just made Brenda and Randy roar with laughter.

"I think they're drunk," Ashlynn said, talking to Spencer.

I lost it. I started laughing. The whole situation. The whole adrenaline dump, every fear I'd felt - and suddenly I had a room full of close friends. It really took an apocalypse to bring people together sometimes. Besides, I'd never seen that kind of snark from Lucy before, and I kind of liked it.

"There," she said, pulling the last strip of tape tight.

I winced, it hurt.

"You have plenty of triple antibiotic ointment, but it's starting to look infected already. I looked around to make sure there wasn't anything stuck in there and couldn't find anything. I want to wash this out twice a day until we know for sure. Maybe keep the bandages off in a day or two and let it dry out?" Lucy told me.

"Ok, boss," I said.

"Good one! See, he's learning!" Randy said excitedly, swatting Brenda on the shoulder.

"Oh, girl, you so have to train them up right… or they turn out like a big kid. I screwed up obviously," Brenda told a very red-faced Lucy.

"So, um… What was the score from the baseball game last night?" I asked them.

"What baseball would that be?" Brenda asked.

"Yeah, who was playing?" Randy interjected.

"Whose TV would we have watched it on?" Lucy asked, poking me in the ribs.

I almost jumped out of my chair. "Hey, there's something I have to do today, for sure. My memory is terrible so I don't want to forget, but I need to go to Mr. Matthews and check on him. He's got a pacemaker and—"

"Oh no," Brenda said, "That's your farmer buddy who has all the corn planted?"

"Yeah," I told her, "I just need to… if he needs help…"

"I'll go with you if Randy or Brenda will watch the kids," Lucy said.

"Ok, if that's ok with you guys?" I asked my favorite neighbors and friends.

"Yeah, sure. Just don't get lost in the woods," Randy dropped me a salacious wink.

"Oh stop it Randy, don't embarrass them." Brenda nudged him.

"C'mon Lucy, let me get you a .22 set up and we'll head on down the trail."

"Are we taking the road?" She asked.

"Naw, once we duck the fence, there's a trail I found when I was a kid that connects our woods to his farm. It's about a ten minute walk fence to fence."

"Ok, bye little man, Mommy has got to run out for a little bit. You're going to play with the girls still, ok?"

The 2 year old gave her a half a dismissive wave as

he was spinning the white plastic wheel. He had twins who adored him playing, what else could be wrong in the world?

"You see that?" Lucy asked me, "He gave me the little princess bye, bye wave."

"Too many cartoons," I told her.

She smacked my stomach lightly, "That's your fault."

"Told you so," Brenda said sweetly.

We closed the door and started walking.

☣ ☣ ☣

We were mostly silent during the walk over to Mr. Matthews's farm. I showed Lucy where to duck the fence; you push through the brush and within about ten feet in you come across an old two wheeled track. Back when our farm was larger, or maybe under Mr. Matthews' family, it was all one big property. I'd found the old road cutting through the woods as a kid and often went exploring down it. It was quiet and you instantly felt ten degrees cooler in the shade. The bad part was the bugs.

I slapped at a lazy mosquito who'd found refuge in the shade and kept moving. Lucy kept pace easily enough, looking confident and comfortable with the .22 she was carrying. It was an old Marlin with a tube magazine. I had seventeen shells in there for it. If she couldn't one-shot kill an attacker, she could spray lead everywhere and hopefully a few would find their target.

"So, the Christian thing. Has it always been like this with you?" Lucy asked me.

"It isn't a thing," I said feeling a little hurt, "It's just my beliefs."

"Sorry, that didn't come out like I wanted it to," Lucy said and fell silent.

I let my mind chew on her question a bit before asking one of my own, "Do you mean, did my faith and conviction grow bigger than it was previously?"

"Yeah, that's it," she said.

"Once my wife died, I went to church a lot more, got a lot more involved. For me, they really did save me and help me pull through one of the worst moments of my life. It was healing somehow. It didn't really stop the pain of loss, but … you know what I mean?" I asked her, not knowing what else to say.

Lucy put her free hand in mine and gave it a squeeze. My uninjured one.

"I kind of feel like, after today, a lot of people are going to find religion; I know I suddenly don't feel the same way I did yesterday, or even last week."

"You still put up with me," I said, breaking the contact.

"No, not you, not us. I mean… Things are suddenly different. That's got to be a shock to people, especially people who weren't preparing for something like this."

"Ahhh yeah, I got you. Hey, here we are." We stopped walking as the trail opened up to a meadow of wild flowers.

"Is that his house up there?" Lucy asked me.

"Yeah, but let's go slow, I don't want to startle him if he's..."

"I know Brian, you don't have to say it."

"Thanks."

☣ ☣ ☣

Mr. Matthews's house was a single story ranch. It had been last remodeled sometime between the Civil War and World War II, if you believed the old man. There

GOOD FENCES

would be a cellar or Michigan basement if I remembered correctly from the handful of times I'd been there. I knocked and got no answer. I knocked louder, though there wasn't usually anything wrong with the cranky old man's hearing. Nothing.

With dread, I opened the door and headed inside the house.

"Hello?" I called out.

Nothing.

I walked in and found him face down on his kitchen table. It almost looked like he sat down to write something and just fell asleep. I walked up already knowing, but I had to check. No pulse and he was cold. I swallowed and stepped back. Lucy checked him as well, before bending over the table and picking up two keys that had been separated from a keyring and pulled a sheet of paper out from under his hand where it had been pinned.

Dear Brian,

I think it's almost morning now, but sometime in the last day or two, my pacemaker died on me. Worst pain of my life and I think I'm building up for the big one. Two keys here are for the barn and my foot locker in the basement. You already know where the will is located and god willing you'll....

"He never finished writing it," Lucy handed me the note with a grim expression on her face.

I read it quickly, and went to grab the will from the credenza, choking back tears.

"I have to bury him, but I don't know..."

173

"I'll help you."

I found the tools in the shed out back, and we found a soft spot in his kitchen garden. I dug until my hand was starting to bleed through the bandages and then Lucy took her turn. She was able to make it big and deep enough for me to get him in. I'd wrapped him in a clean bedsheet before lowering him into the ground. Filling in the hole went twice as fast, but quite a lot of time passed. We were both tired and more than ready to head back to the house. I was too exhausted to read through the will or check out the footlocker. I was running on empty.

The walk back was quiet and when I got inside the cabin, the loud ruckus fell silent as they took a look at my face.

"I'm going to hop in the shower," I said, putting the note and the will on my bed.

The shower didn't do what I really needed it to; I needed it to wash more than just the dirt and sweat of the day off. What I really wanted to do was wash away the guilt I felt. I'd known Mr. Matthews had a pacemaker, and I'd waited to go and visit him. The honest truth was because I thought he was already dead. I had no way of knowing if he'd survived the EMP, and he had died alone. If I would've known he was still there, I would've gone sooner, and maybe we could have helped him or at least made sure he hadn't died alone

By the time I left the bathroom, the kids were back to playing again and Lucy was reading a book, sitting on the couch. Both Brenda and Randy were sitting at the table in the kitchen, books in their hands, reading quietly.

"Hey guys, you know what? I think we need to do something fun tonight. A lot of really sad stuff seems to have happened lately, and maybe it'll be, you know, fun?"

"What you got in mind?" Randy asked.

"I don't know just yet, but I know things are going to get a lot worse before they get better," I told them.

"So what can we do that would be fun? Maybe we could pick on Lucy and Brian some more?" Brenda snarked. "That was pretty fun, wasn't it?"

"Please, no," I said, throwing my hands up in the air.

"Oh no, this could actually be pretty funny, don't knock it till you try it!" said Lucy.

"Wait a minute, I thought it was pick on us, not pick on me!" I told them.

"It is, it is," Randy said looking at his wife and laughing.

"You know, I wouldn't count it as fun, but we could always go set up part of the security system tonight," Randy suggested.

"Yeah, I know what you mean, but I don't think I have that in me," I told Randy plopping down into the closest kitchen chair.

"I know it doesn't sound like fun, but what I really want to do is to figure out some way of watching the property lines to make sure that Toby and Scott don't come back with anymore meatheads."

"But we can just sit around, inside the house all the time. If we cannot can feel safe walking around outside within the farm then we need to do something about it. I really think it would be a good idea for every adult to go around armed and really think it would be a good idea for Lucy to learn shoot and shoot well. If there ever was a time to piss off your neighbors by firing off guns, think the time has finally come." Said Brenda, looking at me for a response.

"Yeah," I said to them, "I'm really not liking the feeling either. I do wonder if there's something we could be doing to help the neighborhood, and the subdivision. I mean, how many of them rely on public services, water, sewage, or is there anyone we can help who's on medication? I just feel like we should be doing a lot more than we are, but in reality, I know we don't have enough resources, and we don't have enough time."

See, that's the problem. You're going to run into an idealist, which isn't a bad thing, but you said it yourself, you want to help everyone. It's physically impossible and the only thing you're going to do set yourself up for a ton of disappointment and heartbreak," Randy said.

"You know, if we're really going to go back and get our stuff tonight, some of us need to get some rest, because we're going to be up till two or four in the morning trying to move our houses without the neighbors seeing us," Randy told Brenda.

"Going to bed early, that could be a lot of fun," I told them smiling.

"It can be," Randy waggled his eyebrows at me and Brenda slugged him in the shoulder.

Lucy put Spencer on the floor, and came over to us, "What I have left in my house I'm not really worried about; if you want I can help you guys get everything of yours tonight and then in a couple days see how things are, then maybe you guys can help me get the stuff out of mine."

"Oh, for sure," Randy said, "We're planning to help you regardless, but there's no reason not to get everything of importance out of there tonight, even if we stash it back by the fence and make a bunch of trips. You don't have to carry it all back here. We can get it loaded on the trailer and drive it in on the quad. If we time it just right, we might even be able to do it without waking a bunch of people. I mean, how many of you are woken up by the sound of cars? Right now it's an oddity, but your subconscious mind might not figure that out." Randy said.

"That makes a lot of sense, but like what Brian was saying earlier, we don't want to advertise the fact that we're going through the fence. We don't want to let everyone else think they can just go and do that too," said Lucy.

"How about this? How about we make a big dinner and those that are going to get up early to go raid your own houses can sleep. You all go do what you gotta do and we can one be here for the kids. I don't know if you wanted me or Lucy or..." I let the words trail off, because this was their stuff, it was my place, but their kids.

We talked it over and it was decided that, with me having a cut up hand, the other three would go instead. Lindsay and Ashlyn were fine with the idea, and Spencer was okay with it, because he was told he could come into my room and find me if he couldn't find his Mommy and he was scared. He was pretty funny about that; he said he couldn't find his mom the night before, so he'd crawled up on top of me and gone to sleep, because I sound like a big bear snoring. Nothing was going to want to come around and eat a big bear, so he figured that that was as good a place as any. That had everyone laughing, much to my embarrassment.

"But I don't snore!" I argued.

"Yes, you do," they all chorused together.

"You okay, I don't mind playing babysitter anyway. Besides, me and the little man here have a pineapple under the sea type of song to figure out."

"Oh, who lives in a pineapple under the sea?" the twins started singing together.

"I just can't win for losing can I?" I asked the group, who were all laughing at me.

☣ ☣ ☣

We didn't end up having fun, but at about 3am, everyone but the kids and I snuck out of the house. I barely woke up when they did, but they let me know when they left, so I got up and checked on everybody. The girls were in the upstairs bedroom and Spencer was snoring softly on his mother's bed. Happy with that, I sat down in the recliner by the couch and tried to rest my eyes.

Sleep always forces itself on you when you really need it, but I found that after the EMP, my sleep was light. That's how I heard the floorboards pop and crackle under little feet, and I sat up. It was almost ready for sun-up, and by this time of year it had to be between five and six o'clock in the morning. Spencer was trying to work the handle to the bathroom, but somebody had shut it tight.

"Hey man, give me a second," I told him, rubbing the sleep out of my eyes.

"Hurry, I got to go," Spencer told me, hopping up and down and holding himself.

I almost tripped and fell on my face as I got the door open. It wasn't funny, but I'm glad the jokers from yesterday weren't around to see that.

"You have to stay by the door," Spencer told me, without closing the door all the way.

I had to hand it to the kid, he had some epic bladder control.

"You there?" Spencer asked.

"Yeah, still here."

"OK," he said, "I'm done now, you can come in."

Not knowing what was expected, I cracked the door. He was trying to reach the sink by standing on the edge of the toilet.

GOOD FENCES

"I can't... Get it..."

I gave him a boost and he sat on the counter, playing with the faucet handles before using about four times too much soap. It was really funny to my sleep and caffeine deprived mind, but I kept my amusement to myself. When we were done I carried him out to the kitchen while he finished drying his hands and arms on my shirt, before pulling himself close to my chest.

"You still sleepy?" I asked him.

"Uh huh," he said.

"Well, I'm going to get the coffee going and peek outside and see if there's any progress. You want me to put you on the couch, the bed... What do you want little buddy?"

"Couch, so I can watch SpongeBob."

"You can lay on the couch, but the TV's broke."

"But... but... I've been good. I'm not a bad boy. I want some SpongeBob..." his breathing hitched and he was working himself up to a big sob.

"Hey now, hey, hey. You guys are here because the power's out. Remember?"

"Yes?" Spencer said in a small voice.

"Well, the TV runs on power. I'd let you watch SpongeBob if I could. We wouldn't even tell your mom!" he looked up and wiped his face, "But I can't because there's no power. Sorry."

"Ok. Can I sit on the couch and we talk about SpongeBob?"

"Yeah buddy, here you go," I told him laying him down on the couch.

I grabbed him the afghan and he wrapped it around himself, pulling the throw pillow close like a teddy bear. I hadn't seen much in the way of toys since they'd been at the house and it made me think to look in the barn or the attic upstairs to see if any of my old stuff was in boxes still.

I got the coffee going in the rising light, and had gotten the pan out for eggs when I heard the quad fire up. I had said I didn't want to make tracks and risk things, but it'd been pointed out to me that I'd been all over that field with the tractors, so one more set of tracks wasn't going to look like anything different than what I'd been doing the previous week.

"And then Patrick said it was his turn…" Spencer was mumbling about the show, "…and SpongeBob said it was his toy."

Since no response was needed I listened to him as I started cooking. I had put a frozen package of bacon on the counter to thaw overnight and I started frying that up first in my mom's old cast iron skillet, and when it was done I set it on a plate to drain and cool. I fried up some potatoes, then cracked and beat a dozen eggs. I poured that in and, before it could finish cooking, I crumbled up half the bacon, added a big handful of cheese and started flipping the conglomerate around in the pan.

I'd always called it a poor man's omelet, but I'd never made one that big. I risked a peek out the window and I saw the quad finally coming, pulling the trailer. If I had to guess, Randy or Brenda was driving and the other was walking beside it with Lucy and their guns. The timing was working out well, and as they finally pulled up to the door I was splitting portions up onto plates and setting the front table, just as the percolator finished the coffee run.

"Oh, God, what's that smell?" Lucy asked, coming in the front door.

"Coffee," I told her, getting the kids' plates ready.

GOOD FENCES

"You are a God among men," Brenda said.

"Don't let his head swell up anymore!" Randy shut the door behind him.

"Hey now, don't start on me. I haven't had my coffee yet!" I told them, and we all had a smile.

They looked tired and I could see how loaded the trailer was. No wonder they had to drive slowly; Randy probably had to lean forward so the load wouldn't make the four-wheeler topple back on two wheels.

"Wow, you get it all?" I asked them, noticing how many garbage bags full of stuff were near the bottom of the piles.

"Yeah, clothing, food, rest of my preps along with the rest of my guns. Lucy here had a fully stocked kitchen, pantry and cold stuff. We're going to have to do that smoker sooner rather than later before all the meat goes bad."

"Not to mention all the meat on hoof," I said, thinking about the pigs.

"Hey, do you milk your goats?" Brenda asked.

"I was going to learn, but I never did. I just breed them so they can increase in numbers. They've been my brush control in the fields. Set them loose for six months, they eat down everything but what you want them to," I laughed.

"Those are Nubians. Supposed to be a good milking breed, and you have kids young enough with the does. You mind if I try sometime?" She asked.

"I don't mind. We're just going to have to bribe them with some sweet feed, they're pigs for their molasses."

"Ok, sounds good!" Brenda said before sitting down and attacking her food with gusto.

Randy was hungry as well, but other than coming into the house and teasing me, Lucy was mostly silent.

I thought about asking her on more than one occasion, but I didn't want to pry or push. Maybe she was just tired. Then it hit me, despite saying they got almost everything, they didn't talk about their trips through the fencing. I waited.

When it became obvious there was something they weren't talking about, or trying to figure out how to talk about it, it was slowly driving me crazy. I was about to ask them what it was, but was interrupted by the pounding feet of two elephants running down the stairs, giggling. Instead of poking and asking the question I wanted, I got two kid sized plates ready.

"Is my Mommy here now?" a little voice asked from the couch.

"Yes honey bear," Lucy said, rising to walk to the couch.

She picked him up and brought him to the table while he was squinting at the now rising sun, shining right in the window.

"Mom, this smells sooooooooo good!" Lindsey said to Brenda.

"Well, don't thank me, Brian is the one who cooked it," Brenda motioned to me with her fork.

"Did you?" she asked.

I nodded.

"I bet you he put healthy stuff in it," Ashlynn said, looking at her plate suspiciously, poking the pile of omelet with her fork.

"Bacon, eggs and hash browns. I would have added more stuff, but I didn't have a lot of time."

When Lucy sat down, she reached for her fork but Spencer was already grabbing it and as amusing as it looked, Lucy's eyes widened in horror as Spencer put his mouth to the plate and started shoveling in the food.

GOOD FENCES

He literally pulled it into his waiting mouth. I laughed, and soon the tension broke. Maybe when the kids were done I'd ask.

"You want your own plate?" Lucy asked her son.

"No, this is good for me," he told her between bites, and I had to fight back a laugh as Lucy gave me a frustrated look.

I got another plate out and got her some more. The rest I figured we'd make into breakfast burritos for lunch.

Everyone ate in silence, and the kids asked if they could go outside and play. Spencer ran from the table and came back with a handful of matchbox cars and asked if he could join them.

"No, not yet. I think we need to check out the farm and the gate to make sure no bandits and bad guys tried to get in," Randy told the twins after a long pause.

"Oh, ok. Think we can play a different board game today?" they asked me hopefully.

"Anything on that shelf, kiddos. You can play whatever's there," I told them.

"You're going to regret that," Brenda told me, shaking her head.

"Why?"

"Because my girls are monopoly masters. Don't let them rope you into any games or you won't get anything done today," Brenda said with a grin.

"I'm going to need a nap," Lucy said in a small voice, "is there any chance you can keep an eye on Spencer for an hour or two this morning?"

"Yeah, sure, I don't mind."

The kids wondered off to find a game and I heard the three of them laugh and head upstairs. That'd make watching them easier. Keep an eye on the doorway and let the twins spoil the little guy rotten. The twins had

183

discovered the rooms upstairs were brighter from the open windows, much brighter than my living room.

"Ok, so spill it, what happened?" I asked when the kids footfalls left.

"I'm going to get a quick shower," Lucy said standing, before putting her dishes in the sink.

I stood there, not sure what had just happened. I waited until the bathroom door closed before turning to Brenda and Randy who were looking everywhere but at me.

"Did I do something wrong?"

"No. We were planning on telling you anyways, but we didn't want to spring bad news right off the bat." Randy said.

"So what happened?" I asked again.

"Lucy's neighbor woke up and came over. He... He pushed his way in the front door. He didn't realize there was anyone other than Lucy in the house. Randy and I were in the kitchen and, when we heard the front door kicked open, we ducked and waited till we could see what was going on.

"He said the way Lucy would get dressed without pulling her curtains was an invitation for him to watch, and wouldn't she really like some..." Brenda shook her head. "it was bad. She denied it, even told him she had no idea her curtains were sheer from the outside. He told her he didn't care, she couldn't call the cops and he'd been watching her for a year. It was bad, Brian," Brenda paused before continuing.

"Both Randy and I popped out with our ARs and hit him with the flashlights. He just froze in shock. When we moved up on either side of her, we asked Lucy if she wanted us to shoot him. He was obviously there to rape and possibly kill her... I mean, the whole neighborhood listened to that damned emergency broadcast… and he probably thought…."

"Did she shoot him? Is that why she's upset?" I interrupted, a lead weight pulling at my heart.

"No, no. She asked us to let him leave. She didn't give the reasoning, but I showed him the door, maybe a bit rough, kind of like how you were scaring the guys yesterday," Randy told me, "Anyways, I watched the door while the girls finished packing and carrying everything to the fence. I had my NVGs on. It wasn't ten minutes later a gunshot rang out from the house. It wasn't loud, but I thought he was shooting at us."

I had a sinking feeling, and I was sinking further.

"So the girls covered me, when we realized all the windows were down and I'd seen him go inside. We walked around the house before we went in. I found him upstairs, dead with a cheap .32 in his mouth. It was pretty horrible," Randy told me.

Wow, I knew it had to have been bad, but that was really rough.

"Is she in some kind of shock?" I asked them both.

"Probably a little more than I am," Brenda admitted, "I mean, it's been two days. If it hadn't been for that emergency broadcast… Would he have treated it like any other Michigan power outage? He was ready to seriously hurt or rape her. None of us expected something like this to happen two days into an EMP."

I had, but not to my friends, not to my Lucy. Then that thought kicked me in the gut. Did I really have feelings for her, more than just a passing attraction? Yes, I decided, I did, and it didn't make me feel as guilty as I did before.

"No free parking!" I heard one of the twins yell, and Brenda got up to head upstairs.

That left Randy and I, who had more to say but waited for Brenda to leave.

"He had a picture book. Photo's he'd taken—"

"What? Was Lucy—"

"No, no, shhhhh," Randy said, his eyes flickering towards the stairs, "None of these women were alive. They'd been abused, but none of them were alive when he took the pictures. I only looked at a couple pages at the back of the book. There must have been forty or fifty different women in that book. That guy offing himself was probably the greatest gift anybody could have given us."

"He was a serial killer?!" I asked, my mind exploding at the thought.

"I think so. I don't know what to do about it, man. I didn't let the women see the book, I left it up there with his body. There's probably stuff in the house that police could use, but…"

"Why do you think he killed himself?" I asked.

"I don't know. I mean, we just ran him out at gunpoint. I didn't know the guy, but Lucy did. He was probably thinking everyone in the neighborhood would know he was going to, uh…"

"Yeah," I interrupted, not wanting him to finish the thought.

"I need some sleep too. Brenda said she'll stay up a bit longer and watch things from the bedroom we're using, then I'll trade off. Maybe later on we can work on those cameras?"

"Yeah, that sounds good. Plus we have to put away the stuff from the quad and trailer," I told him.

"There's never enough hours in the day, is there?"

☣ ☣ ☣

GOOD FENCES

Brenda wasn't kidding. I got sucked into the next Monopoly game when the kids all came downstairs. I knew we couldn't keep them cooped up in the house all the time, and they didn't complain much, but when I did animal chores, they were more than happy to join me to get out in the sunshine. I kept my pistol and AR on me the whole time we were out, but nothing happened. Spencer had fun trying to chase a chicken that had gotten out of the inner pen into the garage and the girls soon joined in to help.

It was the most hilarious thing I'd ever seen and I laughed until my sides hurt.

"Aren't you going to help them?" Lucy asked from the doorway, startling me.

She must have been sleeping hard, because she still had a red mark on her face that matched her hand, and she had come looking for us as soon as she awoke.

"Want me to? They're running off a ton of energy right now..."

"Brian, about earlier..."

"Randy and Brenda filled me in. I'm sorry, Lucy."

She walked towards me slowly. "Will you hold me, for just a second?"

I did. I understood at a fundamental level, that most guys would deny, that both sexes need comfort when their emotional ship has been rocked. We didn't say anything, but I held her close to me as she watched the kids continue to chase Mr. Einstein the chicken, as Spencer had named him. It wasn't a rooster, but I wasn't going to argue, none of my chickens had names. I gave Lucy a quick squeeze when she started to make motions to let go before dropping my grip as well.

"I feel safe here. You know? I thought I did at my house, but I don't think I ever will again. It was just such a...."

"I know," I said, taking her hand, "you don't have to be alone. You've always got a place here."

I hadn't meant it to not sound as deep as it did, but Lucy threw her arms around my chest and almost knocked the wind out of me in a desperate hug. Spencer caught sight of that and came running up on her in the stumbling running manner all kids have and jumped, wrapping his little arms around her legs almost toppling her over.

"Jam pile?" Lindsey asked her sister.

"Jam pile!"

That's how I ended up on the bottom of the pile, my AR sitting high up on a bench before I let them pull me down. Tickle torture ensued. I won that round, but lost the war as Mr. Einstein flew on top of my head. I swatted him away and pulled myself up, all of us dusty and dirty but smiling. We needed those laughs. I got a bucket of feed, which immediately caught the chook's attention, and dribbled some of it all the way to the inner doorway to the coop inside the barn. I cracked the doorway open and threw a handful of scratch in and closed the door.

"You mean, it's always that easy?" Ashlynn asked.

"What?" I asked, not sure what she was saying.

"You got the chicken back in by giving it treats. It's totally manipulating you," Lindsey told me.

"Well, I did it quicker than you three weirdos... Who won that round by the way?"

☣ ☣ ☣

We got the security system started the same day, but it took us three more days to get all the wires run. It didn't give us more than two directions of coverage on the farm, but I could see the gate and the fence along the subdivision. The cameras had built in solar panels, and weren't the most discreet things, but they worked. The monitor in the house hooked up to two coaxial cables that linked all the cameras, and three of the big solar panels in the faraday cage were used to charge batteries to run the monitor and the radio in the room Lucy was in.

The solar panels had been an easy install. Build them up on a frame, run the wires to the charge controller, charge the batteries we'd taken out of Randy and Brenda's cars they went back for late one night… Then the monitor was plugged in via dc/ac converter that was alligator clipped to the batteries. It looked Rube Goldberg, but it thankfully worked the first time we turned it on.

With one person watching the monitor, the rest of us could relax a little bit and we let the kids play outside after a week of no activity. The smoke in the distance seemed to double every day that week, but it looked far off. We weren't getting any ash from it, but I'd started to worry that whatever was burning would meet in the middle of Flint and Saginaw right where we were. It was a bad time too; it had been a really dry spring and summer was in full force, and everything seemed drier than it had ever before. The corn didn't care, it grew regardless, but everything else that was dry probably fed into the fires.

I worked with Lucy a bit on her marksmanship, but we'd gotten mad at each other. Brenda took over teaching her about the guns and firing until Lucy was ready to move up beyond the .22. I gave my AR to her to use and her eyes went wide.

"But, that's huge! It'll break my shoulder!"

That made me laugh, and I explained that it did

have some kick, but not as much as the big guns. It was a really easy one to fire. She took it reluctantly, and soon the ladies came back with grins. Lucy told me that she'd found her new favorite toy and she could shoot the middle out of the ten ring with it. Obviously I wasn't going to give her my baby… so we kept cycling her though different firearms and had plans to start teaching her how to use a pistol.

15

A couple of times over the next week or so, one of us would see somebody come to the fence. They would stand there, letting their arms hang through the barbed wire. Many of them were looking dirty and disheveled. On a day when half a dozen people were all lined up on the fence, I got a bucket out and ran water into it.

"What are you doing?" Randy asked.

"Look," I said, pointing to the left side of the monitor.

"They look pretty bad, don't they?" Randy commented.

He'd taken to staying up the latter half of the night, watching the monitor and keeping an eye out while we slept.

"Yeah, I was going to run some water out to them. That can't hurt, can it?"

"You're better off not doing anything, actually," Randy told me.

Gone was my happy-go-lucky friend. He was being serious, dead serious.

"Do nothing?" I asked.

"How can you? You go out there all showered and shaved, and they're going to know you aren't as bad off as they are. What are you going to do when they all start asking for food? I don't know about you, but I don't have that much stored. I think it'll start a big bunch of suck once we open that door, even a tiny crack." Randy said passionately.

"It's just some water," I argued, starting to get irritated with him.

"Listen man, it's your place, but I think you'd be putting us all at risk. I'd leave them, man."

I grunted, and then put the bucket up on the counter for washing later. You never knew when you'd need it.

☣ ☣ ☣

Two weeks passed since the EMP happened, going into three. We all slowly adjusted to the new life, and worried about Frank, Kristen and Ken daily. The Docs would have been a great addition to the help as well, but it wasn't any of them who eventually showed up, it was Brandon Sanderson and his three sons. They were pushing a hand built cart with bicycle tires for wheels. They looked at the front gate and then started talking, gesturing wildly.

I could see it all over the monitor. At first glance I thought it was the tweakers coming back, but when they got close to the fence I could see Brandon Sanderson's distinctive build. He was tall like me, but where I was wiry, he was more barrel chested. Brenda was called to watch through the window with her scope where she could also keep an eye on the monitor while Randy and I went to the gate.

We walked out there, fully armed. I'd borrowed one of Randy's spare tactical vests, and I kept it right by the kitchen table. It was a mini armory all on its own. Enough to hold six magazines, a small water bottle, a Ka-Bar I kept near the small of my back, sideways so I could pull it with my right hand and then it had basic first aid supplies in one of the dump pouches. There hadn't been any trouble since the night they went and got the rest of the supplies from their house, so I wasn't expecting any now.

"How well do you know these guys?" Randy asked me as we walked.

"They go to my church. I hired the four of them on to do the fence that last week before the EMP came down. Brandon could probably figure out what I was doing if he spent any time in the barn, but he kept his mouth shut and didn't even bat an eye when I asked him to install the driveway gate."

"So he's on the level?" Randy asked.

"I think so. His wife is real sick. Cancer, I think, and him and his sons were hard workers. They'd show up here before I left for work and a lot of times left way after dinner time. I know they really needed the money… but half of the defenses here are from them."

"So you're wanting to let them in?" Randy asked.

I stopped walking, my jaw dropping.

"We've been saying that we need more people. Lucy brought up all the livestock you have that you were going to send to the butcher… It's not like we're going to be hurting for food right away," Randy admitted.

"I thought you were worried about the time I wanted to run water to the neighbors at the subdivision? What's changed?"

"Nothing really," Randy said and we started walking again.

"How's that any different?" I asked, trying not to be annoyed.

"There's 65 houses roughly in the subdivision. Most of them have at least three or four people including kids living in them. So that's upwards of 240 mouths to start feeding and watering. It's a math game. The ones who are still alive over there would soon want more than we could give them from over here. A small group like ours could easily defend ourselves if needed, but we don't want to become the soup kitchen for everybody around here."

"Shit, you're right Randy. I'm sorry, it's just that the thought of kids over there, or even their parents suffering while we could probably help—"

"There's no probably," Randy said interrupting me, "it'll get us killed. You see how crazy some of those folks in that subdivision are. We haven't even seen Landry or the kid since the morning after it happened… and he's nuts. Lucy's neighbor was nuts… What do you think's going to happen when somebody's little baby is crying because their stomach is empty and they're hungry and thirsty?

"Hopefully find them something to eat?" I said, knowing that was lame.

Most people don't know where their food comes from, nor how to produce, hunt or forage for it. The lawyer I'd dealt with at the fence line had said something similar. Why hunt when you could just kill off some of your own animals? You don't need guns, he'd said… Sadly, I knew Randy was right, but I needed to hear it aloud from somebody else. To share my darkest thoughts so I didn't bear my shame alone. I knew that was selfish, but it helped somehow.

"We've talked about this. The first big die off is those on life support, the elderly or on medication," he paused and saw the look on my face, "hey, we couldn't have done anything for Mr. Matthews anyways, not unless you had a pacemaker that was shielded from an EMP and had a heart surgeon on standby."

"What you're saying is that I'm buying my own trouble, aren't I?" I asked.

"Yep. Help those you know and trust and, a year from now, worry about the rest of the world," Randy said.

"That's too much of an isolationist, lone wolf thing for me, man." I told him after thinking about it.

"Ok, maybe not a year, but those guys at the gate… We could really use some help around here and I'm guessing they didn't come here to sell us Avon."

I laughed at that. Sure enough, when we got close the Sandersons were pulling that hand built cart so the rear of it could face the fence. I saw a woman, curled on her side, obviously in a lot of pain.

"Brandon, what's going on?" I asked, worried.

"I was hoping… I mean… You were always so good to us, that last weeks' worth of work made it so I could get Kristy's medicine and make the bills. Now nothing works and I don't know what to do. Me and the boys would be willing to do work, cut firewood or whatever it is if we could stay here for a little bit until things calmed down?"

We talked at the gate for about five minutes and then let them in. I offered to help push the cart, but the sons all politely declined. I never knew their names and made a mental note to find out without looking like an ass later on. Their story came out in a rush, and it was pretty bad.

A week ago, the prisons had been opened up. It was either let the prisoners loose or figure out a way to keep them in food and water. With less and less people showing up, they just threw the switches to manually unlock all cells and ran for their lives as the inmates tried to catch up and rain down their wrath upon them. All of it was told in a hurry by Brandon, whose neighbor had been a turnkey at the prison. He was one of the last men out, with the two slower ones behind him becoming cannon fodder to the angry population.

With services going out and no hope of quick relief, the guards did what they could with their dwindling staff and everyone got their bare essentials done on every day, but every single prisoner was kept in their cell. No outside time, no socializing in the cafeteria, just the same bars they slept in every night. Most of them resented it and once they were set loose, well... it wasn't pretty.

His neighbor had gotten home and started packing. He filled in Brandon and told him to get out of there, but Brandon didn't think it was as bad as the guy was saying. Three nights later, the inmates joined up. Black Panthers working with the Aryan Nation, with the only holdouts being the Muslim population. Those guys faded out of sight quick. They had started going house to house, neighborhood to neighborhood.

They knew that the cops wouldn't be coming, and if FEMA or the military hadn't done anything in close to two weeks, that they'd be home free for quite a while. When Brandon's house had been attacked, the four men were ready and the inmates had threatened from the cover of a car in the road that they'd be back later on that night.

They loaded up Kristy and all the food they could and started walking. I'd seen Kristy was on the cart, but the boxes and bags around her must have been their supplies and food. I readily agreed to let them in and immediately had no clue where I wanted to put them.

"How's Kristy doing?" I asked Brandon, not sure if she could hear me through the fog of pain.

"She's been out of her medicine, can't really eat without throwing up."

"Cancer?" Randy asked softly.

The Sandersons nodded, none of them dry eyed.

"Let's get some food going and we'll figure this out."

"So we can stay for now?" Brandon asked.

"Yeah, we just have to figure out where to get you situated is all." I told him.

Five people, I suppose I could let them have the barn, or they could have floor space wherever they wanted... then it hit me. The hunting cabin. It was too far off the house for somebody to run there in an emergency, but it was close enough that maybe.... Hey, I had the big tractor that Mr. Matthews had given me. That could move it down close!

"Randy?"

"Yeah, Brian."

"Want to help me move that single wide I was going to use as a hunting shack?" I asked him.

"Good idea! By the house?"

"How about between the house and the barn? If we get the rest of the stuff out of your truck some night, we can hook it up to the water so they could do dishes and have a shower. Just... no bathroom. I don't know how to hook it into the septic."

"I do, I'm a plumber, remember?" Randy said, bumping me with his shoulder.

"Oh yeah... Well?"

"I think it's a good idea. If Frank, Kristen, Ken and the Docs do show up, we're going to need more room anyways." Frank told me.

All we had to do was figure out if we really had enough food and figure out how to sneak into the subdivision and unload Randy's truck without people seeing us. More and more people had been walking out to the fence, especially when the pigs and goats were out. It had worried me, but the folks were starting to look worn down.

☣ ☣ ☣

We temporarily hooked up the trailer from the garden hose, the same way I'd done to the house. Since the driveway and turnaround by the barn was compacted gravel by the barn we were able to jack up the house, move things around and lower it on my big collection of blocks. I tried to fire up the Kubota, but it was as dead as I thought it would be. Still, I could scavenge the hydraulic parts, fittings and implements off it. Otherwise, it would remain where it was for now, a toy Spencer and the kids could play with until I needed the room.

Right away, the Sanderson boys went to work, constructing bunk beds for inside the mostly empty trailer. They used up some of my scrap wood pile and then went through all the lumber left over from renovation projects. They'd overheard that there could be more people, so they didn't even bother leaving the living room as a living room. They built five sets of bunk beds, but we had no mattresses for them.

Which also made me think of Mr. Matthews and my inheritance. I still didn't know what he had in the foot-locker, or any idea of what he was going to finish telling me about in his note. I wanted to head over there one day, but with the Sandersons' arrival, I didn't want to leave until everyone was settled in. Almost immediately the boys had asked if they could expand the garden, and I explained that the tiller I had on the Kubota wouldn't mount up to the old tractor Mr. Matthews had given me.

They did some digging and found a shaft extension somewhere in my father's piles of junk and, like magic, it suddenly was good to go. They hooked it up to the PTO and headed out towards my garden. I had about half a tank of diesel, but I also knew Mr. Matthews had a triple container tank in what he called his tank farm. He used it to keep his tractors topped off, and probably the semi that I hadn't known he had. There was a lot of stuff there, and I really should have done more immediately, but I'd spent the last week reading my dad's old foxfire books and one on country living. It was a tabletop book, easily 15x15. It was all reprinted articles and how-to's. In it, there were plans on all kinds of things.

What I'd really wanted to learn was how to butcher and smoke a hog, and then move on to goats. They had plans inside the book for building all kinds of smokers, smoke shacks and how to butcher animals, plus about half an inch of the book dedicated to foraging for food, medicine and vitamins. I just needed to figure out a way to start storing things for the long term, or we were going to have to throw away the food like the stuff I'd finally been forced to clean out of the fridge and freezer… well, it had gone to Ruby and the rest of the hogs, but I didn't want to waste any more.

"What do you think about something like this?" I showed Brandon one morning.

"Do you have any chicken wire?"

Oh boy, did I.

He began cutting down saplings about two to three inches around, and then trimming all the limbs off until he had a dozen poles. He put six of the poles into the ground with the help of Steven, Bret and Brandon Jr. They'd used a post hole digger to get about three feet deep and put the poles in the ground. They cut off the poles at eight feet, so there was easily five feet in the height. Once they were set, they dug two more holes, one in the middle of the outer framework and one on the backside.

The hole in the back was kept as small as possible, probably two feet away from the one in the middle of the new structure. I watched in interest, trying to guess what they were doing. The hole in the middle was widened up until you could fit a five gallon bucket into it then they dug from the big hole until they reached the smaller one outside. Poles were cut and fitted again, secured with nails to make cross beams on each end and two of them that flared into an A shape, the open end by the door. Then they laid poles the other direction on top of that. It was probably overkill, but it looked sturdy enough and when I shook the structure, it didn't budge.

Shelves were formed that way, and chicken wire was stretched over them. They were tacked into place and the boys went scavenging in my trash pile in the barn's loft and came back with an old piece of cloth canvas my father had used to cover his car with back when I was a kid. Brandon Jr. came back with an old screen from a storm window and dropped it on the ground, where the smaller hole was outside.

200

"You going to tell me how all this is supposed to work?" I asked them.

"When I figure it out, I'll let you know!" Brandon said, frustrating me.

Randy had already figured things out, but I was still scratching my head on the two connected holes until they built a small fire.

"Can I borrow a big cast iron pot?" Brandon asked.

"Sure," I said, going inside and finding the one my mom used to make stews.

I hadn't used it much, and hopefully whatever they were going to do wouldn't ruin it. I doubted it would, people had been cooking over cast iron for so long… When I got back out there, there were three pieces of re-rod that had been laid across the big hole and they nodded when they saw the oversized pot.

"Perfect, now let's see if it'll work," Brandon said, putting two scoops of sawdust into the pot that was placed over the makeshift grate.

"What about the other hole?" I asked, noting the smoke coming up from the one outside.

"I don't know if this will be the most efficient way, but I'm hoping it does… Ahhh see!"

Little streamers of smoke started rising out of the pot as the sawdust from the bunk construction first turned brown and then combusted a moment or two later.

"Wow that went quick. That won't work if we're trying to slow smoke something will it?" I asked.

"I know what he's doing," Brenda interjected, walking up with Lucy. "He's making this like a water smoker. There's going to be some heat inside here, but most of the smoke is going to come from wood chips soaked in water then added to the pan there. The outer hole is to feed oxygen to the fire on the bottom."

"Exactly. And I think as long as no hot sparks go flying up, this canvas tarp will be pretty safe to use," Brandon said.

We all agreed, and soon we'd wrapped it up with the canvas, nailing it on in three spots. It didn't have to be super tight, but we didn't want to get flies in there while we were starting things out with food for the first time. The flap for the door was an unsecured piece. You pulled it over, hung the top on a trim nail Brandon had put in, and the bottom was held in place by a large rock. You could feed the fire from only once spot which kind of sucked, but when we ran it for the first time without food in it, I could tell that it wasn't going to get too hot and cook not smoke the food.

The Sanderson boys had re-tilled up a large garden and when they were done they checked on their mother. I hadn't seen her upright since she came to the farm, but I'd stopped in to tell her hello on one of her good days. She looked pale and drawn. I wished there was something I could do, but I knew it wasn't up to me.

"Hey Brian," Lucy called after I'd high fived the guys, "Come here a minute."

I walked over, all smiles.

"Spencer has missed you terribly this week. He thinks you're mad at him," she told me, her face serious.

"I'm not mad at him!" I said, confused, "he's been playing with the twins nonstop and I've been—"

"You've been busy trying to set things up so we can all live. I know. But he misses you and… I miss you too."

Brenda had been walking back at that moment and she stopped and gave me a look and turned and walked the other way.

"You know, you're right. Let me go make friends

with my buddy again and you and I can figure things out. I'm sorry if I've been ignoring you two."

"Good, he's in the bedroom, pretending to be talking on the radio."

"It's not hooked up though, is it?" I asked, sure I'd unhooked it last time I'd used it.

I hadn't used it often, really only to see whether the emergency broadcast had changed any. I put my AR up high on my dresser and headed into Lucy's room. Little changes I hadn't noticed previously were apparent. Lucy had hung her clothes in the closet and her makeup was sitting on my mother's small desk where she used to get ready for work in the morning. Spencer had a trunk inside there. It was open and there were toys spilling out of it, compliments of the attic and what they'd brought back last time.

"Come in good buddy, over, Rodger Dodger." Spence said into a dead handset microphone.

"Hey buddy," I said flopping down on the bed sideways so I could see him.

Slowly, he reached out and put the microphone on my father's desk and slid off the stool.

"I'm sorry, I didn't mean to play the radio," he said, tears starting to form, "I promise I'll be a good boy."

Shit, that I wasn't expecting. I was the one who'd gone in feeling guilty and the little guy thought it was something he'd done wrong. It wasn't, I'd just gotten excited and caught up in getting projects done that I thought were necessary for our survival. But I realized right then that without friends, family and a reason to live, survival wasn't enough. Not by itself.

"You didn't do anything wrong, buddy," I said holding my arms out.

He gave me a shy grin and then came closer to the

203

end of the bed. I picked him up and Supermaned him over me until he started laughing and I set him down next to me.

"It's my fault, Spencer. I got too busy. I love you to pieces, little man and I never meant to hurt your feelings. I promise you I won't let it happen again," I choked that out, but still smiled.

"You do?" He asked.

"I do, I love you to pieces. You're my buddy, I want you to know that."

"You love Mommy too?" he asked in an innocent way that totally disarmed me.

"Yes," I whispered, "I love your Mommy too. She's my buddy too," I told him, not able to lie to the little man, realizing the truth of the words when I spoke them.

I heard a choked sob and turned to see Lucy standing in the doorway. I almost panicked, but Spencer was smiling. Had I crossed the line? She'd asked to take things slow, and other than random hugs and horseplay we'd not repeated the kiss. I'd wanted to, I'd wanted to do a whole lot more than that, but she'd lost her husband a lot more recently than I'd lost my Cathy. Her pain was still fresher and I wanted to give her all the space and time she needed.

Lucy then said two words and tackled me.

"Jam pile!"

16

I started seeing less and less people when it was my turn on the monitors. Not many were coming to the fences any more, and the ones who did were definitely on the survival diet. Gone was any semblance of baby fat, cheeks were starting to hollow out. It was a hard thing to watch, while we ate normal meals. We'd done the math and, with all the extra I'd stored, we'd easily had enough food to last us a year. I had about three months' worth of animal feed before we'd have to do something about that.

"You think it's safe to get the rest of the stuff out of your van?" I asked Randy one day.

"I don't know. I don't want to do it too soon and risk having to shoot my neighbors, ya know?"

"I do. I was just curious; I know there's tools and supplies you've needed and things have been... dead," I finished for lack of a better word.

"It has. I don't know, you're probably right. It might

help if Brenda and I go, or see how things have been lately. I'd kinda like to check on my house actually," he admitted

"Oh, yeah. That's cool then. I was just curious, but I know what you mean."

"How about Brenda and I go tonight? We can have the girls watch Spencer for a bit so you and Lucy can have some alone time?"

Damn, that wasn't what I was angling for, and I didn't know what alone time Randy was referring to. The kind his wife and family had upstairs, or the get to know each other better kind? He was really putting me on the spot and I knew that anything I told him would be repeated to Brenda - who would in turn tell Lucy.

"Sure," I said, taking the easy way out, "We can maybe have one of Brandon's kids watch the monitors?"

"Ha ha ha, yeah right. I'm sending the kids upstairs and leaving you two the downstairs. I thought you'd like to… have some alone time?"

"Dude, don't push it," I said pushing him and then laughing.

"Ok, if you're not ready, you're not ready. I just know she's been talking to Brenda and—"

"What's she saying?" I demanded.

"Now, you know that shit is private, man!" Randy complained as I needled him.

"You know, Brenda knows… I'm just… curious. Would it help me if I knew?" I asked.

"I think you already know. I just need you to put on your big girl britches, man up and—"

"My big girl britches? I'm not the one who wears pink frilly robes," I said laughing.

"That was one time, and I was half awake when I did it." Randy said, a little hurt.

GOOD FENCES

I laughed even harder, drawing the attention of Brenda and Lucy. Brenda came over to sit down at the table, but Spencer called his Mom and she went the opposite direction.

"We're talking about your husband's cross dressing habits," I said, giggling.

"You should see him in my leather…"

That shut me up. Like a faucet that had been turned off, my laughter dried up as Randy looked at his wife incredulously, his jaw almost hitting the ground.

"Whoa, TMI, TMI Brenda…. So give me the dirt. Randy is telling me you two are going to give me and Lucy some alone time. You obviously know more than I do so…" I held up my hands as if to plead or pray.

"Oh, so you want your best friend's wife to set you up, fill you in on the inner secrets of a woman's mind? Betray a girlfriend's confidence? Is that what I'm hearing you ask?" Brenda said, smiling at me.

"Yup."

"Good, I just wanted to make sure. Uh… make your move dumbass. You had her heart the night you two were wrestling around on the bed. She told me if Spencer hadn't been in the room you would have been staked and claimed," Brenda told me.

"Staked and claimed?" I asked incredulously, wanting to hear the rest.

Footsteps started approaching and I turned to see Lucy walking towards us.

"It's a paranormal romance thing. We read the same books." Brenda whispered back.

That made no sense at all to me, but whatever. I was happy, but there was one problem I could foresee: no preacher, no wedding no… God forgives all sins if you repent. Good deal, because I was hoping to sin at least once tonight. My face was burning red when Lucy took the seat next to me.

"Poor Spencer, he doesn't like to go to the bathroom alone... What?" She asked the silent table.

"Uh, Brenda and Randy are going to check things out at their place later on. They said the twins would watch Spencer for us." I said that and waited for her to explode or cry or...

"Good, I hope he doesn't give them any problems," she was also red in the face.

☣ ☣ ☣

Dinner was a quick affair. I made sure to make something quick with easy cleanup. Fresh veggies for stir fry, rice and some diced radish for some kick. It wasn't how I usually made things, but I didn't have a grocery store to make sure I had all the right ingredients. The Sanderson boys finished off the last of the food before taking a plate back for Kristy. Brandon told me she was out of it most of the time and he asked if there was a place he could use when it was time. I nodded and told him we'd figure it out.

The twins had been instructed well and told Spencer he was going to sleep in the middle of the floor tonight, and they'd read him all the books they wanted. It was obvious to everyone in the crowded house that the grownups were trying to give Lucy and I some time alone. I tried not to get too red in the face. It'd been over three years for me, and I'd married the first woman I'd fallen in love with. I was more than a bit nervous, but as soon as everyone was out, Lucy pulled me into the bedroom.

"Do you love me?" Lucy asked, closing and locking

the door behind me.

"I do," I admitted.

"Would you marry me someday, when things are safer?"

"Yes."

"Good," she said, striking a match and lighting two candles.

In the flickering candlelight she pulled her clothing off slowly, one piece at a time. I stood and watched her, mesmerized. When she was finished, she stalked over to where I was standing and started pulling at my clothing.

"You sure you're ready for this?" I asked her, trying not to let my hoarse breathing be too loud, too noticeable.

"I've been ready for a bit now. I was just waiting on you," she said as her soft hands caressed my chest.

☣ ☣ ☣

Gunshots. I awoke from a dead sleep, Lucy's nude form laying across me, as if to steal my warmth. I pushed her off gently and she stirred awake.

"Somebody's shooting out there," I said searching for my clothing.

"Here," Lucy flicked a lighter on and found the candles, the matches from earlier probably for effect.

I got dressed as quickly as I could and ran to the monitors while Lucy ran upstairs to check on the kids. It wasn't true night vision on the monitors, but with enough moonlight you could make out things. Everything had a green cast to it, and I could see the grass laid down in one spot as something thrashed.

"Oh shit. Watch the kids, grab your gun out of the safe." I yelled and pulled my vest on and got my AR ready.

I didn't slow down to grab my Glock, but I was out the door almost at a dead run. The thrashing form in the grass was at the house just north of George Landry's, at either the lawyer's or his neighbor. I prayed it wasn't Randy or Brenda, and I prayed hard. The only time I slowed was going through the gate and then I was off again. I wasn't going for stealthy, I was running wildly into a firefight to save my friends.

Firefight, now there's a word. I hadn't heard more gunshots. Just the four or five that woke me up. Had there been more that I didn't hear or register in my sleep? I literally stumbled upon the corpse before I even saw it. It was one of my pigs, and it'd been shot through the neck. I checked the barrel of the AR for any debris from my fall and listened, letting the night calm down because of my wild run.

"Who's there?" Randy's voice boomed out of the darkness.

"It's me," I said standing up.

"Me who? Turn around."

I did and heard the click of a safety and froze.

"Sorry about that, I have my NVG's on," Randy said, coming under the fence by Landry's backyard.

"What's going on? Who shot the pig?" I asked.

"Well, we uh… It wasn't us," Brenda said.

"I sort of pulled a 'you' and things went south." Randy admitted stopping in front of me.

The NVG's made him look like some weird alien bug, and he kept scanning around behind us.

"You pulled a me?" I asked.

"George Sr. saw my pen light while I was digging through the truck. Apparently Jr.'s cast was supposed to come off and he was asking to borrow a hacksaw or something," Randy said.

"You didn't loan him one did you? After trying to get your van thrown out of the HOA?" I asked hardly believing it.

"No, worse," he said softly.

"What did you do?"

"I cut it off for the kid. George was thankful, but they were looking pretty sickly. Apparently a bunch of people heard about that guy's suicide. He'd had a ton of food, apparently he was some sort of conspiracy theorist on top of everything else. Had a ton of MRE's. Anyways, they'd been eating all of that and he was asking me to talk to you about buying some animals when I heard a shot. I ran out and a guy with a rifle shot at me, so I uh…"

"He froze and I lit him up," Brenda finished.

"The neighbors are pissed. Apparently the couple who came to investigate said we shouldn't have stopped him from killing the pig. They'd had to watch them grow up, and felt entitled to…"

"Aww shit man. No." I said.

"Yeah. We ran before more people with guns showed up and escaped out of George's backyard. I don't know if you want to stay out here and watch the fence tonight, but I sort of think… Wait," he said, pulling the NVGs off and looking at me in natural light, "Did your date go well?" He was grinning in a way that left no doubt as to what he meant.

"We had a couple of dates, we're cool man," I admitted.

"A couple of dates? Randy, you are such a slacker you no good, low life—" she started belting him on his arm.

"Hey now, neighbors. Let's be serious," I whispered loudly.

"Right, yeah. Ok, so… Do we give them the pig? Do we take it back? Do we stop people from crawling under the fence? Brandon Jr. said he's run people out of here more than once, and they always head west," Randy said.

"I don't know man, part of me says yes, but I really don't like that these people think that they can just come in here and take our—"

"That's why I stopped you with the water," Randy interrupted, "It's going to get worse now, I think."

"Do you think they'll come through tonight?" I whispered.

"Probably not, but maybe a couple to look for the pig," Brenda said quietly.

"I'll stay out here, I've got a few hours' worth on these batteries before I need to recharge them. Then I'll sleep in the daytime. What do you think?"

"Sounds good. I'll bring the quad back here so we can load the pig somehow, we'll hang him in the garage and process tomorrow."

"Ok. You'll know if I run into trouble," Randy patted his gun.

"Let's pray you don't."

Brenda and I walked back; she headed in to let Lucy, and whomever else was awake, know that things were OK. I stopped in the dark barn and found my quad and got a tow strap. I pulled out and debated the headlight. In the dark, the noise alone would give me away but if I went too slowly, they could pinpoint me if they wanted revenge. I debated my options and decided to pick my way through slowly till I could silhouette Randy in the moonlight.

17

Butchering the hog wasn't as difficult as I thought it would be, and we smoked two of the hams on the top shelf, leaving room for slabs of meat all the way down. The book that described the process of butchering a pig was quite a bit like butchering a deer, just a lot more parts on the hog you could eat, if you chose to. I fed the entrails to the chickens and tossed the rest into a hastily dug hole with the head. Then I made my cuts and fired up the smoker.

One thing I learned that morning was that the smaller cook hole was very efficient, but I had to keep adding wood to it until it had a good bed of coals. I made a note to ask Brandon Sr. if a larger hole, at least at the bottom, would be a big deal. I could fit larger chunks in there… But since it was already cooking, I kept it going while Brenda and Lucy patrolled the parameter.

We'd talked that morning about heightened security. I don't know if the neighbors saw what or who happened to whomever it was that Randy and Brenda had had to light up, but we were all concerned about backlash. Randy decided to man the gate with one of the Sanderson boys, and we all were on edge. I had my eye on the kids while I worked, and I'd taken quite a bit of time showing them what we were doing and why. The twins thought it was boring, but Spencer hardly left my side at all.

"Can you make chicken nuggets like that?" he'd asked me more than once.

"If you like them smoked."

"Yuck!"

"You like jerky?" I asked the kids, "Or how about smoked ham?"

"I like them on sandwiches," Ashlynn said.

"It's sooooo good," Lindsey told me.

"Well, this is my first time, so we'll see how this goes. We didn't soak or brine the meat, so it's going to be like people did things in the olden days!"

Then Ashlynn produced an old soccer ball from some of the stuff they'd brought over, and the kids soon had a soccer version of keep away, running all over the hard packed gravel of the turnaround between the house and the trailer. I watched them play and felt kind of cheated a little bit. During my childhood, there wasn't a ton of kids to play with until I'd gotten to school. Back then, there were no subdivisions, in fact, our only neighbor was Mr. Matthews. I couldn't be resentful towards the kids though, it was just my situation.

Feeling thoroughly lazy, I did feel a bit guilty. Food and kid patrol wasn't as difficult as walking the perimeter or trying to watch out for angry mobs of mutant zombie wannabes.

Two shots rang out, and I let out a shrill whistle.

GOOD FENCES

Scanning, I didn't see anything, but I knew those shots had come from the gate. We'd talked about this also, so when the girls ran up, I sent them inside the trailer with Mrs. Sanderson and one of the boys who'd stayed behind to watch over their mother. I went into the house and double checked the monitor and saw the outlines of a small mob of people at the gate. The fence was clear, and I could see Lucy, who was learning from Brenda, move into their pre-arranged spots to cover the fence. If a big firefight broke out, then they would decide if they could back us up if they could. With me, and the Sandersons minus one son, we'd all converge on the fence.

Randy and Brandon were already there as I worked my way closer. Brandon Jr. and his older brother were jogging to catch up with me. I patted my hand up and down in the air to let them know to slow down, keep low. They seemed to understand, and noticed that I was using the cover of the trees on the North West side of the drive to make it up towards Randy and Brandon.

I'd taken to wearing my .45 on my hip instead of concealed, for comfort and ease. I had the AR as well; I didn't have my vest handy, but I did have a spare 30 round mag stuffed in my back pocket. Sixty rounds. That may sound like a lot, but I'd always read that even the best trained police miss six for every four shots in a heated gunfight.

I hoped I wasn't about to get involved in my first one.

☣ ☣ ☣

"… was just trying to get some meat. He didn't know it was a farm animal!" A belligerent neighbor shouted, his words carrying to me through the wind.

215

BOYD CRAVEN

In another half a minute I'd be standing near Randy, but I could only hear his words as if a whisper.

"Our pigs are pink, you idiot?"

Murmur from them until Randy yelled "… wild pigs are hairy," Randy's voice was shouting volume.

"Back off," this from Brandon.

Two figures started climbing the fence, somehow ignoring the barbed wire until one of them screamed and jumped backwards, scarlet drops falling from his hands.

"Listen, what's it going to take to buy some food then?" an angry voice shouted, and it was a voice I recognized.

"George, what are you looking for?" I asked him, finally caught up with Randy, the two boys taking up positions from concealment behind me.

"We want to buy some food from you guys. You obviously are a pretty good farmer, you don't look malnourished to me," he said.

"I might be willing to barter for some food."

"Barter? You have an entire field of corn!" somebody in the group shouted.

I tried to do a quick count, but people were moving and shuffling around. The smell of unwashed bodies was overpowering, and I could definitely tell from the scent that they'd run out of toilet paper a long time ago and hadn't found an alternative.

"The corn won't be ready for another month. I inherited the equipment to harvest it, but no. I'm not going to just give you guys' food. You can either barter for it, or work for it." I told them on the fly, hoping I wasn't pissing off everyone from our group.

"Barter? What are you looking for?" a raggedy woman asked.

"I don't know, what have you got? I don't mean to

216

be coy, but I don't know what you have that would be useful to me. I like guns, bullets, gold... or I could use some extra help come harvest season or putting in a new garden area," I told them.

"Do I look like I'm in any condition to shovel a ditch or swing an axe?" an angry man shouted.

"Hey, I'm ok with helping you guys out, but somebody went through my fences and killed one of my pigs and shot at one of us. I'm not really in a charitable mood right now!" I shouted back.

"Yeah, and one of yours killed Cindy's husband. What's she going to do now?" the raggedy lady in the back yelled.

"I don't know, is she here?" I asked.

People looked around themselves and murmured back and forth before the guy who'd been screaming at me started back up.

"It isn't right, he was just trying to get food for a few of us. You guys murdered him!"

"No, no we didn't!" Randy shouted.

The change in direction made a few of them snap their attention to him.

"He raised his rifle and took a shot. He died because he was trespassing, stealing and tried to MURDER ME!" the last two words were shouted.

"Oh, so it was you who shot him?" a voice jeered.

Randy hesitated, then nodded. I knew it was a lie, it had been his wife, but in his shoes, I probably would have taken the heat as well.

"I didn't want to do it. But what would you do if somebody was pointing a gun at your face!" Randy said in a softer voice.

"You guys are running around like soldiers anyways! Those guns and pistols. I'd put in a complaint to the HOA if it would do shit, but nothing has so far," A voice I recognized as the lawyer said and I saw George Landry turn a dark red.

"It would have if you idiots had helped me like I asked!" George snarled.

"Wow," Brandon laughed, "No wonder you guys have such a bad rap with Brian here. When you guys aren't back stabbing each other, you're trying to get the farm shut down. Now that you need the food, you want the farm to run the way you want, huh? How many of you have gardens? How many of you are hunting the state woods to the north of your subdivision?"

Another murmur, but the voices were not as angry. I caught snatches of conversation. Someone was saying they just should regroup and take what they wanted, others were discussing the idea of hunting. Two women walked up to the gate and held up their hands as if they were in school.

"Yes," I pointed to one of them.

"What kind of work are you talking about, when harvest comes?"

"Preserving the food. Obviously some is going to be canned, some dried out and some… Well I can't say frozen… sorry. A lot of it is going to be eaten right away though and, I'll be honest, corn and wild game isn't a great meal when it's all you've had for months on end, but it'll keep you alive for a while. You," I pointed to the second lady.

"Two questions about hunting and bartering. If I were to trade you a gun, what would I do about hunting? I don't really know about hunting at all and the only way I know is to shoot them. I just… my kids are hungry. They've started crying everyday about the bellyaches. I just want to help feed my babies—" her words broke off

GOOD FENCES

into sobs.

"We could just cut the fence and take what we needed!" George yelled and about half the group cheered.

I raised my rifle and he went very still. I walked to the gate and stuck my flash suppressor through it an inch until it was less than a foot away from Landry's schnoz. Oh I so wanted to pull the trigger, I so wanted the man to pay for everything he and his son had done to me. The repeated harassment, the way he illegally forged documents to screw me over. How he got his son off - even though his son didn't seem to be a snake the way his father was as far as I could tell from our short conversation. His broken ankle was literally the only contact I'd had with George Jr., and I still felt bewildered at the prospect of forgiving him. Could I forgive his father as well?

"George, you really don't want to give me any more excuses to shoot you. You have tried to systematically ruin my life since the car accident. I don't know if you were trying to save your son, or you were overcompensating for his misdeeds, but trust me George, you don't want me as your enemy anymore," I told him, flicking off the safety.

George gulped and took a step back. Everyone had gone silent.

"Oh, you didn't hear about that?" I spoke to the group at large. "The year before the subdivision was built, George's son T-Boned my car. I was in the hospital for weeks. My wife died of a broken neck, or a crushed skull. The police told me the kid admitted he was texting and blew through the red light. George had the charges against his son quashed with his money and influence. Then he had my insurance canceled by backdating and forgeries. He's pretty good with forgeries. Do you guys

219

realize the last few complaints to the police had almost everyone in the HOA as a signatory?" I asked them.

There was a pregnant silence and some were looking back and forth at each other with stunned expressions. George fumed.

"Then to top things off, after my wife died? I got fired when I tried to sue his insurance company. Yeah, I used to work for him; I've known the guy almost two decades. What's he do? He builds a subdivision right next to my farm and then tries to get it shut down. Those of you who signed those complaints, you'll get nothing from me, ever. Those whose signatures were forged, well, take it up with George because I doubt I'll do shit for you unless you can convince me it happened." I was letting all the anger and hate boil out, and I didn't miss the concerned looks from Randy and Brandon.

I realized I'd leaned forward, so my gun was almost touching George's forehead and I put the safety back on and backed away. I knew that in theory that what I'd done was stupid; somebody could have grabbed the barrel and pulled the gun to take it off target and then I'd have been forced to fire on them to get it back. I didn't want a massacre, but part of me wanted a little bit of vengeance. Just a little.

"If we were to turn our backyards into gardens, or even the community park, would that be enough for us to plant and feed us?" a quiet man who hadn't shouted at me yet asked.

"That I don't know, but I would have done it as soon as you heard that we'd been attacked and the power was going to stay off for a long time," I said.

"You can grow some things that'll help out a lot, actually," Brandon offered, and everybody turned to look at him, including me. "Potatoes. People have lived on those in Ireland when no other food was around. Sure it isn't healthy, but it fills the belly. If we continue to have another hot summer through fall, I bet you most of you can get a quick crop in."

I made a note to ask Brandon about it later. I didn't know a thing about growing potatoes!

The people started talking amongst themselves and I saw two people break ranks and start walking away. It was the men who'd tried climbing the fence. I wished I had a handheld radio to warn the girls, but I didn't. They'd have to keep an eye on the fence and I'd tell them about those two.

"What would it take to turn all the land we have in the sub into something we could grow food on?"

"Well..."

"Brian, come here a second," Randy said, starting to walk backwards.

I followed and after about thirty feet he looked at me, "You know, I don't know how comfortable I am with having some of them work for us. You've seen what half of them are like. What about the rest in the subdivision? What about the other sub where Frank is?" Randy said, and his eyes took on a hurt look when he mentioned Frank.

"What should we do?" I asked him.

"It's your place, but you've always kind of let this go like it's a democracy. That mindset might lead to a lot of problems, but I have to respect the fact that you don't have all the answers. I don't either. Would it hurt if we took the tractor and tiller over there for a day or two? If we had a couple armed guards? It would save a ton of these guys from shoveling by hand and most of them don't look like they are any kind of shape to do something that strenuous." Randy suggested.

I'd been thinking along those same lines and told him so.

"So you don't think that's a sucky plan? Because I'd rather have them looking at us like we're helping them, but not like a food bank or place to raid," he finished.

"I was wondering how to turn it into that, but I got carried away with George," I admitted.

"Who wouldn't? For all his money and influence, he's now a refugee, the same as them, and it's driving him crazy. I'd be tempted to put a tumbler through his skull myself."

"Thanks, man," I whispered as we walked back to the gate.

"So, are you folks serious about improving your situation and not stealing or poaching from us?" I asked.

For once, most of them nodded.

"Listen, I have an idea but first... I have a lot of poor feelings for George, still. I'm not going to paint you all with that brush. It's not how I was raised and I now kind of feel guilty for doing that... But... I'm willing to bring the tractor out there for a day, maybe two, and till up everything I can. It's an old, big tractor, so any front fences or gates would have to be removed for me to do anything in the backyards. If you can take care of that, I'm willing to come out and do what I can to help. It will give us all some sort of peace of mind, won't it?"

I saw two different figures in the distance, behind the mob, and my heart soared. I recognized the camo the one was wearing, and the woman walking beside him. Both had packs and ARs held at the ready. Kristen and Ken! I smiled widely as they took up positions to the back and right of the group, so if they had to fire on them, their misses would go into the woods and not through us.

GOOD FENCES

"Then why won't you take your fences down and do it?" George asked, his voice timid.

"Because I have livestock. Soon, I won't have feed for them and I'll have to let them into a bigger area. That's why this whole farm is fenced now," I answered.

"Why do you need the gate all barbed then?" he replied.

"To keep assholes like you out. Listen, you want my help, pull those gates and fences down in your front yards. I'll be out in three days to help you guys."

"What if we don't want to leave?" an angry man shouted from the back.

Ken shot about five feet behind the man, skipping the round off the pavement. I smiled as half of them hit the ground and the other half froze.

"What is this?" the raggedy woman demanded, turning to notice the two figures holding guns behind them.

"Flanking move," Ken answered, "Thanks for waiting for us to get into position. If you don't want to be put down right here, listen to the man and don't piss in his face about help or food. He doesn't owe you fucktards anything."

I almost laughed. Fucktards. Ha ha! Move they did; one by one they turned, whispering to each other, and started walking. It wasn't until they were moving as a group that I noticed that they all had the listless shuffle I'd come to associate with zombies after watching too many episodes of The Walking Dead.

I waited until they were out of eyesight before unlocking the gate and letting Ken and Kristen inside. We all hugged and I introduced Brandon Sanderson.

"See babe," Ken told Kristen, "All the fun shit happens around this guy."

223

BOYD CRAVEN

☣ ☣ ☣

Ken and Brenda ended up being my security, and over half of the neighborhood had dismantled or were dismantling their fences. I started with the community park, which was a couple of acres of green grass and park benches. I knew there must have been a ton of weed killer sprayed on it in years past, but it was starting to almost get too tall to till without mowing first. I ended up spending four days there and, in a fit of taking the high road, I even tilled George Landry's backyard for him. Every front yard was turned into tilled land, but many houses were unoccupied as the residents had died from lack of medication, care or suicide. I was finishing up when I saw a limping figure walking towards the tractor. I couldn't quite make out his face, but I stopped and waited when it became apparent they meant to talk to me.

I idled it down and killed it when I saw it was George Jr. I felt conflicted, and I could see Brenda and Ken working their way closer, to make sure they both had good fields of fire.

"Mr. Cartwright, I've been talking with my Dad," he said softly.

"Yeah?" I asked, not knowing what to expect.

"He told me about what you said, when you pulled the gun on him and almost shot him at your gate."

Oh, that, not my finest moment of self-control. I tried not to feel horribly guilty about it, but I did feel some all the same. "Yeah?"

"Listen, he said when I broke my ankle that it was the first time you'd talked to me after the accident. I remember as a kid, you would always come out for the family picnics and bar-b-q. I always looked up to you.

224

GOOD FENCES

What I did, I feel horrible. Nothing can take that back, and if I could go back in time, I would. The truth is, I didn't know how to talk to you about it. I know how much Cathy meant to you and I was texting my girlfriend, wishing I had the same thing you did and—"The kid's chest hitched and he started crying. "I'm sorry, I've wanted to tell you for a long time, I'm really, really sorry. I never meant to hurt you and kill her and I can't take it back…"

Dust got into my eye again, and I wiped the moisture away. No, I'm not blaming it on dust this time, I cried. I started crying so hard Brenda left her position so she could get closer to see what was wrong. Call it the mothering instinct, or the fact that she was pretty badass anyways.

"George…" Shit, how could I say it? I forgive you? I'm not mad? None of those really felt like the truth and I struggled to speak through my own sobs. It felt like a boil had been lanced and most of my anger and hatred were working themselves out in one big shot. It was overwhelming; how do you forgive somebody who fucked up and killed your wife? I remembered the conversation with Pastor White and decided to just do it. No matter how much it hurt, I'd do it.

"Georgie," I said and he looked up, "I believe you. I know you didn't mean to."

That wasn't the same as forgiveness, but that might come with time.

"Truth is, I'm more mad at your father about his behavior afterwards. Every time your name would come up, I'd picture what he did to me and fly off the handle." I admitted.

"Do you think someday you could forgive me?" he asked, his voice wavering.

"I think so," For now, let's just—"

"Don't you bother my son!" his enraged father screamed from the Landry's house.

"See you next time," I told him, my tears starting to slow.

"Yeah, next time," George Jr. gave me a half a smile and left.

18

Kristen had been staying back with Lucy and the kids quite a bit since she arrived, teaching her to shoot and playing with the little ones. Spencer had started calling her Aunt Kris, which was cute. But the little man still hung at my side whenever I was around. In the past weeks we'd started hearing transmissions out of Kentucky, but we didn't have enough juice to respond or be heard.

A few of the neighbors tried ducking the fence at night but, with increased people, we now had more than somebody watching the monitor; we all took turns patrolling the farm. We had more than a few gawkers who might have been neighbors or strangers walk up to the gate, and a couple even tried to climb it before we came out of hiding and scared them off.

This had me concerned, but what I was really worried about was the prison gangs and refugees. I knew I had to check on Mr. Matthews' place, but I feared it'd been taken. Ken, Randy and I decided to go check it out one night, using the NVGs that Ken and Randy had. I would go in the dark, but I'd done that most of my life and what I missed, I was sure my buddies would catch.

The fated night came around and half the crew stayed up so we could continue patrols and have enough coherent people away to propel raiders while three of us snuck over to Mr. Matthews's house. Ken had a ton of experience, and we'd made some modifications to some of the fencing entry points and cleared lanes for fire.

"How can you see the path?" Randy whispered.

"I used to run this two track as a kid. Only place I could duck out on chores when my dad was in a mood or I screwed up." I said with a smile.

"It's kind of creepy, but quiet," Ken admitted.

It was very quiet. Too quiet. I smelled wood smoke and heard voices long before we left the meadow at the edge of the woods.

"Four men, one of them in a white tank top, two who look like they came from a Nirvana concert and one who's got a makeshift brace on his leg," Ken said after sneaking forward to check things out.

"Fucking tweakers," I spit, "It's Scott and Toby I bet."

"Front door to the house is smashed open, looks like they have some sort of bonfire dug into the dirt on the far side of the driveway," Randy said.

I held back from cursing.

"Want me to take the shot? It's an easy one." Ken asked.

The cold way he asked me if I'd like him to kill them chilled me. I knew Ken was a badass dude, but he was also a warrior, something that I wasn't. I tried to be more like a peacemaker.

"No, let's see how bad things are. Do you think

we can get them down without having to kill them?" I asked.

"Sure, it'll be messy, but sure. You two cover me." Ken said and handed Randy his AR as he pulled his .45 out.

We crept closer, but not in line with Ken. We were more cover fire if things went south. He used every shadow to his advantage, and I only could keep track of him when I saw a flicker of movement. He was like a bug eyed ghost. A ghost who literally tore into the four of them like the Tasmanian Devil on PCP. I couldn't make out who he was hitting, punching and kicking, but I could see him sweep the legs of the first man, using a knife edged swing with his fist, which hit the second in the temple. Both dropped and the other two turned to stare at their friends for the half a heart beat until Ken crushed one in the ribs with a knee and did a superman punch on the last guy.

Two seconds. Damn!

Randy and I broke into a run as soon as they all started falling and I made it there as the first one jumped back to his feet. I butt stroked him with my AR and watched him fall again, hoping I hadn't crushed his skull. He dropped like a sack of shit and Randy and Ken took off their NVGs as the fire made them almost useless.

"Looks like some fucked up trailer trash here," Ken said, profane as always.

I rolled the man I'd butt stroked over and saw Scott. His chest rose and fell, and blood was running out the side of his nose. I rolled another onto his side and made sure. Yup, tweedle dee, tweedle dumb and Toby. Great.

"What do you want to do with them?" Randy asked.

"You two keep an eye on them, I'm going to clear

the house and make sure nobody else is around," Ken said, kicking dirt over the fire.

It went out in smoke, leaving me night blind for a few moments, but Randy and Ken put on the NVGs and started scanning. Ken was only gone a few minutes when he came back out and motioned for me to come with him. He pulled off his NVGs and held up a zippo and lit it. In the flickering light I could see the mess that had been made in Mr. Matthews's house. Dishes were broken or piled in the sink dirty. Empty wrappers and boxes were everywhere.

When I'd left the house, I hadn't thought about taking anything right away, because in the country, I hadn't thought anybody would do something like this. I was wrong. Gouges and holes had been made in the sheetrock, probably by a knife and, as we walked down the hallway, I could smell the stink of an unflushed toilet, long abused and left alone. He took me to Mr. Matthews's bedroom and held the zippo up high.

A nude woman was bound and gagged and her arms and legs were tied to the bed. The stench of decay was strong and Ken took a step closer and stumbled. He aimed his .45 at the floor and almost dropped the lighter. My eyes took it all in. The woman on the bed had had her throat slit. There was another body, and she was thrown on the ground beside the bed. Her skin had started to turn colors, and I could only guess she was once white when I saw the red hair. She'd been stabbed dozens and dozens of times. Sickly I realized they'd been raped, tortured and murdered.

"Do you want to keep them alive now?" Ken asked.

I started walking back to the front door, needing to clear my lungs, needing to get out of the house. I'd have to go back in at some point, and check on the footlocker

GOOD FENCES

in the basement that Mr. Matthews had thought so important. But later. I just made it outside when the overwhelming urge to puke hit me and I staggered off to the side. It was horrible and painful and, when I was done, I could barely make out the darkness, because of the stars floating in my vision. When I breathed more they faded, leaving me angry in a way I'd ever been angry before.

"Are they awake?" I asked Randy, walking towards them.

"Yeah, the dude you conked is almost out of it, the rest are up." Randy said, noticing me holding my AR up, pointing at them.

"Scott, on your knees." I said kicking at his feet.

"Fuck you," he said.

My next kick was between his legs and he rolled over, making gagging sounds.

"If you don't get up on your knees, I'm going to kick some fucking sense into your thick skull." I said, aiming a soft kick into the soft part of his side.

Scott struggled, but he made it up on his knees, using his hands to brace himself.

"What do you want?" he asked me.

"Two answers. First question… why do you think you could break into this place and trash it the way you did?" I asked.

"Nobody was living there, and after momma died we left the park to go find some food. There's still plenty there," he said as he felt the flash suppressor touch the back of his neck.

"Question two, are you guys responsible for the dead women in the house?" I asked.

He chuckled and Toby looked at me and smirked. I could barely make it out in the moonlight but I wanted to be sure.

"Why?" I asked them.

"Because we could," he answered after a pause, and started laughing.

Randy was looking at me and Ken in confusion, but I couldn't spare the time because I pulled the trigger, almost literally blowing Scott's head off. The two tweakers and Toby started running. A flash suppressor is good, but what flash there was ruined my sight for what seemed a heartbeat when Ken started firing. Four shots, three men face down, not moving.

"What's going on?" Randy asked.

I knew I'd just killed a man in cold blood, in anger to boot. In my heart I knew it wasn't murder, though I would pray for forgiveness. Instead, I looked at it like putting down a rabid dog. I know it would come back to me in my dreams, but I'd done what I thought and felt was right.

"Go look in the bedroom, and watch the floor, don't trip like I almost did." Ken said, taking his AR back from a disturbed Randy.

Ken slung his AR and put a new clip in for his .45. If I was blinded by my AR shot before, I was dizzy with the almost four foot of flame that the 1911 had shot out of its barrel in the darkness. I noticed the meadow and woods around us were silent, even more so than before.

"We have to do some kind of cleanup if we're planning on using this place." Ken told me.

"I know," I said.

"You want to do it tonight?"

"Oh God, can I shoot them too?" Randy lurched out of the front door and vomited in almost the same spot I had.

"No, not tonight," I said over his retching sounds, "Tomorrow is good enough."

GOOD FENCES

☣ ☣ ☣

In the sunlight, it was even more gruesome than at night. At night, you couldn't see blood and brain matter sprayed across the grass. You couldn't see the torn holes where the bullets had hit. I almost lost it again, but remembered what they had done. It seemed easier, but I don't know if I could be the one to move the women. Somehow, they reminded me of Cathy's accident, and that was hard.

Two of the Sanderson boys and Ken and Randy walked over with me in the daylight. I took the key to the big barn and unlocked the padlock. A Krieg. I almost laughed when I noticed it wasn't shot like mine. At least the fools had learned that much. I got it open and pushed the big doors to the side, letting light in, revealing a semi-truck and trailer, two bobcats, a backhoe and two combines, one shiny and new and the other a relic from the 70s. Brandon whistled.

"Some inheritance, man." He patted me on the shoulder.

"I figure only a couple things will work in here, and we're going to need that combine unless we get a ton of labor. There must be close to 80 or 90 acres of corn to harvest soon." I said.

Brandon was familiar with how to run a backhoe, which surprisingly started right up. He drove it out and started digging a hole not too far from where the bodies had fallen.

"Ken and I will…" he motioned to the house and I nodded.

"I want to check out the basement. He thought there was something important down there. Never finished his thought in the note."

233

I headed into the house, holding my breath until I reached the kitchen. The smell of rotted food and dirty dishes was strong, but it was nothing like the charnel house reek of the bedroom. To get to the basement, you had to go through the kitchen and into the back mud room where another door led down. I'd never been allowed down there as a kid; Mr. Matthews told me it was too dangerous down there.

I opened the door and turned on a penlight I'd borrowed from Randy and almost fell when I encountered two sets of eyes staring at me from the bottom of the stairs. The basement walls were stacked rock, mortared in place, but hanging from the wooden floor beams and joists were half a dozen animals, obviously stuffed. I shone the light around the basement and whistled softly.

In one corner, there was a rodent-eaten pile of animal furs, a work bench and some hand tools I'd never seen before. I looked around for a foot locker, but didn't see one. I took another few steps in and looked around the dark, cobwebby space. Another bench full of tools caught my attention. They were hand tools, not the unusual bladed ones. Underneath it was more of a large trunk than a footlocker, with another Krieg padlock. I unlocked it and set it up on the bench but found I couldn't open the trunk under the bench.

I found two handles and pulled it out. I was confused by what I was seeing at first; rusty metal traps, some spring loaded, but a bunch of them square, varying in size. In the back were two books sitting on top of everything, with a raccoon pelt protecting them from the metal. One was leather-bound and the other was an old book on trapping. Suddenly the unusual contents of the basement made sense to me.

I'd heard the stories Mr. Matthews used to tell my

dad about running his own trap line when he was a kid, but I didn't think he did that anymore. Was this his treasure trove from his childhood? I decided it probably was, according to the look of age and cobwebs. I spent some time going around and looking at all the tools. When I was done I looked at the furs and realized most of them were old and falling apart, so yes, this was likely his old stash.

"Everything ok down there?" I heard Ken yelling from the top of the stairs.

"Yeah," I yelled back.

We had to take these traps back. I wasn't going into the fur business, but I knew now how I could help out the neighbors with these traps. They were re-useable and would cost little to no effort to use them. I was sort of ashamed I hadn't thought of it sooner. In Boy's Life magazine's I used to read as a kid, they'd talk about animal traps, snares and stuff. It would definitely be a great help.

If I could let Ruby and one of the younger sows breed, I'd be able to increase my hog population but I'd need to find a way to feed them...

Then it hit me. They could eat all the leftover or spoiled food. They could forage for themselves in the fenced in pens and, most importantly, I could go gather wild fruits and nuts in the state land to feed them in the dead of winter. I'd keep breeding stock and kill off what I didn't have enough to keep alive for the winter and then preserve or barter the meat off. I'd seen calculations on how much food a person needed for a year, and if I didn't have to dig into my preps for more than rounding out a meal I'd be happy.

"We're going to need the truck," I yelled up the stairs, knowing I'd also have to unload half of the stuff before two people could carry it upstairs.

☣ ☣ ☣

Brandon had already filled in the hole and was driving the backhoe to the barn. I was excitedly telling the guys about my find and what I was thinking in regards to adding to the meat and helping out the neighbors. Randy grudgingly agreed and when the barn was locked up, we headed home. Randy and Ken were mostly silent, having to bear the brunt of burying the women. They would probably have similar nightmares to my own, but for now, we walked in peace.

"Does anybody here know how to trap?" Brandon asked.

None of us did, but I held up the leather bound journal.

"I think I'm going to do a bunch of reading. Maybe my dad has some books on it?" I said.

It was a somber party that returned to the farm, and we let ourselves in the gate and waved to our sentry and headed back to the main house to wash up and grab a quick bite to eat. I checked on the fire, added more wood chips and went to the barn where I could hear two excited feminine voices. I walked in to the funniest sight ever! One of the Sanderson boys had made some sort of platform with a ramp leading up to it, about 3' tall. There were three pieces of wood at the end of the ramp, shaped in a V. One of my mother goats had her head stuck through the V, and a fourth piece kept her from pulling her head back through.

The goat didn't worry though, she was happily trying to lick some sweet feed off of Brenda's hand and Lucy was sitting with her head almost in the goat's butt, trying to milk it. I snickered. It would have been even funnier if she was trying to milk a buck, but I didn't say that out loud.

"I think you should probably do that from the side," I said, coming up behind her and wrapping her in my arms.

I'd moved into the big bedroom with her, letting Spencer have my old room. It had been an easy transition to becoming a couple after that first night alone together, and neither one of us had one damned regret.

"You know how to do this?" Brenda asked in an accusatory tone.

"When I was a kid I my dad did. I watched him. We only had goats for two years though, they always got out or climbed on my dad's tractor." I told them.

"Show me," Lucy demanded.

I walked over and grabbed a bucket to sit on and made sure the stainless crock pot was under the goat and started to slowly feel her udder. She was still full of milk, and the girls probably had been going at it awhile so she might be a bit sore. Usually he would milk in the mornings and Mom would manage the rest. To say I was a bad milker would be an understatement though. I started up high on a teat and used my fingers in a circle to gently pull down, trying to remember of it was more pressure at the top or more pressure at the bottom.

The goat bleated at me, pissed, but I got a few drops out. I changed up my technique and more came out a couple times later.

"Let me try," Lucy said, using her hip to almost knock me off the bucket and into the dirt.

I let that go, but I'd have to pin her down and tickle her for it later on. That usually led to good times, so I saved my revenge. Brenda smiled and got another handful of feed and the goat lost interest in what we were doing. I watched for five minutes and Lucy had gotten the hang of it rather quickly. She finished and showed me the pan of goats' milk and I had to smile. Something she could do on her own, something she could be proud of. I even remembered my mom buying books on soap and cheese making when they were thinking of expanding their goat enterprise. Hopefully they were still on the bookshelves.

"You go girl," I teased and bumped her back, almost causing her to spill it.

"Stop! This will be the first milk we've had in a while!" Lucy sniped.

"Well, I didn't know you wanted some. We've got dried milk in storage," I told her and got the look of death.

Ooops! "Ok, I'll be back later."

19

As summer turned into fall, we started tuning in to Rebel Radio more and more. Blake and Patty were a wealth of information. I found out that the set Randy bought was quite a bit more powerful than my dad's unit; Randy said it was something to do with the crystals. We moved the set out into the living room where the kids had been doing coloring books and puzzles on an old writing desk. Randy and I would sit and listen for hours and both of us were surprised when I asked about trapping that it was Patty and not Blake who first answered.

Her and her late man named Neal had become somewhat experienced trappers and she told me what they'd learned in a short period of time. I used her experiences as well as what I read in the two books from Mr. Matthews to start trapping my own game. The first raccoon I killed was a fat old male and I was walking proudly down the western fence line when I stopped. I really didn't need the meat.

I was passing the lawyer's house when a thin woman, barely five foot tall and clearly malnourished came out. Her dress wasn't immaculate, but she'd taken great efforts to look presentable.

"Mr. Cartwright?" She called.

"Yes ma'am?"

"Can I… I mean, I'd like to barter for that there food I can get," she said.

I was willing to give it away, but I was curious. Where was her husband?

"Ok, uh, what do you have to trade?" I asked her.

She pulled up her dress, showing me her bare body beneath. My eyes popped open and my jaw dropped. Had it really come to that?

"Don't, you don't need to do that." I told her, and she thankfully pulled her dress down.

"It's been how I'm keeping my husband and I alive. Don't you… you don't want me?" She asked, starting to cry.

Shit, I'd read about things like that, but I'd never seen it happen before. I was thunderstruck. She was prostituting herself out - with her husband's knowledge, apparently.

"Here," I said, pushing the raccoon through the wire, the barbs snagging small tufts of fur, "I don't know how to cook him, but I imagine if you're hungry you'll find a good way," I said.

"Oh um… Thank…" she started crying, but she took the animal. "This doesn't feel like charity, you'll want something else from me later on, won't you?" The tears still fell.

"No, I'm really not all that bad of a guy. I'm going to start trapping small game for us and to see if I can help

GOOD FENCES

you guys out. I can't promise to feed everyone this way, but I will do what I can, when I can."

"Why didn't you earlier?" she asked, wiping her eyes.

"Because half of you were trying to get me thrown off my own land when I was here first. Because I prepared and you didn't. Because George is an asshole and I painted you all with the same broad brush strokes. You weren't there for the gate confrontation, were you?" I asked her.

"No, Pete wouldn't let me go. He said it was really ugly. You almost killed George."

"Yeah, yeah I did. I don't like that man." I told her.

"He's dead, you know."

That floored me. "What?"

"He hung himself a day or two ago. George Jr. buried him in the garden in the back, next to his potting shed."

"Oh God. I think I'm going to head that way."

She nodded to me and turned, carrying the raccoon by one leg in front of her and marched to the house. I walked down the fence line and stopped three hundred feet away to look at the McMansion that had fallen into disrepair. The edges near the house had tall grass, but the rest of the yard had been meticulously weeded after I'd tilled it up. I wondered what I'd say to Jr. What would make things right?

"Hey, Mr. Cartwright," his voice startled me so bad, I almost dropped my rifle.

"George? How you doing, kid?"

"I guess you heard?" His voice was flat and emotionless.

"Yeah, I'm sorry if that means anything to you."

"It does. Thanks," Jr. said, stepping over rows of late

241

veggies and potato plants.

I looked at him; he didn't look as pathetic as he had when I'd first put in the gardens for them. He looked a little older, more fit… Definitely thin, but he didn't have the markings of youth on him anymore. George Jr. leaned on a hoe and stared at me, lost in thought.

"You know, it's a good thing you guys found all those potatoes on the railcar," I told him, trying to break the awkward silence.

I'd heard about it from Brenda who had talked to a neighbor she was somewhat friendly with while on patrol one night.

"It was good luck, I just wish we would have looked there sooner. As it was, most of a whole railcar was rotten. It was a mess," he said.

"Yeah," I didn't know what to say.

How can you talk to a kid whose father you hated, especially when the father is now dead and there's no one left alive to blame? I didn't know but I stood there, not wanting to leave just yet.

"Where did you find all the seed packets at?" I asked him.

"Some at the closed up hardware store a mile from here."

Ahhh yes. Goldie's Hardware, fish tackle, booze barrel. The man who used to run it had died a few years back and all of his kids lived out of state. They'd paid somebody to board it up so vandals wouldn't break in. Apparently somebody had broken in, but they weren't stealing from anybody, not really.

"Good. Any news to share?"

"You're supposed to be the one with the radio," George said, and I wondered who'd let that slip.

"There's nothing local. It's all FEMA bullshit, listing

to NATO operations scooping people up and putting them into camps. People liberating the camps. Really sad, depressing news. You haven't heard anything?"

"We had a few people move into the abandoned houses. They were pushed out of their places by some gang. Other than that, somebody shot a deer yesterday on the state land. Pete's wife is offering—"

"Yeah, let's skip that."

"Trust me, I did," George Jr. said and I started chuckling.

"Nothing big, just this gang?" I asked him.

"Yeah, I guess they've moved from one sub to the next. I heard it was the one a few miles further down the road. Folks here are worried that we're going to be next," George said, scratching his nose before leaning back on the hoe.

"What have you all been doing for water?" I asked him, curious myself and wanting to talk about something more pleasant.

"The drainage ditch. We boil it now, after a bunch of people got sick, and a couple died. Tastes like crap, but you don't shit yourself to death."

"Ouch. I'm sorry man. Listen, if you have enough potatoes to bargain with, want to trade for some corn in another couple weeks?" I asked him.

"Sure. Now that dad is gone, I should have more than enough. I'll probably see about working some for you in trade for some meat, or do some hunting. My canned stuff is almost out, but it's just in time for this stuff," George pointed to his garden.

"Ok, well, I'm going to get going. I'll see you."

"Later, Mr. Cartwright."

With a heavy heart, I walked away. Things were grim, but if we got the harvest out, we'd be in really good shape.

BOYD CRAVEN

☣ ☣ ☣

I called everyone in so we could have a sit down and talk. Everyone showed up except Brandon Sr. He was sitting with his wife. I relayed my conversation with George Jr. and a few of them seemed shocked at the suicide of his father. I didn't know the old man's reasoning, nor did I want to. It could have been anything. Guilt, shame, feeling helpless, feeling hated or maybe simply wanted to give his son a better chance to live on their limited resources. No matter what though, the part of the conversation that had stuck with me was the gang taking over things.

It was the second time I'd heard about them and I had no clue what, where and why. Most importantly, it sounded like the subdivision where Frank lived. Randy was rocked by that news and we decided in a heated debate to head in that direction. We'd be sitting ducks on the road, so I showed them my proposed plan. Two or three of us would go overland, which would be slower, but four miles wasn't that horrible of a hike. When we got close, we'd use a large storm drain that drained the edges of a field underneath the road. As a kid I used to play in them when it wasn't springtime, always when I tried to play hooky from school or was in trouble with my parents.

We could follow the ditch right back into the subdivision itself. We'd find a spot, observe for a while, and then come home. Easy, right? Not when I mentioned I wanted to go.

"No way," Lucy stated, with a tone of finality.

"Why not?" I asked, "I'm the one who knows the way."

"I could do it easy enough," Ken said.

"I kind of figured on taking you along anyways."

"Who else would go?" Brandon Jr. asked.

"I don't know, Maybe Randy,"

"So this is a boys' club only?" Brenda challenged.

"I mean…" I looked around the table and threw up my hands, "I'm open to suggestions."

"Kristen, Ken, Brenda and me," Randy said pointing at himself.

"Why?" I asked.

"Kristen, Ken and Brenda are expert marksmen. Ken has military training. Me? I don't trust Brenda to be alone with Ken, Lord knows what she'd get up to with him in the tall bushes—"

A playful smack stopped his words and Brenda turned four shades of red, glaring at her husband.

"Why leave me here?" I asked.

"Well, it's kinda your place. Plus, we need you and Lucy to watch the kids. I trust you all," he said to the Sandersons, "but Brian is kinda their second father. If something were to happen to Brenda and I, I'd expect him to raise them for us."

That was touching and the objection I was going to voice floated away into the ether. Lucy looked at me and nodded.

"I don't want you to go. We're supposed to play cars tonight, remember?" Spencer said bouncing and jumping onto me in a crushing version of a bear hug.

"Ok, ok. You guys convinced me. I'll stay back." I told them.

Lucy visibly relaxed and the Sanderson boys looked relieved.

"Good, besides. You lost at cards yesterday, you have dishes!" Kristen told me, laughing.

"Do you think this should be a night trip?" I asked.

"I'd like to get there close to dusk," Ken said, "If we wait too late, we risk not seeing any activity. Only two of us have NVGs and I'd like to save those for walking back, so we don't walk into an ambush."

"OK, you're the expert on that."

"Good, let's suit up," Brenda said.

In a flurry of activity, the four of them got their camo and gear together. Their nerves prevented much in the way of hunger, so at about dinner time, they all got a quick bite to eat and then split, with Ken leading the way. The house was almost quiet when Brandon Jr. cleared his throat.

"Yeah?" I asked him.

"Uh, can I take the kids out to the barn and teach them how to milk the goats? I know it's a little early, but there's more light," Brandon said, but he was red in the face, and not from anger.

"Uhhh, ok," I said, feeling confused.

"Come on kids, you're going with Brandon to play with goat babies!" Lucy said in a cheerful voice.

They followed Brandon and his brothers out, the other two heading for the gate and one to check on their dad. I sat down at the table and considered my egg salad on sourdough sandwich.

"Hey dummy, the house is empty," Lucy said, undoing the buttons of her shirt before disappearing into the bedroom.

"Yes Ma'am!"

☣ ☣ ☣

After we made love, we both washed up and headed back to the kitchen to sit. From the window by the doorway, I could only just make out a goat on the stand..

GOOD FENCES

So they were still out there. I smiled and looked at my sandwich I'd neglected to eat. I took a bite and marveled at the flavor. The mayonnaise was home made. One cup of oil and one egg. Whip it. Easy right? Only if you have an old hand crank mixer. Luckily my mom did. We'd been experimenting with adding onion or garlic into it for flavor by crushing it in a spoon, and then using the droplets of oil or moisture and mixing it in. This batch was by far the best.

"Hey, that's Brandon Sr.," Lucy said, already halfway done with her sandwich.

"He don't look happy," I noticed.

"Do you think it's Kristy?" Lucy asked.

I nodded.

Brandon walked in and sat down across from me, his grief stricken expression telling.

"Did she pass?" I asked; we all knew she hadn't had long left, even if she'd still had the medicine and chemo.

"Yes. She was real lucid and then straightened up. She kissed me and told me there was no more pain. She sat in my lap and fell asleep. I felt it when she quit breathing. She just…"

"Easy, Brandon," I said standing up putting a comforting hand on his shoulder as he bent over and cried.

I knew those tears, I knew what it felt like. God had taken another angel home. It hurt. We waited and, when he finally took the offered Kleenex, we sat back down.

"So, the offer, is it still there? For her grave?"

"Of course. You pick a spot." I told him.

"I think she'd like the top of the hill, between the corn and the back of the property. Under that big willow tree?"

"That's fine. How are your boys taking it?" I asked.

"Much better than me. They've known for a year this

247

day was coming. It's easier on them I think," he told me.

"Lucy, let's go get the kids so Jr..."

"Why don't you, in case Jr. Wants to talk?"

"Ok," I told her and took my sandwich with me.

The sandwich wasn't an acknowledgement that I didn't care, it was fuel. The same way that the gas went into the tank of the quad, tractor or truck. Even thought I was fueling my body, the constant toll and struggle sure was draining. Bad news after bad news. It was depressing to turn on anything on the radio except Rebel Radio. We'd taken to start taking notes on survival tips and life hacks, and not all of it was coming from Blake. When he wasn't online it was anybody and everybody who could be heard.

Survival was the thing that tied us all together, and it sounded like the information was making a big difference for a ton of people. A lot of the tricks I knew from boy scouts and farming, but there were some that were just too cool. For example, a kid on the west coast ran out of water and was having a hard time finding fresh water. Salt water? Oh yeah, everywhere. He found a sunny spot out of sight and dug a hole in the ground, then put a stockpot in the middle of the big round hole. Small plastic tubing from his fish tank bubbler was clipped to the side, and the rest of it was pulled out of the hole and weighted down.

He said he found the clear plastic somewhere in his father's garage, though he wouldn't say what happened to his family. He'd stretched the plastic over the six foot round hole, weighted it down and buried all the edges with sand and put enough rocks in the middle to dimple the plastic over top of the pot. Every few hours, he could come back and get several mouthfuls of pure water out of the bubbler tube, distilled from the sun. On rainy days, he put out every container he could, but it hadn't rained much.

Little tricks and life hacks like that were flooding in from all over, but the part that really bugged me about the radio broadcast was loved ones looking for others, and for the hour after Blake logged off, everyone talked about loved ones lost. The losses were horrendous and it was heartbreaking, and a little reality couldn't do more than sap my spirit some.

Spirit! That's what I'd been missing. I paused my walk to look up at the stars that were starting to show. I had been missing my church and, though I thought of my spirituality often, I think I had been missing the good news and the raw faith. Somehow, I decided, we'd figure out a way to fix it.

"Brandon?" I asked pushing the door open.

The kids were sitting on the dirt floor, pushing cars. Brandon was putting the goat up, his movements slow.

"You ok, man?" I asked him.

"I think so," he said softly, without meeting my gaze, "I knew it was coming, prayed for it to come, but now that it's here… I just want my Momma back." He said, silent tears pouring down his face.

The twins looked up and stood, helping each other. They pulled Spencer to his feet and whispered something to him. Spencer started the running wobbling toddler sprint and when he was halfway there, the girls took off on their own. When they were in range the two almost ten year olds practically tackled Brandon Jr. in a flying hug. He let out a surprised laugh despite the near sobs and hugged them back.

"I got this, you go be with you dad and brothers," I told him, "and when you guys are ready, and I'll give you a hand with stuff."

Kristy's death didn't bother me as much as I felt it should, but I really didn't know her. She'd spent her time at the farm in the sickbed or knocked out by the pain. It was almost a blessing to the family that she went so peacefully in her husband's arms. I think Brandon Sr. could accept something like that a little easier than if it was painful and ugly.

"Come on kids, I have to watch the monitors," I told them, corralling them towards the door.

Spencer paused long enough to collect the matchbox cars, and then he took off running to catch up.

"Don't worry buddy, we're holding the door for you."

20

Ken, Kristen, Brenda and Randy made it back to the house after we'd gotten the kids to bed. I had been halfway dozing off, but Lucy was already awake, watching the monitors. She let out a small gasp and I bolted awake.

"What is it babe?" I asked, "Trouble?"

"No it's... Ok, It's our guys coming back in. I saw the fence opening and couldn't really make out people behind it until the gate moved."

"Ok, good. Probably doesn't help they are wearing camo and the night monitor gives everything a green tint."

"Right?" Lucy said, stretching and yawning.

"Was Brandon ok when you last talked to him?" Lucy asked after a minute.

"Yeah, he seemed relieved. Sad. He's taking things a lot better than I would," I admitted.

"She'd been sick a long time," Lucy said.

251

"I know, I don't think that makes anything easier."

"Probably not," she told me, standing up.

I stood as well and headed out to the porch. The night was the darkest I'd remembered in a while, with the clouds hiding what little moonlight we'd normally get. Adjusting to no power and no lights hadn't been as horrible as I'd thought it was going to be, at least in the summer time. We'd had running water, thanks to the windmill, propane to cook with for the stove and oven, and some firewood stacked and ready for the winter time. We'd need about five times more, otherwise I'd be hooking up the two propane wall heaters I'd bought and stored.

Michigan winters are either mild or raging snow or ice storms. There is hardly a day that there's middle ground as far as temperatures. It's either cold, or ouch-my-breath-is-freezing-my-nose-shut cold. -30F isn't that unusual in the central parts of the state, whereas the lake sides are a little warmer, and they get lake effect snow. The past two winters had been brutal, with three to four feet of snow staying around until March. The ground stayed frozen and wet for a while longer.

Mr. Matthews always wanted to turn the soil and get started as soon as he could, and I guessed that job would fall to me. The coming week I'd be learning how to run his combine. I'd sat on his lap once as we did harvested, and he'd hired a truck to drive by while it was going. Once I knew how to run the machine, I'd need to have a truck or other tractor ready with a big trailer to get it done. Storage could be done in the crib or the silos at Mr. Matthews's old place, but I didn't think there was going to be enough storage, and we'd also have to set some aside for replanting. I'd leave a small stand up for it to finish drying out, and that could be my seed stock

GOOD FENCES

for the next season.

"Hey," I said when the four of them came into sight, their footfalls easily heard in the silent darkness.

"Hey," Randy said, his voice pinched.

Everyone else was silent and they looked at me uncomfortably.

"What?" I asked.

"Are the kids asleep?" Randy asked.

"Yeah, they're out cold."

"Good, I'd rather talk in here after I clean up real quick," Ken told me.

They all started to file in.

"How bad was it?" I asked Kristen.

She shook her head and whispered, "Really bad," and headed inside.

I took a moment staring out into the skies and then headed in. After trips to the bathroom and some washcloths to make them feel more human, they joined Lucy and I at the table. In the candlelight, I saw dark patches on Randy's shirt.

"Are you hit?" I asked him, concerned.

"No, it's not my blood," Randy said softly.

I waited. I waited some more. Ken tried to start speaking a couple of times, but it just didn't happen.

"Dammit, what's going on?" I asked.

"The rumors were pretty well true," Kristen said after a long pause, "Almost one whole subdivision gone, most everyone killed."

I swallowed hard and Lucy took my hand, giving it a squeeze.

"What happened?" I asked, starting to get upset that they were drawing it out so much.

If we were in immediate danger, there were things we could do, we could also head into the state land be-

253

hind us and hide if needed… The kids, Lucy… I wanted to protect them, and dammit, I needed to know. They all took a breath at once and it was Brenda who finally spoke.

"We found Frank's neighbor's wife. She literally ran into Randy in the dark. When we calmed her down, she told us a lot more than what we'd seen with our own eyes. The gang came in three pickup trucks they'd stolen from somewhere and started going house to house. They kicked in doors, dragged people out and shot them on the front lawns. After a while, they started saving the women," Brenda said in disgust, "tying them together and to the trucks. Most were too traumatized by the sound of it to fight back. Parents, husbands and children executed in front of them? The lady we talked to was one of them, part of the harem, the gang had called it.

"Whenever they found somebody who'd start shooting back, they'd concentrate to gun them down, or burn them out of their house. As people were trying to give up, they were shot and killed. It sounds like this went on day after day. Most people who could get away after the first night did, but not everyone who did had any place to go other than to their neighbors, or hide outside the neighborhood. They tried to band together a couple of times, but the gang found some military hardware from somewhere and just threw grenades and cut them down with assault rifles," Brenda finished.

"What about the woman?" I asked them.

"She died while we were trying to give first aid. She'd been part of the harem and had been beaten so much, and she was probably suffering malnutrition…" Brenda said.

"Did they get the whole sub?" Lucy asked.

They nodded.

"Do you think they're coming this way next?" I asked.

They nodded.

"The woman we tried to help told us that she'd heard them talking about the farms out here, and another sub-division of 'Skanks' to play with," Kristen said with a shudder.

"How long do you think?" I asked Ken.

"I don't know. They're eating the supplies from the houses they didn't burn down. There's at least forty of them, so between thirty or forty houses worth of food... It can't be that long, people have been scraping by since the power went out. I can't imagine there's a ton of food for them to get. My best guess? From what we saw, maybe another week or two."

"Damn!" I swore, "We have to get the corn harvest started and now we have to decide how to either bug out and leave everything behind, or figure out a way to run them off." I said.

"Don't forget about the neighbors," Lucy said, standing and starting to rub my shoulders.

"They're in even worse shape," Randy said, "About half of them don't even own firearms."

"Huh?" I asked, "How would you know?"

"Because of a HOA meeting. George was trying to have guns banned from the Home Owners Association. Half the people who were there, shouted him down. It was the only time I'd ever seen George not get his own way," Brenda told us.

I chewed on that. George didn't like hunting; well... he hadn't liked it. I had to remember to use past tense. I suppose he thought of that subdivision as his own little kingdom, and wanted to see how much he could push and threaten people. I already knew he used forged signatures plenty of times. I wouldn't have put it past him to use some of those tactics into bullying the folks from the neighborhood.

"Wow. Well, at least half the families will be armed," I said, "maybe we can get them together and we can all…"

"It's crazy," Lucy said, "There's forty of them."

"But I doubt they're military; just thugs, drunks and murderers." I countered.

"Who went to jail for beating, raping and killing," said Lucy.

"Do you want to pack up and leave? I have a working truck. If it looks that bad, I mean…"

"No, no," Lucy said, my shoulders sore as she worked on them, probably relieving her own tension and bruising me black and blue in the process, "It's just a lot to work with. A lot to take in."

"I've got an idea," Ken said, "In the military, we use force multipliers. It's a fancy word that means something that allows you to kill way more of the bad guys than you normally could. When we were in Mr. Matthews's barn I noticed a pile of chemicals. Any of them bags of fertilizer? Or was he an organic farmer?"

"No, he'd talked about going organic, but he said it'd be triple the cost for about 1/3 of the money. I never pushed him on it, because he was pretty good about soil testing every year and amending the soil to keep it healthy," I told him.

"Good. If we use the element of surprise, then I think we can take them, mostly in one fell swoop."

"How do we do that?" I asked, incredulously.

"Remember Timothy McVeigh?" Ken asked the table. We all nodded.

"Oklahoma City Bomber. From Michigan. Was supposed to have been a member of the Michigan Militia?" Randy asked.

"Yes. Remember what he used?" Ken asked.

"Yeah, a fertilizer..." my words cut off in a moment.

I remembered why the fuel depot at Mr. Matthews was so far away from the barn now. Shoot, he'd told me that once when I was a kid!

"Ammonium nitrate and fuel oil," I finished.

"Right. We don't have fuel oil, but we do have a lot of diesel, which is a cleaned up version. Do you think he has some bags of it?" Ken asked me.

I nodded, I'd seen them. They smelled bad, but there had been two pallets worth of them in the very back of the barn, covered by a tarp.

"You know how to do this?" Randy asked Ken.

"I know how it works from EOD. Usually, I was figuring out how to *not* make it go boom. I think the reverse applies just about the same way though," he gave me a wicked grin.

"What about the women in the harem?" Lucy asked, "We can't just blow them up, too."

"I don't know if there's going to be any of them left," Brenda admitted.

"So why don't we do something about it now?" I asked, "Go in there and shoot them from a distance? I don't know, how bad it can be? Forty or fifty guys?"

"Those are overwhelming numbers," Ken said, "We'd be cut down, even if all they did was charge us. We need to take the bulk of them out and then kill them. I don't think they'd move the harem with just three trucks. Unless they found more working vehicles, they'd probably leave a few men behind to watch them - if they kept them alive."

"Damn," I swore again.

"Hey, where's the Sandersons?" Brenda asked.

I hung my head; forgetting to tell them had been inexcusable.

"Kristy passed tonight. I guess it was about as gentle as it could be," Lucy said, giving my shoulders a break.

"Oh man, that's too bad," Ken said.

"Yeah, figure we'll do a funeral service and burial tomorrow. Brandon Sr. already had a spot picked out the last I talked to him. They knew the time was close," I said.

"We have to talk to the neighbors," Randy said, "After the funeral. We need to get them on board; even if they can't shoot, they can help us set up and help us watch."

"Yeah buddy, we'll do that tomorrow."

☣ ☣ ☣

Randy and Brenda paid their respects once we'd dug the grave and left for the subdivision, while I tried to remember the words to the service. I couldn't, so instead we said the serenity prayer and the Sandersons shared what a great mother and wife Kristy had been. The cancer may have been what killed her, but it never changed who she was or what she'd meant to the family. After we filled in the hole the Sanderson boys went and got their rifles and two, of the three went out the front gate, staggering themselves almost a quarter mile apart.

Close enough to hear gunshots clearly, but far enough away that they could relay information a little more quickly. It was these moments that made me really want some sort of portable communications, but the agreement was that at the first sight or sound of motors heading our way, each boy was to fire off one round and start heading back towards the farm. A crude early warning system, one we'd tossed around in our talks early in the morning. They'd link up with the last brother at the gate who'd let them in, and then we'd get ready to defend.

Part of preparations was to drag fallen trees towards the main gates. I planned to lay a few across the road just past the entrance, sealing off access by small vehicles and trucks. It wasn't foolproof, but it would give us and the people in the subdivision some time. We agreed that if our fences were breached, we'd all head west, leaving the animals and supplies behind. If we didn't take out most of the group before they even got to the fences, then we'd almost surely be dead anyways, Ken had told us.

Brandon and Lucy kept an eye on the kids while Randy and Brenda went going door to door to warn and offered help. Brandon wanted to do more, but he really wasn't in any shape and I felt for the guy. I hoped maybe having the kids around would be therapeutic, and help him keep his mind off of Kristy. It might make it worse also, but it'd keep him busy and not dwelling on his loss.

It was a hard call to make, but when we talked, he understood and agreed. He did say something about the root cellar dug into the hillside, but I told him how flimsy the door was and he shrugged his shoulders. It wouldn't keep people out, but maybe it could be used as a hiding spot. It could, but there wasn't much more room than a small corridor of about six feet wide by three feet deep. Just enough for me to hang a rope hammock during the hotter parts of summer.

"Coming through," Brandon yelled, opening the gate as I dragged my third large tree out.

With only one chain, it was hard getting it positioned, and I more than once wished I had a front end loader like the one on my Kubota. The third tree would do it, and provide almost ten feet of obstacle crossing on both sides of the road and shoulders. It'd taken a lot of cursing and cussing, but we were going to stop them and stop them right there.

"Ok guys, I'll be back, I'm running to Mr. Matthews' to pick up a load or two." I hollered over the idling engine.

I got the nod and took off. For a minute I worried that I'd forgot the keys when I did the automatic check most guys get accustomed to doing, but I found them. With a sigh of relief I headed out down the road, passing first one brother and then the other, who only came out of cover to wave. A little past that was the twisting drive to Mr. Matthews's house. I turned the tractor in and headed up. I stopped at the equipment barn and backed the tractor up to a small trailer with short sides. I think he'd used to haul extra implements on it when he needed to, but it'd be perfect for what I'd wanted it for.

I backed up to the pallets, and loaded four bags of fertilizer, then went in search of his fuel cans. I found them after about half an hour of searching and drove up to his fuel farm. I filled my tractor back up and both five gallon cans, not knowing if that was enough. If it wasn't, my tractor plus the Kubota would have more than plenty for Ken's surprise. I knew why he kept things so far apart, but I sweated the whole trip back to the farm, both from having the two fuel cans next to the fertilizer, and the fact that I was driving around loud and proud. Everyone within a mile or two could probably hear me, and my back itched as I imagined a target on it.

I did make it back without incident and parked by the barn. I went in to trade with Brandon and give

GOOD FENCES

him the key, so he could do his part next. If things went well, we'd have a big hole dug into the hillside near the road approaching the farm. Ken explained the theory of shaped charges, and this one was no different than C4 in regards to things. When Timothy McVeigh had lit off the Oklahoma City bomb, the barrels had been pointed up. Most of the explosive forces were concentrated in that direction. See, the bottom and tops of those barrels were the weak points... So by burying a barrel on its side, only leaving part of one end exposed, it would create a blast that would go up, but we'd planned on putting these on their sides where most of it would go sideways and, with good timing, we'd fry all three trucks at the same time.

Brandon was heading to Mr. Matthews' house to get the backhoe. He'd have his sons for protection, and he was armed as well in what really amounted to a civilian's version of a tank. As long as they couldn't shoot at him through the glass, he could keep the rear counter weight pointed at them and use the bucket to push, squash or crush a truck if it slowed down enough. Besides, he had his deer gun as well, and quite a bit of elevation, because Mr. Matthews had one of the largest backhoes I'd ever seen.

I waited with Lucy and the kids, watching the monitor and waiting. I'd field stripped and cleaned my AR and .45 a couple of times by the time I finally saw the backhoe heading slowly towards the gate. Two brothers were walking beside it, close to the tree line for cover, and Brandon Jr. opened the gate long ahead of them. I could hear the backhoe's steady rumble and winced. It was a lot louder than I'd anticipated. It didn't take him long to move it into place and park it halfway to the house. It'd be an impromptu shooting platform for

261

Brenda, who was by far our best ranged shooter.

We all sat down to a quick dinner of ham, sour-dough bread, carrots and green beans. It was one of the best meals we'd had, and we all made sure to eat plenty. We'd all been using minimal food from our storage, as much as we could, but we wanted and needed our strength for the battle to come. For that matter, if the neighbors were going to help us, it wouldn't hurt to get them well fed and healthy too, even if it meant leaner times for us. If they were too weak to lift and fire a rifle, then they really can't be counted on to help.

I pondered on that, and listened to Randy and Brenda telling us about the subdivision's reaction.

"Most of them said they would help. They heard that you're going to be helping with the meat situation a bit, but I'm guessing that's from traps mostly?" Randy asked.

"Yeah, I think so, but we don't know how long it's going to be until we're attacked. I wonder if we ought to slaughter two of the younger feeder hogs and bust into some of my grain supplies so we can give them something nourishing in payment. In advance maybe," I finished.

"That's going to make food really tight, isn't it?" Brenda asked.

"For our stored food? Yes. But if we get out of this ok, we're going to have more corn than we know what to do with. Enough to barter and trade for stuff we're going to need. Clothes wear out, shoes and boots too, like Ken found out," I said pointing to the duct taped toe on his right boot. "I want to give this stuff away, but it's the only thing we have of value to trade and we don't know how long this is going to go on."

"Could we pick ears of corn now and eat them?" Lucy asked.

262

"Well sure…" I said.

"How about this? We do the two smaller hogs, and let the neighbors come in and pick a couple grocery sacks worth of corn. We can still keep an eye on things, and they would be close by if they were needed to help with the attackers."

"Lucy, I love you," I said, standing and kissing her deeply.

I only stopped because Randy hooted and the twins were making gagging noises form their end of the table. I laughed.

"You know what, we might as well eat it now instead of jumping into our stored stuff."

"Here's what I'm worried about," Ken said, "We ran the tractor and backhoe today. Do you think they heard it and are going to come looking for the noise? Are we giving ourselves away? We don't even have the ANFO mixed up, and I think we're going to have to make some noise once we start doing it. Plus… we still haven't found any dynamite or blasting caps."

"Wait, what? I know where you can get some!" Brenda told us. "That George kid, when they got into that hardware store for seeds and tools, he remembered hearing that there were some locked crates in the back room that said dynamite on them. I bet you that it has all we need!" Her voice was excited.

"Dang, how do we go that way? I just blocked the road!" I grumbled.

"We wouldn't need much," Ken said smiling, "two sticks maybe, and some caps. The easiest way I heard was to use a smaller charge to light off the bigger one. Two sticks might be overkill, but I know it'll do the job."

"Why would the old hardware store sell dynamite?" Lucy asked.

"Because," I said, "sometimes farmers plowing the fields find a rock they can't pull out. It's a big boulder that's slowly made its way to the surface. So you drill a hole, put in the dynamite with a long fuse. Light and run like hell!" I grinned.

"I'm hoping with blasting caps we won't need to mess with fuses," Ken told us.

I nodded. I knew the basics from my father, and had used it once. Almost any wire would work, as long as it could hold the load, and then you hooked it up to a switch or just hooked one end up to the battery, and let the exposed wire on the second side touch when you wanted it to go boom. I think we used my dad's old John Deere battery the one time I was allowed to use it. We had plenty of charged batteries.

"Ok, so tomorrow's plan, we need to get people inside here, get them food and get them fed. One or two of us will have to watch them, but we also need to get that old fuel drum I have in the barn out there with the supplies, and get it mixed and ready. Somebody has to go to the hardware store and see if we can break into those crates and, last but not least, we need Intel and a good way to find out when they're coming. Damn, this sounds impossible," I grouched.

"That's because you're thinking in your head how YOU would get it all done in a day. If you hadn't noticed, we're all in pretty good shape here and none of us are hurting. We're skinnier than we were before, but other than that fat between your ears, it's probably good for us," Randy joked and I shot him the bird before he continued, "besides, if we split up into small teams, we can get this done in a hurry. Much faster than you'd think."

"Ok, then I guess I'll drive the tractor out tomorrow to—"

GOOD FENCES

"No, I can do that," Ken said, "I got a pretty good idea on mixing the ANFO. I think we'll need you watching the neighbors with Lucy. Either that or Randy and Brenda."

"You guys pick, I'm starting to get tired." I said.

"You can count on me and my boys," Brandon told them, a smile starting to touch the side of his mouth.

"Ok. Not to sound too cheesy, but Go Team!" I joked, and was surprised when the silence was broken by Spencer:

"Go Team!"

Soon we were all chanting it, smiling and laughing.

☣ ☣ ☣

The Sandersons kept an eye on the roads, much the same way we had done before. The four of them were spread out more than a mile away from the front gates, knowing how and when to alert the others and ghost into the woods. Ken drove the trailer out before first light, when we assumed the cretins would be asleep, and filled the barrel with the noxious mixture, mixing it thoroughly with a shovel before putting the lid on tight. He buried everything but the lid, which was about waist level with the road, and headed back to the farm before the sun had properly come up. My job was food. While Randy and Brenda went and spread the news through the subdivision, I slaughtered two of the smaller hogs.

They were about 140lbs apiece and probably a good 2/3 of them was pure meat. The pigs that I'd been going to send to slaughter before this all happened had suddenly become essential to our survival and previously we'd only slaughtered them as needed for ourselves. Taking two out of the herd was going to hurt, but it

265

wasn't something that'd make us starve if we could bag a couple of deer. I planned on keeping my rifle with me when I drove the combine, remembering how often that Mr. Matthews said he almost had to run them over to get them to move out of the way.

Then they could hunt the freshly harvested field when the deer came back for gleanings. It was a cycle that most of the critters had grown up with and I wasn't about to break it, I'd just push back hunting season to feed the family.

Since Ken was familiar with explosives, he was given a hand drawn map, a pry bar and a heavy hammer, and took off on the quad to go get the dynamite and blasting caps or fuse. Things were starting to come together nicely when I heard Brenda yell, "Hey country boy, need some help around here?"

I looked up and there was Pete's wife, holding hands with her lawyer husband, followed by Randy, Brenda and what had to be most of the survivors.

"I didn't think you liked guns?" I asked the lawyer.

"I'm here to help with food or anything else you need. I guess I've sort of changed my way of thinking for a lot of things, but I don't have the tools to help. Arguing in a courtroom is sort of pointless now," he looked me in the eye without a hint of pride.

I looked at them all in shock. "You all came here to help?"

"We're neighbors. We work together or we die together," George Jr. said.

I almost choked on what was either a sob, a gagged on a June bug. I blamed it on a June bug. Damn, that hurt. For a long time I'd wanted to keep them all out, to keep them from eating up all the food that we needed for survival. The only thing that kept me from losing it entirely (June bug, June bug!) was the fact they'd tried to storm the gate and take it by force and, if I'd let them do that early on, they would have literally eaten all the food and left us high and dry.

One lady I only vaguely recognized from church spoke up, "I lived in that sub down the road. What you're doing... I left there because of those animals. I'd rather die than go back to them. What you're trying to do, it's a good thing."

Now I couldn't blame the June bug. Guilt washed over me and Randy and Brenda took over. Lucy called to me in concern and came running with Spencer on her hip. I wasn't crying, but I was gasping at air, trying not to. It was a shock and I've been an emotional mess ever since the event happened. Actually, that isn't quite true, since Cathy died if I really want to be honest.

"C'mon guys, first things first, let's go pick ya'll a couple bags of corn. It should be about perfectly ripe now for a big bar-b-q, let's let Brian work on them hogs before they go bad and we'll have a cookout tonight!" Randy yelled.

There were cheers and they all pulled plastic bags out of their pockets and were led up the hillside.

"What's wrong?" Lucy asked, reaching my side.

"Things just hit me funny. You know, they're thanking me and all of you for bringing them in and giving them food, for making a plan to try to save us all," I said.

"Well, that's all true," Lucy said, moving Spencer to her other side.

"What about in the beginning? We ran them off at gunpoint, even shot one of the neighbors when he..."

"He shot at Randy. Self-defense. Besides, back then we couldn't have helped them all. There was no way. I know it's not kind to say, but... the die-off actually helped stretch the resources they had long enough for this corn to come in. I think after we beat this gang, we're going to find that people are more forgiving than you think. Besides, don't you have a bar-b-q to get ready?" she asked, pushing me with her free arm.

I almost fell into the buckets of pig guts but laughed. The spell was broken and I felt ok again.

"You're right. I thought that, but I don't know. It feels good to hear somebody else say that. I just—"

"You try to save the world, dear," Lucy told me, "and I love you for it."

She turned and walked back towards the house. I paused to consider that. If anybody would have been asked what my biggest character flaw was, that would have been it. In a no grid situation it can be fatal in some circumstances, but maybe it didn't have to be a flaw. Maybe it was a positive aspect in the weird new world.

I worked on processing until both pigs were hung. I fired up the smoker and hung the hams from the top frames, adding large cuts and slices of meat on the shelving. I was just finishing filling it and was adding the soaked wood chips when the group came back laughing, bags bursting full of corn.

"You get everything you need?" I asked them.

Nods and people yelling yes. We found an old kettle in the barn, cleaned it out and filled it with water. Propping it up with some cinder blocks, we built a fire underneath it until the old cast iron started glowing and the water boiled. One by one, people dropped in two ears of corn each until the large pot was almost overflowing. I waited for about twenty minutes and started pulling the shucked ears out with tongs and handing them back to the folks on the broad leaves they'd pulled off to serve as plates.

GOOD FENCES

I made a gross side note to self; should those broad leaves should be saved for TP? It was more to discuss with the group, but not when we were eating!

When everyone had eaten their two pieces, they took turns throwing the cobs over the fence by the bar for the chickens and pigs. There was almost a riot of porcine bodies attacking the fresh corn and the few kids from the sub cheered and laughed. It took Randy, Ken and I to pull the big pot off so we didn't put the fire out by spilling it... but then we laid several sections of rebar over the bricks.

I hadn't been smoking the pieces for very long, but it would add some amazing flavor. The ladies helped me cut sections into strips and we started cooking them over the rebar that was acting as a grill. I pulled out a big jar of salt from the stash and made sure it all got a liberal dosing. Processed foods have salt added to them, but one thing that we would have to mention to folks here is that they needed almost all they could get now. The first piece was taken off the fire and I gave it to George Jr.

He nodded, choked up. I gave him the bro nod back and went back to work. I couldn't say it, but I'd forgiven him. It had taken me a long time and a lot of heart-break, but later on when there weren't witnesses or dust to get into my eyes, I'd tell him. Everyone lined up for their turn for food. The portions weren't large by our standards, but it was more than they were used to. The high density fatty meat would provide them with a lot of nourishment and I hoped we'd have a few days to get them all ready before things went south.

Ken was going to be the one organizing fortifications and fields of fire. He was also going to make sure those who couldn't fight were kept back and safe. Some folks were going to be digging what would be foxholes in and out of the fence near the road. If the gang kept pushing on towards us after the explosion it would be up to the twenty something riflemen we'd been able to scrounge up.

As dusk fell, I felt good. I didn't feel so empty. Spiritually, I was feeling good again. Everyone had eaten their fill, and there was pork left over. We put that back in the smoker with what was left of the hams for another day and I said my goodbyes. I walked folks to the fence and showed them where we'd prefer them to come and go, and they all acknowledged that at the first sound of gunfire, they were to come running to help defend.

Since I hadn't checked my traps yet, I went north along the fence line until I found my first set in the 'string' as Mr. Matthews called it. There was another nice fat raccoon in it. I reset the trap with the setting tool, walked the dead 'coon to the fence and checked on the rest. It was a good night and, in all, I got three more raccoons, one rabbit and one opossum. More than I could comfortably carry. It took me two trips and I was staggering from exhaustion when I brought the last of it in.

"I'll have my boys clean those and get them in the smoker. Those coons need to be boiled a couple times first though." Brandon said.

I nodded and we put the big pot back on the make-shift fire pit.

"I can get it," he told me.

"Listen, your wife just…"

"I need to keep busy," Brandon interjected simply.

I nodded in understanding and headed in. Lucy was waiting for me at the kitchen table, the soft glow of the monitor the only illumination in the downstairs.

"Where is everybody?" I asked.

"Sleeping. We were going to post a watch, but the last two days…"

"If they didn't come tonight, we're probably safe?" I asked.

"That's what Ken thought. He's going out at first light to set up the dynamite and the blasting caps," she told me, standing and stretching.

"Spencer give you any trouble going down?" I asked.

"No, he actually fell asleep on his bed all on his own. Said that someday when he's bigger, he's going to be just like you," Lucy said, putting her arms around me.

I hugged back, smelling the sweet smell of her body near mine.

"Ok, let me rinse off and then I'm going to pass out," I told her, already trudging towards the bathroom.

"Don't you fall asleep on me yet!" Lucy called softly.

"Oh?" I asked.

"I got plans for you tonight," she told me with a mischievous grin.

If I survived the night, I thought, smiling to myself, I could survive anything. The gang would be no problem.

21

Ken and Kristen would be the ones to light the charges at the first sight of the gang. Kristen would give an abort signal if the women were traveling with them, but otherwise the timing and the boom were on him. He couldn't sit right on the charges, which made timing tricky, and I only had about three hundred feet of wire that we'd cobbled together. It would have to be enough. The plan was for them to blow the small convoy and then ghost into the woods and do a flanking action while they snuck back in from the eastern fields, a ways away from the road if possible.

Two days we waited. The construction of the foxholes had been almost effortless when Brandon reminded me we had the backhoe, and that was knocked out in half a day. The rest of the time was preparing, watching and listening. I also cooked everything I'd caught on my trap lines, and we feasted on corn. One thing I learned that I hadn't known, was that you can soak it in water, then grill it with the husk on, or you can pull the husk back to the end, not remove it and then smoke it for a couple hours. You use the husk and the end to hold it over the fire to finish cooking. That way took a lot more time but it ended up being my favorite, especially with the pork grease dropping and releasing smell and flavor when it hit in the wood chip pan.

Two days of solid food. Folks were starting to move with a little spring in their step. They rested as much as they could, so the dense calories were used to help repair and rebuild tissue, but it would be a long process. On the third day Ken went out to the traps, and I was almost excited at the prospect having another day of worry and uncertainty. We were all worried that nothing had happened yet, and were surprised that a forward observer or scout team hadn't been checking us out already.

"How would we know?" Ken asked and that stopped the conversation.

We had discussed that it wasn't military trained peeps and they would probably just come all at once and try to take the place by force. The same way they'd done over and over again, by the sounds of it. Lucy would hide with the kids near the root cellar when the explosion happened, so they would already be halfway to the fence if we yelled for a retreat. It was centrally located on the property, so even if the attack came past the road block and through the fences, she had a lot of room to escape with the kids.

I was sweating and musing all of this when a loud explosion ripped through the air. In the distance I could hear gunfire, far more than just two people could offer. A moment later, I saw the plume of smoke in the distance.

"Let's go!" I shouted and ran towards the backhoe.

I paused long enough to give Lucy a kiss and an 'I love you', gave Spencer a quick pep talk on being a good listener and kept going. The gunfire seemed to go on for minutes, then it slowed and stopped. We all got into positions and waited. I guess it was about ten or eleven in the morning, so there was more than enough daylight. I hoped that Ken and Kristen made it back.

I picked up movement and swung my AR towards the eastern fence as two shadows went between the wires. I flicked off my safety only to put it back on when I recognized the buzz cut on the blocky figure. Ken. They double timed it to my location and both hunkered down.

"There were six trucks, not three," Kristen said.

"What?" I asked.

"Six trucks with at least fifteen people between the truck and the bed. All armed," Kristen panted.

"Did you get them with the blast?" I asked them.

"Probably at least two trucks, maybe three. They started firing into the woods almost before I could move. I got winged," Ken said, showing me the scrape across his arm.

"Tis only a flesh wound, ya baby," I joked.

Ken chuckled but Kristen groaned.

"So we're looking at maybe... sixty guys left?" I asked.

Ken nodded.

"Where did all the extra people come from?" I asked, almost in a panic.

"Hard to say, maybe they merged with another gang. We have to be ready to bug out, this could get really hairy," Kristen aid.

"With the stalled traffic, how long do you think till they get here?" I asked.

GOOD FENCES

"I think they slowed down to check the dead, get their supplies. That's what it looked like when we took off running."

I nodded; it made sense not to leave weapons behind. I was surprised, but not much. It was a pretty rough world, and any resource, no matter how small, could mean the difference between life and death.

"Here they come," a voice floated out of the darkness from one of the fox holes and engines could be heard.

Our plan was so simple I doubted it would work. We'd blocked the road knowing they had two targets. One was the farm, and the second was the fatter prize: the subdivision. They weren't expecting much in the way of the farm we had reasoned, because there was probably a big family or extended family at most, and what would they be able to do against overwhelming odds like the gang? We'd divert them the way we wanted them to go, towards the locked gate. From around covered positions, we'd fire on them until they quit moving.

Simple right? Didn't work out that way so much. Above me, I heard the sharp crack of Brenda starting to pick at targets from far off and the neighbors with rifles, along with our group who was nearby, started shooting. With Brenda, I knew every shot was finding a mark, or it needed to. The plan was for one of us below to start reloading magazines until we engaged ourselves. Shit! I started as soon as an empty dropped down and had just gotten it topped off when I heard Ken start to shoot. I tossed the full mag up and got into my spot behind the tread of the big backhoe.

Bloody, angry men started firing back at us.

"Keep your heads down," Ken yelled, "fire when you have a solid target."

His advice was spot on. I had a lot of ammo, but nowhere near what would be needed to sustain a big fire-fight. I'd made sure all of our people had everything they needed and, with Randy and Brenda bringing a bunch, we were pretty good for .223 or .556. In fact, I'd loaded two magazines out of my ten with the AP ammo that I'd gotten from Kristen. The rest of the neighbors had a hodgepodge of weapons, but some of them only had one box of shells total, that they had for hunting purposes. Some had shotguns, which was probably why they weren't firing yet. All of them had been given ammo from my stash, and I prayed it would be enough.

The gang started to take cover behind the trucks, which they'd parked at angles, as soon as they saw the roadblock. They'd been openly attacked already, and had found out who the bushwhackers were. Uh, duh! Us! They weren't horribly organized, but it became apparent that the assortment of weapons they were using wasn't something they'd worked with or trained with much. For example, I peeked my head up as a guy with what looked like an M16 started spraying lead all over. In a second or two he was completely out and still standing. I saw two bullets hit him in the chest, seemingly from two different directions, judging how his body was flung apart in half a heartbeat.

Another gang member was shooting a pump action shotgun, but the range he was firing at us from was so far out I doubted he was getting the spread he was hoping for. I doubted he was using slugs, because the rail on the top of the gun indicated that it was either a duck gun or a trap gun and, if he'd thrown some big lead through it, he would have torn off the choke tubes, or blown the front of the gun off. Another one was firing a handgun at a range that I'd only use a rifle at.

I lined up targets, no use thinking of them as humans at that point, and fired. Some were hits, some were misses and lead made pock marks on the heavy counterweight of the backhoe above me.

"Brenda, you ok?" I called up.

"It's a turkey shoot," she hollered back.

The gang must have thought that the only fire coming at them was from Kristen, Ken and I. I hadn't even heard the glass shatter above me. A shout went up as one of the defenders stood a little too high and got hit in the neck, while his foxhole buddy screamed for help. Fire, repeat, fire repeat. It was almost monotonous and inhumane.

"Grenades!" someone shouted as round spherical globes were tossed over the fence.

Somehow, they'd used the chaos of the battle to sneak two or more people up in a position right next to the fence. They'd been missed, and had used the heavy cover at the side of the road to move in close. The grenades hit near the gate, near the foxholes, and one dropped right into a foxhole right next to the right gate post. The explosions rocked the gate and flung bodies as it tore into them.

"Oh shit," I screamed, trying to find a target.

From cover, I could see somebody duck behind a tree, to the far left of the gate. He went to make a wild overhanded throw when I saw his head turn into pink mist at the exact same moment I heard a shot from above. Brenda had got him, but the explosion on that side of the fence was a lot more violent than I had expected from one grenade.

"Damn," Kristen swore, changing magazines.

We fired on, and I had to break to start reloading mags, but the fire coming across was quite a bit lighter than it had been moments ago. Were they regrouping?

Retreating? Engines fired up, but the men didn't hop into the beds. I quit reloading and put what I had into the AR and charged it. My gun was made to shoot quite accurately and, in the hands of Brenda, it would probably be as deadly as anything out there. I, on the other hand, was a mere mortal and, although I'd been making accurate shots, I worried about what I was going to do. I fired on the tires, and first one truck and then another was disabled as the tires were flattened. Ken patted me on the shoulder and started firing as well. If they were moving the trucks but the men weren't leaving, whatever they were doing was not a good thing for us.

"What do you think?" Kristen asked Ken.

"I think there's something coming. Why move the trucks?"

The firing from the other side stopped by another degree as men started pushing the trucks out of the way as an air horn sounded. At an almost fevered pace, the drivers and men pushing tried to move the trucks as the flat tires lost their beads. We fired on the men pushing, and then we started firing on the drivers but, as something approached, the men who were still alive and pushing abandoned the trucks and dove for cover.

"Jesus," Ken breathed, as an old Kenworth semi pulling a gravel dump trailer came barreling down the road.

Everybody in our group started firing on it as it plowed through the trucks and the gang members that hadn't moved fast enough. It looked like sheet metal had been bolted or welded to the front, making a shield. The driver's window was a narrow slit, with rusty looking sheets of steel covering most of the flat glass. My blood ran cold as I changed magazines for the ones I'd put a strip of red tape on. The two magazines that I'd not used yet. I charged the AR and started firing.

GOOD FENCES

"What is this? *Mad Max*?" Kristen yelled.

I didn't answer. I aimed for the front cowling of the screaming truck that was a scant one hundred yards away, and closing fast. I started firing, seeing holes every time I could fire. The gang must have picked up or absorbed another one because our scant Intel didn't have any of this going on! Smoke or steam erupted, but the truck didn't slow. I spent the remainder of the magazine shooting towards the tires, hoping to make it lose control. All that momentum, all that force. We weren't ready for that! I pulled the charging handle and was going to try to aim for the fuel tank when Ken tapped me and yelled into my ear.

"Go for the driver, the sheet metal—"

The truck was almost kissing the gate when I opened up and peppered the entire cab of the truck. I didn't know if any of my shots found the target, but the truck roared through the gate like it was nothing. The swinging gate literally took the heads off of people who were positioned too close to the swing of it in foxholes. I kept firing until the truck jerked hard to the right and tipped. The sound it made was horrible. Grass, gravel and rock from the driveway flew up as the dump trailer gouged deep furrows in the land. Many of our people started fleeing and quite a few were shot as the gang moved towards the now open and unmanned gate.

"Shit," I cursed, "I'm out," I said pulling the mag and started reloading with the ammo I'd brought again.

Brenda's shots had been slow and well placed. Now it sounded like she'd gone with a full auto. I knew hers wasn't, so I could only assume that it was her firing as fast as she could. Kristen as well was laying down a deadly barrage of fire, but the numbers were too overwhelming as more thugs joined in the fight in the wake of the semi.

"We have to fall back, leave this place," I said grimly.

The gang was sitting in our foxholes, shooting back at us and, other than hoping they ran out of ammo first, there wasn't much we could do. None of them had advanced as far as the turned semi, but it wouldn't be long.

"No, not yet," Ken yelled.

I got my magazine topped off and started on another even though things were getting hairy all around us, and potshots were being taken at the backhoe pretty regularly. I knew when the big push by them or our retreat came, I'd be out of luck if I had an empty gun. So I worked as quickly as I could, bloodying my thumbs at the quick and careless reloading. I wiped them on my shirt and stopped after three magazines and charged my AR. The gang was advancing, running low towards our position, and I could see somebody pulling the pin on a round globe.

"Grenade," both Ken and I yelled at the same time, and ate dirt.

Kristen was pushed under Ken's dive beyond the second set of tracks, and I went between the tracks under the big digger. I hoped Brenda had seen or heard, but things had gone silent above us and I prayed it was because she was reloading. The explosion rocked me, almost lifting me off the ground with the concussion, but I wasn't hit by shrapnel. A sharp pain ripped through my head during the explosion and then everything went silent.

I crawled to the edge of the tracks, feeling dizzy. Either things were moving, or I was wobbling more than I realized. A leering face with teardrop tattoos under the eyes was smiling back at me from no more than four feet away. He pulled a cheap AK knockoff up and, as his finger was finding the trigger, four holes appeared in his chest and shoulder. He fell back. I rolled on my back to get my gun up and looked. Ken was holding a thumbs up at me as if in question. I tried to hold one back up to him but I felt myself passing out.

☣ ☣ ☣

I woke up to hear gunshots. Weird, I'd been deafened by that blast. Maybe it was only temporary? I tried to roll to my stomach and puked when a wave of nausea ripped through me. I knew what the problem was, and I didn't have time for a concussion, but it was what I had to deal with. Ken motioned for me to stand up and when I did, I almost fell again. He wasn't taking cover like we'd been moments ago. Moments? How long was I out?

"Don't silhouette yourself," he said, pointing.

My hearing was coming back, good.

The gang was fleeing towards their trucks as what looked like two military hummers with .50 Cal's on top spewed shells faster than men could run. The men the shells hit seemed to explode wherever it hit them. A leg? Gone. Arm? What arm? Take a shot through the chest and the gang was lifted off their feet with a hole blown all the way through them, their internal organs flying through their cavities.

"Who is that?" I asked.

"I'm hoping it's the National Guard and not NATO," Ken said, "keep it frosty."

My legs wobbled and, as I started to fall, Kristen grabbed me and eased me down.

"How bad is it?" I asked them.

"You look like you hit your head," Kristen said, "Other than that, cuts, bloody thumbs—"

"How bad is the community?" I asked her.

She looked down at her feet before turning to look back at me.

"I don't know," she said in a small voice.

I knew I was passing out again so I made sure I didn't hit my head. I leaned back against the treads of the backhoe as I saw two feet hit the treads from above. It was Brenda's boots. I could tell by—

22

oft hands checked me for wounds. My ears were being examined and cleaned with a wet cloth. I tried to open my eyes, but I was too dizzy. Sleep. I wanted Lucy and Spencer and I wanted sleep. A kiss on the cheek, a soft body lying next to me on my bed. On my bed?

I tried to sit up, but it made my stomach revolt and a bucket was put in front of me. When I finished I chanced opening my eyes and saw all of my friends in the doorway or in the bedroom with a stranger in uniform. I was sweating buckets from being sick and nauseas and embarrassed. How long had they been staring at me?

"Hey," I said.

"Hey baby. Don't move fast," Lucy said from the side of the bed.

I looked down and Spencer was curled up next to me, his thumb in his mouth, and snoring softly. In his other hand was a piece of notebook paper. I ignored

283

everybody and stared at the paper until I could make out what was drawn on it. I squinted my eyes and could make out three stick figures. One was taller than the others, one came roughly to its chest and there was a small one. They were all linked stick hand to stick hand.

I couldn't make out the names beneath it but I knew what it was.

"How long have I been out?" I asked.

"A couple hours," the man in uniform said, "you took quite the beating out there somehow. How did you hit your head?"

"Grenade I think. Lifted me up and sideways. Didn't know I hit my head." I told him.

"You've got a line of stitches running across the back of your head now baby," Lucy told me, her hand brushing my arm.

"What happened? Is everyone ok?" I asked, trying to make out faces.

Randy, Brenda, Brandon and his three boys, Kristen, Ken, and the twins were sitting in the corner with coloring books. Spencer and Lucy were by me, along with George Jr. He was standing just outside the doorway next to the soldier.

"It was pretty bad," Ken admitted, "We lost ten people, most of it to the gate breach and grenades," he looked down.

Ten people. The neighbors had provided twenty shooters, and another ten in support personnel for reloading magazines. In one fell swoop, they were down by a third while we were safe. I sat back, wincing as I could felt the line of soreness.

"Who stitched me up?" I asked.

"One of my guys. I'm Lieutenant Costello, and we've got our medical team looking everyone over. Of the survivors, you're one of the worst hurt," he said.

"Who are you guys?" I asked.

"My men are active duty mixed with National Guard, come down from Camp Grayling. We're to secure the state and put down looting wherever we can and we're supposed to link up near Detroit, Ann Arbor and Dearborn."

My head swam but I got it, we got lucky. Real lucky. The alternative to not fighting a losing battle is to lose and die. We would have died if it hadn't been for these guys.

"We're a bit off the highway," I told him, meaning it as a question.

"We followed up on rumors of the released prisoners," he told us all, "Rumors had us pushing west towards your farm here. The first two communities we checked had been completely destroyed, the inhabitants tortured and killed. We heard the explosion from miles away and came to investigate. It was pretty clear to us who were the good guys and bad guys. Unfortunately, two of the men killed were from friendly fire. I'm very sorry."

His face was stoic, but I could see that he was upset by that. Lucy handed me a Dixie cup half filled with water. I took a sip and fought down my gorge.

"If you hadn't shown up when you did, we'd all be dead," I told him.

He nodded and continued talking. "Your friends and neighbors told us about the sacrifices and problems you all have been going through. Your wife Lucy has been telling us that you've been feeling guilty about—"

"We're not married, not yet."

"Oh, well… uh… she said that you've been feeling guilty about not being able to do more and help more. I want you to know, your community has done better than most I've seen as we roll south through the state. Don't doubt yourself, and don't blame yourself for your losses today."

Dammit, he *had* been talking to Lucy, because he was hitting every guilt trip I was preparing myself to experience. I looked to her and she smiled at me and gave my arm another squeeze.

"But I could have done things differently, maybe it would have made a difference," I said.

"No, from what it sounds you did what you had to do until harvest time. I just wanted to thank you personally because..." he looked behind him and Pete the lawyer walked up into the doorway. "You saved my little brother, even if he's a liberal retard, no load, pencil dicked, puss nutted, pansy ass mother fucker."

I'm sure he meant that as an insult but we all busted up laughing. Within seconds I was reaching for the bucket again and when I was done I was still laughing as my head spun.

"Oh, and about the husband and wife thing; we have a Chaplin with us," the lieutenant said, walking out of the doorway.

Everyone broke out in cheers and dizzily I looked at Lucy and smiled. I would, I do.

☣ ☣ ☣

The guard unit bivouacked at the farm. They moved the trees blocking the road and their combat engineers reinforced the gate and got it re-hung for us, before they righted the semi and towed it out of the driveway. What did they get? A community to rest in for a few days. The best corn on the cob in the state of Michigan, some smoked ham, wild game and company. We didn't have much to share, but they loved every bit of it. There really weren't as many soldiers as I would have thought, perhaps twenty or thirty, but I spent most of that time laying on the bed. On the last day of them being there, Randy, Ken and Brandon came into the bedroom and dragged me to the bathroom.

"I don't know if I can do this," I said, miserable from the dizziness.

"Dude, we all get cold feet once in a while, we're just here to make sure it's a wedding and not a funeral. Lucy would—"

I laughed as I stripped and got into the shower. Once they heard the water start they walked in and sat on any open surface they could.

"I'm not talking about that, I meant washing my hair. I'm wobbly and my head is killing me," I admitted.

"Ohhh….." Randy said.

"I've got something I have to do real quick. Yell if you need me," I heard Ken say.

"Ok, will do." Brandon told him.

"I thought only girls did this?" I heard Brenda ask from the doorway.

"Don't want him to fall," Randy told her.

I let the water wash over my head. It'd been a while since I'd had a shower, and a sponge bath wasn't the same thing as nice hot water. It hurt at first but soon the sheer joy of being clean overpowered the sharp pain. The hot water made my already wobbly muscles relax, loosening up the tensions I'd been feeling.

I turned the water off and an arm poked through the back of the shower with a towel.

"Coming out," I warned them, wrapping the towel around my middle.

"Ok, we're out of here. You fall, yell." Brandon said.

I heard the door close. I took a step out and almost slipped but the grab bar saved me. Standing on firm ground, I toweled off and sat on the closed toilet seat, feeling my stitches and pulling my hand back to see if there was any blood seeping. Nope, it looked safe.

"You ok in there?" the banging on the door startled me. Ken's voice.

"Yeah, just about to come out. Ya'll didn't put some clothes in here for me did you?" I asked, looking around.

"No," they both answered and giggled like school-girls.

"Damn."

I wrapped the towel tighter around my waist and opened the door and headed to the bedroom. The group minus Ken, Kristen and Lucy were all there to jeer me. I could take a joke and wolf whistle like anyone so I scurried quickly and shut the door to my bedroom. It was empty, thank God.

What I found though, was my suit had been carefully laid out on the bed with a note:

Hurry up and dress. My men are pulling out of here at 14:00 and we'd like to give you enough time.
  Lieutenant Costello

I got dressed as quick as I could, but couldn't find my dress shoes anywhere. I shrugged and put on my least worn work boots and looked at myself in my mother's dressing mirror. I looked thin and drawn compared to my usual rangy look. Food, worry and comfort had been tossed out a long time ago, but I looked like a survivor. I debated adding my .45, and decided it wouldn't hurt. I got my concealed holster and put my gun in it. You just never know.

GOOD FENCES

☣ ☣ ☣

I wasn't surprised to see Ken and Kristen standing hand in hand next to Lucy who was looking back for me and the twins were holding hands with Spencer. I smiled and walked as steadily as I could. The Chaplin married Ken and Kristen first, and then it was our turn. I repeated the vows and when it was done, I was almost knocked over by the kiss. All the pain, all the worry, all the guilt. Gone. It was the best day of my life. My friends, who were more like my family, were beside me. They all cheered and a louder roar came in behind them. I broke the kiss and saw the neighbors over by the community cooking pit and the smoker, and they were cheering.

I could smell the food. I'd been told that several deer had been taken and the neighbors were cooking it up.

I found out they'd donated a fair amount of potatoes to be cooked on the lowest rack of the smoker, and they'd been in there since the previous day. It rocked me. I'd started off putting up bigger, taller fences to keep the neighbors out, but since then, we had fought together, we had suffered together and it looked like we were sticking together. I couldn't give everything I have away, I'd learned that, but what we had done was teach those who wanted to learn that survival isn't easy, but it's doable. And in a day or two I was going to learn how to drive the old combine and Ken was going to pull a trailer to catch the kernels.

It would be a boring diet for a while, but Americans had existed on corn and game for a long, long time. I had ideas of doing more, but for now what we had was probably going to be enough. Once I'd been given a plate of food, I sat down next to my beautiful wife, and George, Pete and Lieutenant Costello took spots across

289

from me at the kitchen table.

"How you doing?" Costello asked me.

"Pretty good. Little wobbly still." I admitted.

"Yeah, my medic said you're probably on light duty for quite a while. Don't get into any boxing matches," he said with a grin.

"Don't plan on it," I grinned and shoveled some heavily salted pork in my mouth.

"Good. Listen, I'm going to be leaving you with three portable handsets. Your little solar gadget there won't charge it. You'll have to figure something out..."

He continued, but I was thinking about the panels I'd kept in storage. Not the backpack panels, but the boxed ones. We'd never put them up, because everything we'd had was fried and the little one charged the battery for the base radio just fine.

"Ok, thanks. I've got something that'll work." I told him.

"I can't promise you won't be raided again like you were, but hopefully with these and the equipment the looters left behind you'll have a bigger tactical advantage," he told us.

"Actually," Pete said, "do you think it's probable that there is going to be a next time? Won't word spread and they'd want to leave the farm alone?"

"Maybe. C'mon guys, I have to go. Nice meeting you all."

The Lieutenant stood and I followed him out.

"Thanks for the hospitality," Lieutenant Costello yelled, "We'll be back in the area in a few months to check in on you all."

"Thank you Mr. Costello," Brenda yelled.

"Hey Abbott!" somebody from the community yelled and I busted up laughing.

GOOD FENCES

"There's always one in every crowd," the Lieutenant growled, "Mount up!"

I stood there and watched them leave, my arms around Lucy, with Spencer holding onto both of our legs in a crushing hug.

"You think we're going to be ok?" Lucy asked me in a rare form of uncertainty for her.

"Yeah, yeah I do," I answered and hugged her closer.

--*THE END*--

ABOUT THE AUTHOR

Boyd Craven III was born and raised in Michigan, an avid outdoors-man who's always loved to read and write from a young age. When he isn't working outside on the farm, or chasing a household of kids, he's sitting in his Lazy Boy, typing away.

http://www.boydcraven.com/

Facebook: https://www.facebook.com/boydcraven3

Email: boyd3@live.com

You can find the rest of Boyd's books on Amazon:
http://www.amazon.com/-/e/B00BANIQLG

WITHDRAWN

Made in the USA
Lexington, KY
17 February 2016